The Alkoryn Chronicles

Part II
Land of Eternal Stars

The Alkoryn Chronicles

Part II
Land of Eternal Stars

C. J. Gleave

COSMIC
EGG
BOOKS

Winchester, UK
Washington, USA

First published by Cosmic Egg Books, 2017
Cosmic Egg Books is an imprint of John Hunt Publishing Ltd., Laurel House, Station Approach,
Alresford, Hants, SO24 9JH, UK
office1@jhpbooks.net
www.johnhuntpublishing.com

For distributor details and how to order please visit the 'Ordering' section on our website.

Text copyright: C.J. Gleave 2016

ISBN: 978 1 78279 840 8
978 1 78279 839 2 (ebook)
Library of Congress Control Number: 2015930436

A CIP catalogue record for this book is available from the British Library.

Design: Stuart Davies

Printed and bound by CPI Group (UK) Ltd, Croydon, CR0 4YY, UK

We operate a distinctive and ethical publishing philosophy in all
areas of our business, from our global network of authors to
production and worldwide distribution.

1

Kindred

Across the desolate landscape the dusty silhouette of a small army became visible. From a distance only their glowing blue eyes could be detected. Through the dust, perhaps one hundred men hove into view. At their head, a dark-robed man, his attire unique. Unlike the other, armoured, soldiers, his robes were finely stitched from a glistening black fabric. He was accompanied at his right hand by a tall, strongly built sentry, modified for optimum fighting capacity, from whom a cold, blue light radiated in the gaps between the sophisticated armoured plates. Over his armour hung a heavy, jet-black, hooded cloak. He had two sheathed swords by his sides which lifted and fell in step with his mount as he rode, as if they had little weight to them.

They travelled on tall, hoofed, lizards, also jet-black in colour, whose scales glittered in the stark light of the nebula stars, their flat faces twisted into a permanent grimace.

* * *

A single shooting star sailed across the dark sky as Ugoki, a young Rhajok'Don, a race native to Stygia, lay on his back, relaxing on a cliff-side ledge; one of many chiselled from the natural rock formations. Wood-smoke from a small fire puffed towards the constellations as if light grey clouds had gathered above, quickly dissipating to reveal the glittering, jewelled firmament once more. The velvet night was dominated by an interstellar nebula; a vast cloud of dust radiating a bright orangey-red, expanding out to a coral mist on the edges. Big, bright stars shone through the dramatic gases.

His workday finished, as usual, Ugoki retreated to the high

cave openings. These were his most treasured moments, listening to the flames crackle and the splashing from below as young Rhajok'Don children played in the geothermal mud spring. The peaceful surroundings and the sweet smell of sugar wood allowed him to drift in and out of a relaxing nap.

* * *

The loveliest voice he had ever had the pleasure to hear awoke Ugoki from his snooze. As he sat up the dried mud cracked away from his thick, grey skin. He looked out over the edge at the fire-lit village and saw his betrothed, Kinoko, out in the bramble fields, a basket, made from grass and mud, full of kernels, and another empty basket by her side. He smiled, content to watch her from afar and to let the wind carry her low tones to his ears.

A second Rhajok'Don female made her way out to Kinoko. Brushing the shrubs aside, she collected the full basket, carrying it back to the village. Walking past the children in the large, warm, mud bath, she disappeared into the huge, clay, communal house: a half dome, connected to the side of the cliff, it was also the large lobby for the cave network.

Kinoko was still working industriously, filling the remaining basket with more of the plump, juicy berries; a short, light-purple bramble and the staple diet for the herbivorous Rhajok'Don.

Ugoki climbed to his feet, he was of a heavy stature, even for a Rhajok'Don and was wearing the common attire for a male of his race; a simple loin cloth, made from tough grass strands, kneaded together with rubber, then allowed to dry and cut to shape. He dusted the remaining dried mud from his massive, muscular body before retreating into the cave tunnels. The underground passages were lit with sugar wood torchlights, permeating the caves with honey sweet incense.

As he entered the large communal mud-house, he saw a circle of females sat under the cone ceiling. Splashing about at their feet were younglings, including the most recent addition to the Rhajok'Don village; Ugoki's niece, a tiny, squealing calf, who had found her wet nurse's nipple and was now suckling happily.

The males of the tribe sat in the centre of the straw floor, ringing a mountain of seeds; grinding the grains using jagged rocks with which to crush the kernels in stone bowls. A few others were ripping strands from a hard, tubular grass that grew close to the surrounding forest.

That day Ugoki had done some maintenance on the house as a small water hole had pushed through the mud walls. He had reinforced it with grass and held it together with sap from the local rubber tree. As he walked past his patchwork he checked it and saw that the interlaced finger indents had dried and left a secure fix. Just as Ugoki was about to smooth the wall with a rough stone, Osok, the chieftain, walked through the entrance. Osok also wore a loincloth, an unusually modest adornment for a tribal chief. He was only distinguished by his embellished horns, jutting from his chin, long, sharp and filed into ridges.

"Ugoki, nice work again," he said, commending Ugoki on his suitable craftsmanship. Rhajok'Don weren't the most dexterous of races; their crafts were crude, yet practical, and usually revolved around hand kneading.

Ugoki bowed his head respectfully, acknowledging the compliment with quiet pride. He began sanding the wall and when he was satisfied it was smooth enough, he sat down next to the seed pile and began grinding grain with the other males. Staring out to the mud pools, Ugoki appreciated the life that flourished there. The geothermal springs were highly fertile parts of Stygia and many types of mosses grew around the edges, spreading outwards towards the cliffs, and in the other direction, towards the adjoining agricultural fields.

A child ducked his head under the surface of the mud, then came up spluttering and wiping his eyes. "I made room for you!" he called, projecting his voice towards the communal dwelling.

"Oh, I've bathed today!" Ugoki replied.

The boy pulled himself out of the sticky mud bath and covered in wet mud ran over, throwing himself at Ugoki and giving him a big hug. Public shows of affection were common amongst the Rhajok'Don.

Ugoki, caught unawares by this sudden exuberance, knocked the bowl, toppling grain onto the floor. He chuckled, warmly cuddling the boy before setting him on his feet. "I'm busy, go play with your friends," he told him.

"I just wanted to hug you," Nis'Ka said before running off excitedly, leaving muddy trails on the flourishing mossy ground.

An hour later, and a much reduced seed pile, Ugoki decided it was time to find his partner-to-be.

* * *

His large toes sank into the moss and moisture oozed out, leaving water marks on his oversized nails. As he neared the bramble fields he could see Kinoko working hard. She was wearing only a simple tunic but she needed nothing to enhance her natural beauty. For a moment, Ugoki recalled again the wonder and joy that had swept over him when, having shyly revealed his feelings for her, he had found them reciprocated. Kinoko completed his life in a way he could never once have imagined.

"Want some help?" he offered on reaching her.

Kinoko glanced up at Ugoki, a smile washing away her focused concentration on her task. "Please. There's plenty of room." Her rough, gruff voice, similar to all females, was slightly higher in pitch than that of a male.

Ugoki dropped down to sit beside her. Grabbing the basket, he held it up to catch the kernels as she rustled them off their stalks.

Kinoko's eyes caught his and another smile lit her face. Her black pupils hid a gentle soul behind them. She raised her head, brushing her small chin horns against his in traditional greeting. Kinoko knew that the caring Ugoki would make a perfect life partner for her. She snuggled her head onto his shoulder, cherishing the feeling of belonging that doing so gave her. Her gaze took in the cliff bottom greenery, thriving on down flowing nutrients, so uncommon in Stygia. Ugoki put down the basket, pulling Kinoko closer and stared up at his cliff-side retreat. From there the view over the landscape, lit with the warm undertones of the sun below the horizon would be glorious. Stygia was the Land of Eternal Stars, where the sun never rose.

"I think we have enough now." Ugoki got to his feet, basket in one hand, tugging Kinoko up with him with the other. Arms around each other, the two slowly made their way back to the village. Scattered fires on the cliff ledges, above the community dome, filled Ugoki with tranquillity as well as that sense of well-being that comes in the secure comfort of home.

A few last stragglers still lingered in the mud pool. "Children – inside now," Ugoki called as they passed. "It's sleeping time." They waited as the youngsters climbed from the pool and ran, laughing, inside, before following them in.

* * *

The familiar squeal of the flying, feathered, tree lizards signalled a new day in the village. The first awake was Ugoki's nephew, Nis'Ka, who poked at his father amongst the sleeping, snuggled pile of Rhajok'Don. Reluctantly Osok shed his rest and pulled himself from the sleeping villagers, his efforts slowly waking the rest of the tribe.

Ugoki was snuggled close to Kinoko, hugging her from behind. "Tomorrow! Just one more day – I can hardly wait," he whispered, his broad lips close to her upright, tubular ear. He nudged his blunt horn against her cheek.

A slow smile spread over Kinoko's face as she opened her

eyes. "Let's spend today in the forest," she murmured.

Ugoki pressed his face into her silky, black hair. "That, my love, would be perfect."

Kinoko turned in his arms, butting her face against his cheek. "Doing anything with you is a perfect way to spend the day."

Ugoki tightened his hold on her. "I love you, Kinoko. You have no idea how much," he said. Then he grinned, launching a tickling attack.

Kinoko giggled, darting to her feet. "Come on, lazy bones. The forest awaits." They made their way to the breakfast hall and collected stone bowls filled with a runny, light-purple, porridge, and a round of the hard bread made from soaked bark. They spooned the porridge up using the bread, grinding the food easily with their strong teeth.

* * *

Breakfast finished, they made their leisurely way towards the south-westerly side of the uniquely adapted tai-qay tree forest. The tai-qay, the most common tree in Stygia, which grew slanting sideways, adapted to a world with no sunrise. Its large sheeted leaves were oval, smooth and a very deep teal in colour. The forest expanded for about a mile to the northwest, with the younger trees always at the edges.

Ugoki and Kinoko went deep into the woods, where the trees were so immensely large they had fallen to their own greed for sunlight; the limited life cycle evident by the rotting barks. Ugoki stopped under one of the curved, towering trunks and tore off a moist strip of bark, passing it to Kinoko.

Kinoko took the offering, smiled her thanks and popped the tasty wood, a staple part of the Rhajok'Don diet, into her mouth.

They continued through the fallen leaves and luminescent mushrooms until they reached an almost straight passageway between the trees, with just a few fallen branches lying across it.

"Let's charge together," Kinoko suggested. A common pastime for Rhajok'Don was to race each other through the forest on all fours. She leant forward, placing her hands into the leafy undergrowth. Her fingers clenched inwards against her palm, allowing her padded knuckles to cushion her hands. Ugoki followed suit and he too leant forward onto all fours.

"Ready?" he asked, and before he had finished, Kinoko had already charged ahead and was leaping over the first branch. "Hey!" Ugoki laughed, charging after her.

Quickly catching up, he pounced on her and they rolled in some fresh mud. "Tomorrow, we'll be life partners," he told her, holding her gaze with his own, his love for her written across his face. He rubbed his cheek against hers, one side, then the other. Nudging her neck with his horn, he softly gave a quick outward breath, almost like a short snort from his flat nose.

A sudden rustle from the canopy of the highest trees alerted Ugoki and he lifted his head to track a flock of featherless birds, which, disturbed, flew quickly into the sky. A few moments later Ugoki's nephew came bounding towards them. Coming to a halt, he used his short horns to rustle some leaves over them before charging off into the forest again. Ugoki fondly watched him go, smiling as Nis'Ka once more ceased his run a short distance from them and strengthened his rear kick by clopping his feet against a small tree, which bore the marks of having been salvaged for bark. Moments later, he ran deeper into the forest and Ugoki turned his complete attention on Kinoko again.

* * *

An hour had passed when a deep bellowing, honking noise sounded from the village. It was the alarm call of a watchman sat on the highest ledge.

"That's the alarm," Ugoki said, shooting Kinoko a surprised glance. "I wonder what it could be?"

Kinoko nodded. "Come, we need to get to the caves."

"Nis'Ka!" Ugoki called. He waited but there was no reply.

"He should be back at the village by now," Kinoko reassured him. "You know we don't let them play too far away from home."

Ugoki was far from happy but since there was little he could do, he put aside his concerns and the two Rhajok'Don charged towards the forest cave entrance leading to the tunnel network behind the dome. As they bolted through the wide, chiselled channels, the honking echoed off the walls.

"Retreat to the caves." The voice of the chieftain bellowed over the alarm.

They caught up to the rest of the clan and quickly arrived at the inner dome; a retreat into safety.

"Eshaki, What is it?" Ugoki shouted, spotting his sister, the ranking matriarch. "A herd of males?"

"We don't know. The watchman saw a mounted group of men, not Rhajok'Don, foreigners we've never seen before. They were riding unusual beasts, heading towards us, beyond the south eastern mud pools."

Ugoki could see the fear in her eyes and in the way she was breathing in short, almost panting breaths.

He struggled to control his own anxiety. "Not Rhajok'Don? How many?"

"Maybe one hundred."

The watchman hurried down from the high cave and joined the rest of the Rhajok'Don in the inner retreat. "They can't get through the mud pools; they're chopping their way through the forest."

Eshaki squeezed herself through the milling, bewildered clan. "Nis'Ka. Was he with you?" she asked, scanning the assembled Rhajok'Don frantically.

"The last I saw of him, he was in the forest," Ugoki said hesitantly. "I called for him when I heard the alarm." He shook his head. "When he didn't answer, I thought he must have gone home already."

"He's not inside," Eshaki's voice cracked.

Ugoki saw tears swimming in her eyes. "Let's check the dome," he said, charging towards the communal house with Osok and Eshaki following close behind, their feet scuffing the dry mud as they ran.

At the dome, Osok immediately rushed to the door, calling for Nis'Ka. When the boy failed to appear, Osok grasped Eshaki's hand in his own meaty fist, giving it a reassuring squeeze. "I'll stand watch," he told her. "Don't worry. You know Nis'Ka. He's probably in here somewhere, completely unaware that we might be worried."

Eshaki managed a small smile but it was plain to all that she wasn't convinced. "I think I'll wait here with you," she told Osok."

"He'll turn up soon," Ugoki added, although, truth to tell, he was also far from sure.

Osok dipped his head, acknowledging his support. Ugoki had the feeling that Eshaki barely even registered what he had said.

Eshaki watched as the mounted men came into view, chopping at the undergrowth as they rode. As the distance between them closed, she bravely stepped forward in the hope of a peaceful interaction. But her heart fell as she took in the heavily armoured men. These, she realized, were not peaceful emissaries. The Rhajok'Don had no knowledge of weapons. Their play fighting traditionally involved only hands, feet and horns. These invaders, with their armour and weaponry, were alien to her.

As they rode to a stop, another, smaller group, appeared from within the trees. Eshaki estimated there were about eighty men. Cold fingers of fear stroked down her spine. Her people! How could she save her people!

A high-pitched squealing reached her ears from within the

army mass. It was a sound that froze her heart. A single soldier came forward, Nis'Ka dangling in his grasp; chained by a collar and held at length on a metal stick.

"Nis'Ka!" Osok bravely ran out of the dome towards the army. Eshaki, having immediately recognised her son's call, and with a mother's urgent reaction, was already running towards the enemy.

"No!" Ugoki tried to grab her but he was too late. Desperately, he followed after her.

The Commander's eyes radiated a fluorescent blue from under his hood. He pointed at Osok. "He's useless," he told his guard flatly. "Dispose of him."

Pulling one of his swords free, the sentry raised it, aiming the point at Osok. The sword pulsed blue and a bolt of blue gel shot from the blade. Osok watched helplessly as his death flew through the air towards him. Horror filled his eyes and every nerve strained, urging him to run, even though instinct told him running would do no good. He would die with honour, he decided, standing his ground.

The substance splashed onto Osok like a contagion, spreading evenly over his body. Gradually, the blue was replaced by saturating red as the stuff consumed his flesh.

A thin, keening wail erupted from Eshaki as she slumped to the ground, her terrified gaze locked on Osok as the goo, quickly encapsulating him, began breaking down his organic material. Slowly he dissolved into a pool of thick, red organic matter.

Stunned, Ugoki force himself to spring to life. He was not going to stand by and let his sister die next. Lunging towards her, he grabbed her under her armpits, dragging her back towards the cave. "We need to retreat into the caves," he panted. "Whoever these men are, we can't fight them."

Eshaki's head fell to one side. Ugoki realized his sister was unconscious.

From the shadows of the cliff-side caves, the Rhajok'Don

villagers watched as ten of the mounted army, led by the sentry who's weapon had so cruelly ended Osok's life, embarked towards the dome. The hooded men withdrew their swords and began hacking at the hard mud casing of the dome-shaped house. The dwelling fell, crumbling away beneath the blades to reveal the large cave entrance beneath.

The Commander ordered his men to dismount, signalling for two of them to go inside. Without hesitation, the soldiers entered the pitch-black cave. They were greeted by two, large, Rhajok'Don males, who charged the soldiers, driving their horns deep into the men's torsos, causing lethal internal damage. The enemy posed little opposition in the confined space against such colossal Rhajok'Don. The bodies were thrown from the cave and they slumped lifelessly on top of each other.

"Smoke them out!" The Commander shouted.

As ordered, the soldiers lit blue, sludge soaked torches, throwing them into the cave entrance. The dense purple smoke, both toxic and blinding, swiftly made its way through the network of tunnels, choking the Rhajok'Don inside, causing a stampede for the openings carved into the rock. Smoke now billowed from torches at numerous openings, spilling outwards and drifting upwards into the dark atmosphere. Those few who could not get to the cave openings collapsed in the tunnels. Even the blaze of the many home fires was choked by the density of the smoke. Ugoki was grateful that fate had smiled on them and that the attacking army's plan had not worked out quite so well as they might have hoped, as most of the Rhajok'Don were able to draw clean air through the cliff openings. Pulling in a deep breath and holding it, he poked his head through the smoke and glanced left. The far forest exit was not smoking yet. Quickly he ran back into the caves, checking the other openings until he spotted Kinoko. "Find the females and young ones," he broke off, overcome by a coughing fit. "Take them to the forest exit. Once you reach the forest, run east and do not stop. Hurry!"

Kinoko wasted no time on words, giving him a sharp nod, she began rounding up the women and children.

"We seem to have a problem!" The leader's voice called up to the hiding Rhajok'Don. "You're more resilient than I thought." He pointed to the guard holding Nis'Ka captive. "It seems I'm in need of a little persuasion to get you to come out."

The clan were unable to make sense of the invader's language, but his tone was all they needed to understand.

The guard pushed the crying boy forward. Nis'Ka shuffled his small toes through the lichen, falling to his knees. But the guard kept on pushing him to move whilst lifting the neck chain, forcing Nis'Ka up onto his toes in an effort to release some of the pressure on his throat.

Ugoki stared, horrified, grateful that at least his sister was spared this savagery so soon after being forced to witness the terrible death of her partner. He breathed a silent prayer to the powers that be that, even though he stood, helpless, unable to stop the violation of his nephew, the women and children were escaping to freedom through the far caves.

The Commander snatched the metal cane from his subordinate, forcibly pushing Nis'Ka to his knees. The poor boy staggered forward, the chains rasping against his hands. He fell onto his face and lay, a small, broken figure, allowing the ground to soak up his tears. "Mamma," he mumbled.

A sudden jerk on his chain brought him into a kneeling position. Nis'Ka offered no resistance, beaten and defeated as he dangled on the end of the pole.

The Commander shortened his hold, coming closer to the trapped boy. He grasped his black hair, still feathery with youth, and with pointed fingers, he scratched the boy's scalp, pulling his head back. Nis'Ka looked up at the glittering stars in silent appeal. Watching him, Ugoki saw that he appeared to phase in and out of consciousness; a defence mechanism of sorts, he supposed. His crying stuttered, tears running from his inky eyes, loosening mud from his face as they tracked down his cheeks.

"Ahh!" Nis'Ka writhed in pain, a scream of excruciating agony ripping from his throat as, abruptly, the Commander lunged. Sharpness pierced his eye, the pain exploding into his head. His torment eased fractionally, numbed by an adrenalin overload. His head was tugged to the left. Opening his eyes, he realized he only had vision remaining in the right one. And then terror seized him, locking him within its grip, as what he saw with his remaining sight was the ghastly image of his left eye being pulled from his skull. That image was what he carried with him into the merciful arms of oblivion. His tormentor malevolently chuckled as he pulled Nis'Ka's eye free from its cord. He held it up in front of him like a trophy. Letting go of the chain, he allowed Nis'Ka's frail, inert body to collapse into the dirt. Parading in front of the caves, he held his prize aloft. Suddenly he stopped, raising his claw to his mouth, he bit into the raw flesh as if it were a succulent delicacy.

Ugoki's stomach heaved. Never had he felt so paralysed and so useless. *Nis'Ka*, the boy's suffering was a knife in his guts. His two hearts pounded, anger blazing behind his eyes like an out of control brush fire. Slowly, he came to his feet. Squaring his shoulders he emerged from the cave opening. Letting his head fall back, he gave out a deep, fierce, howling roar. Behind him, a low murmur ran through the villagers; this was a sound no Rhajok'Don had ever before heard. Ugoki turned to his kin. "We'll charge them," he growled. "On my signal." He started to pound his hands on the stone ground, as he did so, he began a low, deep, rhythmic grunting. Other male voices quickly joined him and the chant rapidly increased in volume.

The enhanced sentry raised his swords above his head and they began to pulse a fluorescent blue. He gestured toward the mounted troops, calling something in his strange language, and Ugoki saw eight more men dismount. He pointed his swords forward, signalling to the soldiers to position themselves in a semi-circular formation, one next to another, their swords touching.

"But – can we charge them, are we strong enough?" A male Rhajok'Don asked shakily.

Ugoki drew himself up, instinctively taking command. "You saw what they did to Nis'Ka. There is no other option. Fight, and maybe some of us die. Or – do nothing and we all die." He swung around to face the exit. "Our families need this distraction," he added and charged.

The entire male population of the village followed him, storming from the caves. Some jumped down from the lower openings, forming a stronghold at the bottom of the cliff. Lining up to face their enemy, they dropped to all fours. Again, that strange cry issued forth from Ugoki as he and his kin thundered into the barrier of soldiers.

Immediately two Rhajok'Don were taken down by the powerful sentry, the fearsome soldier gutting them with his evil weapon with no more effort than Ugoki would have expended on slicing some slushy bark. So fast his movement was just a blur of motion, their opponent brought his swords up, crossing them in front of himself. Blue goo shot from them, forming a deflective field in front of him. The oncoming Rhajok'Don, dazed by the shield when they charged into it, made easy pickings.

"Ignore the blue one!" Ugoki roared at the top of his voice. "Go for the leader!"

The stampede swerved, charging directly at the Commander who was, belatedly, realizing his army of one hundred men was not equal to the ferocity of a few dozen Rhajok'Don. He spurred his lizard into action, retreating from the front-line as the tribe stormed the next line of defence. The Rhajok'Don rolled over the army, giving no quarter as the enemy went down like a line of grass at harvest time. Two soldiers who had escaped the first wave of ferocity drove their swords home into the belly of a Rhajok'Don who fell mid-leap to a lifeless heap on the dusty ground.

Ugoki drew to a halt. Lifting himself onto two feet, he gazed towards the far cave, where purple smoke was rising above the trees, hoping desperately that Kinoko and the women and children had managed to get to safety.

From the corner of his eye, he saw the soldier he most feared had pulled back with a few men of his own and was leading them to a flanking position at the rear of the Rhajok'Don. He roared trying to alert his kin, but it was too late, the attack was already under way. The enemy slashed at the feet of the Rhajok'Don, crippling them and sending them plunging to the ground, where they made short work of despatching them. Ugoki could see a dozen already felled and more dropping as he watched.

He roared again, "Rear kick!" To the complete surprise of the soldiers, his brothers at war stopped dead, lashing out with their strong legs and feet. Soft grunts and painful yelps drifted to Ugoki's ears as the Rhajok'Don savagely struck the oncoming enemy, their powerful limbs connecting with armoured faces, knocking them to the ground instantly. His gaze found the deadly, blue-glowing sentry who was rapidly firing the pestilent goo from his swords, disintegrating another dozen Rhajok'Don in a matter of minutes. A terrible fear lodged in Ugoki's chest. Half of his tribe were gone and he was running out of ideas.

"All charge the blue one!" Ugoki knew it might be the last order he ever issued, but they had to try. If it worked, they would take out the most lethal and deadliest soldier.

Holding his breath, he watched as the remaining Rhajok'Don smashed into the sentry with staggering force. His desperation increased as some of his kin went down immediately on impact with the killing shield. More fell to the pestilence as the sentry fired his swords at them, the blue infection spreading to further Rhajok'Don as they ran to help their fallen colleagues and they too putrefied into the soil.

Thankfully, the shield did not protect the fighter on all sides, leaving him vulnerable to attack from behind and, at considerable cost of lives, he was overwhelmed and toppled forwards. The Rhajok'Don immediately set to, trampling his fallen body but, as hard as they pounded him, nothing breached the alien armour. Finally, a Rhajok'Don struck his fist to the soldier's throat and, mercifully, the sentry ceased to glow. Ugoki let his breath out in a long, slow hiss. Thank the powers that be for that one weak spot. Behind him, he could hear the Commander ordering his remaining soldiers to retreat and swiftly they galloped off in the opposite direction.

"We did it!" One young Rhajok'Don rejoiced and began chanting, "Ugoki!" He powered his arm into the air with each chant. "Ugoki!" Two more joined in and the chanting grew faster. More voices rang out. "Ugoki! Ugoki! Ugoki!"

Relieved and happy though he was, Ugoki's thoughts were all for the woman and the children. He left his clan to their chanting and scrambled into the still smoking caves.

Holding his breath, he ran through the tunnels to his usual retreat. He scanned east, to the far cave, hoping to see some sign that his kin were still free and running to safety as he had instructed. To his dismay, what he saw was something very different.

Moving away south was another army, meandering through the sparse greenery at a slow pace. Behind them stretched a mournful tail of chained Rhajok'Don women and children.

"No!" Ugoki howled, his face slack with crushing disbelief. "No!" His scream of anger echoed across the plane.

Bowed down by her heavy neck chain, bruised and battered by her rough handling, her face stained by the tracks of her tears, Kinoko heard Ugoki's anguished cry. Glancing back towards her decimated home, the one thought that kept her on her feet and moving was that Ugoki was still alive. While the breath of life still flowed, she told herself, a spark of hope remained.

* * *

The ground was cold, flat and murky. The Rhajok'Don struggled along, sunk in despair. Some of the children had fallen and now found themselves dragged through the mud, helpless to regain their feet. Their mothers tried to help them but at each attempt they were thrust savagely aside and threatened at the point of the soldier's swords.

The industrial landscape of Kraag'Blitz rose up before their tired eyes in its full unremitting bleakness. Glancing around, to their horror, they saw many armies gathered, all with Rhajok'Don trailing behind them.

Kinoko's numbness was apparent even in her thoughts as she looked around, wondered where she had been brought to and why? After marching for hours, she was so weary her legs folded under her and she slumped into the soot-ridden mud. She had no more reserves: no energy left to get back up on her feet and allowed herself to be tugged jerkily past the tall factories all around her. Silent tears chased their way down her cheeks to mix with the dirt. Finally, she closed her blurry eyes, unwilling to face the brutal reality of her surrounds for a moment longer.

When she opened her eyes again, she was strapped to a large chunk of metal that jutted upwards. Her back faced outwards and her clothes had been removed. All around her were her chained and caged kin. Some naked, some weeping, others just stared down at their hands and feet and a few more clutching their bodies as a way to feel comfort.

"You were unconscious when you arrived. You will be punished." The unknown voice of an oppressor addressed her.

She didn't understand the words. But she understood the intent as she heard the sound of a whip crack against the ground. Fearfully she turned her head to see a segmented black whip, blue sections, shining with an unnatural light, lay between the pieces. Kinoko inhaled deeply, squeezing her eyes closed. The first searing stroke was the worst. "Aarrgh!" The scream tore from her throat. The second felt as if it had melted into her skin. She screamed again, shuddering violently, scalding tears chasing each other down her face. She endured the third lash, closing her mouth and tensing as much as she could. The pain was insufferable. With the fourth blow, her limbs grew heavy and she distanced herself mentally from her body, as if it wasn't hers anymore. She stared up at the clear, inked sky, her eyes wide, flooded with tears, her brow furrowed as she pleaded with the stars to save her. But no salvation came from those cold, distant orbs. She hung her head; she was defeated. And so were the Rhajok'Don.

2

Resistance

From the cliff ledge, Ugoki looked down at the destruction of his village. The communal house was nothing but a pile of dirt with a few grass stalks sticking upwards. Rhajok'Don bodies lay on the mossy ground, some sinking into the mud bath which was now coloured red with blood. His eyes scoured the scene, searching for Nis'Ka's body but the smoke and darkness made finding anything nigh on impossible. Had his young nephew also been taken? Ugoki's thoughts ran round and around in his head, as if looking for a place to hide. He sighed heavily, hoping the young Rhajok'Don had survived his ordeal. Steeling himself, Ugoki raced through the tunnels, jumping over bodies where they lay; he had to know – one way or the other – he had to at least try to find out. Reaching the place where Nis'Ka had fallen, Ugoki halted his frantic rush, staring blankly at the earth. There was no sign of the boy, all that remained was a rapidly congealing pool of blood.

Trembling with exhaustion, his spirit aching with grief, he let himself slump onto the blood soaked lichen as his kinsmen, like silent ghosts, drifted to his side to sit with him.

Finally, Ugoki roused himself. "We can't stay here." He shook his head slowly from side to side. "They'll be back."

One of his kinsmen, Masuka, tugged at his arm to gain his attention. "Where do we go?"

"We'll travel west, through the forest, try to find another tribe. Hopefully they'll give us shelter." Try though he might to disguise it, he could hear the lack of conviction in his voice. Holding back the urge to just get to his feet and run, run as fast and as far as he was able, he marshalled his thoughts. If he didn't find some answers, and quickly, the remainder of his tribe would die. He met Masuka's frightened gaze. "Go, quickly, and search for any survivors." His eyes flickered over the rest of the small group. "Split into pairs and cover as much ground as you can thoroughly search. We meet back here.

Thirty minutes later, the survivors reassembled.

"Nothing... there's... no one out there left alive." Masuka, the eldest kinsman's voice trembled with shock.

Ugoki kept his head bowed, unwilling to witness his tribesmen's pain. "Gather all the food stuffs and necessary items you can carry. Be swift. The longer we stay, the more chance there is of those murderers returning."

Within the hour, the small band of Rhajok'Don set off, wearily towing their scant provisions, moving silently towards the furthest edges of the forest.

* * *

As they tramped through the woodland, the trees gradually grew bigger and the foliage became denser and as they approached the centre, the ground turned to muddy decomposing bark and leaves. This was a tree graveyard; a place where the tallest trees had fallen, leaving an opening, allowing for the ground to fertilize and reseed. Once the opening was large enough, the saplings could take advantage of the limited, hazy sunlight once more and the forest life cycle would start over again.

Shortly after entering the dead space, Ugoki became aware of a scuffling to the south. Quietly motioning his men to wait, he went to investigate.

Concealing himself in the undergrowth, he peered gingerly towards where the noise was coming from... to see a middle-aged man appear from behind a tree, carrying a basket and stick. Ugoki recognised the man's build, it was similar to those who had attacked his village, yet, this man looked harmless. The events of the past few days, however, had taught him not to take any chances. He threw himself forward on all fours, making himself as fierce as possible.

The slender man jerked around as he heard a branch crack behind him, stumbling backwards into the blossoming brambles. "Please! Don't... don't hurt me! I'm a friend."

To Ugoki's surprise, the man spoke Rhajok'Don. Slowly, he relaxed his posture and stood up. "You know my language."

"Yes." The man pushed himself to his feet, ripping the sleeve of his olive tunic in the process. "I'm Connor," he said. "I'm part of a Resistance group. We're on your side. We fight the Zygeth as best we can with our small force."

Ugoki stared at him. "My tribe was attacked by mounted men. They destroyed my village and took all the women and children. They were these Zygeth?"

The stranger nodded hurriedly. "Yes, that's what they've been doing for many, many years. They allow you to re-populate, then they take you away to slavery." Connor stretched his hand towards Ugoki in a gesture of peace. His heavy-lidded, subdued, but friendly, grey eyes swept over Ugoki. "We want to help your people."

Ugoki imitated Connor, stretching out his hand also. Suddenly the sound of four Rhajok'Don, charging through the undergrowth as they raced towards them, reached Ugoki's ears.

"Wait!" he called and the Rhajok'Don stopped immediately.

Masuka stepped forward. "You were gone for so long, we grew concerned."

"I'm fine," Ugoki hastened to reassure his kin. "You'll never believe..." He pointed to the man they had stumbled across. "He speaks Rhajok'Don."

Connor casually walked over to greet the new arrivals. "Hello," he said, managing a nervous smile.

"How do you understand our language?" Masuka asked.

"Your language was originally known by the founders of our group. We go on teaching it because in order to help the

Rhajok'Don, we must be able to communicate with you," Connor explained.

"How many of us have you known?" Ugoki asked.

"We've fought beside a number of tribes – we've even succeeded in preventing one village from being taken. Since then our numbers have dwindled, and the Rhajok'Don moved on. A few stayed with us." Connor shrugged. "But they've all gone now."

An idea came to Ugoki – maybe he could join the group; strike back at these brutal invaders – revenge the massacre of his village?

"Come, Ugoki, we must go," Masuka said, beckoning him.

For a long moment Ugoki stood, undecided. Then he gave himself a mental shake. He could not abandon his tribesmen now, nor could he force them to go along with him, into a dangerous situation. Reluctantly, he turned to the stranger who so quickly had come to feel like a friend. "Connor, I honour you, but I must go with my kin now." He held out his hand and Connor shook it this time.

"Stay safe." Connor nodded as the Rhajok'Don departed.

* * *

Another day passed before they reached the forest's edge. As they emerged, in the distance, purple smoke could be seen drifting from a number of locations. More villages had been destroyed. The sight tore at Ugoki's heart and gnawed at his gut. Increasingly, he was becoming convinced that he could not simply stand by and let this go on happening.

Picking their way through a recently demolished Rhajok'Don village, their eyes met with total devastation. All that remained of the buildings were piles of rubble with trails of smoke issuing here and there through the debris. The dead males lay in haphazard piles around which a dark cloud of buzzing insects hovered, biting at the mangled bodies and amputated limbs. A few scavenger birds feasted on the fresh meat. The five refugees gazed emptily at the scene of atrocity. Ugoki looked away feeling helpless. A hatred such as he had never known burned in his breast.

Grimly, they set about cremating the bodies: the funeral pyres burning long into the night. Finally, as the fires burned down to ash, they assembled a small camp and numbly and in virtual silence shared a small meal before settling down. As his kinsmen crowded together seeking sleep, Ugoki sat staring up at the stars, dulled tonight by the smoke. His thoughts were all of Kinoko. How, he asked himself over and over, could he find a way to help her? If he did nothing she would be lost to him forever and the idea of life without her was something he could barely stand to contemplate. No matter which way he looked at it, only one solution presented itself. His only chance of finding and helping Kinoko was to join the Resistance. Ugoki scrubbed his hands across his face. He had men who relied on him. But Kinoko also relied on him. He sighed out loud; his kin would manage without him. They had handled themselves well in battle – they could take care of themselves. Come morning, he would retrace his steps and seek the Resistance. Having made his decision, he lay down next to his kin and drifted into an uneasy sleep.

* * *

The next day, he was first to be up and as he paced around the camp he struggled with what words he would use to tell his kin that he was leaving. Taking a small sack of crushed oats from one of the packs, Ugoki tipped some into a pot and added water. He stirred the sludgy porridge until it was ready, then shook the huddled Rhajok'Don awake.

"Here." He handed round stone bowls from which steam curled into the air. "Breakfast." The tribesmen awoke quickly and were soon making short work of their food.

Ugoki cleared his throat. He glanced at his men. Somehow, although he knew exactly what he wanted to say, the words would not form themselves. "I want to go back," he blurted. "I can't hide and pretend this isn't happening. I'm going to join the Resistance and fight. Masuka stopped eating, his mouth hanging open, disbelief painting his face. "What? We need you!"

Ugoki put down his bowl and got to his feet. He was silent a moment; slowly, he shook his head. "As the eldest you have authority," he told Masuka. "You have enough experience to lead this tribe and rebuild it." He placed a hand on Masuka's shoulder.

"Ugoki! I believe we'll better ensure our survival if we all stay together."

"I will not leave Kinoko to those monsters!" Ugoki said sharply.

Masuka put down his bowl and lowered his head. "I understand and I respect your decision."

"Then this is where we part ways, my brothers." Even as he spoke, the conviction was growing in Ugoki that he had made the right decision.

Resuming his seat, he picked up his porridge bowl once more, refusing to acknowledge the awkward silence that now hung in the air. Once in a while, one or other of the Rhajok'Don would glance at him before quickly looking away. Ugoki resisted the urge to make small talk. The sooner they accepted the idea of him leaving, the better.

After breakfast, Masuka knelt down before Ugoki, with the others following suite. "You'll be remembered as the hero who fought our enemies with great force," he said, his mouth twisting into a tight smile. "But more than that, you'll be missed by your brothers. Go! Follow your destiny. Go with our blessings and revenge the great wrong done to our race."

Ugoki ushered the small band to stand before solemnly knocking horns with each of them. "Goodbye, my friends. Spirit willing, we may yet meet again," he told them. Turning, he headed away from his kinsmen, back in the direction they had come.

* * *

A hard day's walking brought Ugoki to the same place he had first seen Connor. Having now arrived, he realized he had no way of finding the man unless he happened to come back to the same spot. As he was pondering what to do next, he heard a rustling of leaves and the distinct crackle of someone walking over dried sticks. Darting to his feet, Ugoki swept his eyes around the area. Cautiously, he moved towards the noise. Peering through the foliage, he spotted Connor, his basket half-full of plump, ripe berries.

Becoming aware of another presence, Connor glanced up. "You've returned." He peered over Ugoki's shoulder. "I see you're alone?"

Ugoki nodded. "Yes. I want to fight; I want to stop what's happening to the Rhajok'Don. You and your group offer me that opportunity."

"The others? They don't share your conviction?"

Ugoki paused. He shook his head. "I think they're still in shock. And, afraid. They just want to put distance between them and what happened."

Connor's expression turned grim. "Yes. I understand that. But running won't stop it happening again. What we need are warriors, like you. There is only one thing which will stop the Zygeth – and that's making them realize that the price of continuing is too high." He slapped Ugoki on the shoulder, a big smile washing his face. "You've made the right decision." He stretched out his hand in greeting. "Come, I'll show you around?"

Ugoki nodded slowly.

* * *

He followed Connor along a trail littered with dried, fallen leaves. Beneath the leaves, Ugoki knew, the forest floor teemed with insects, hidden under the sludgy, decomposing bark and the parasitic, surprisingly moist, bio-luminescent fungi.

Five minutes south of their position, Connor came to a halt and started to move aside some of the undergrowth, revealing a door. The heavily bolted, circular entry lay horizontal and was camouflaged by sticks which projected out beyond the edges, allowing it to remain concealed once closed. Compost covered the sticks for added protection. Three sturdy handles poked through the sludge, one at the top, one at the right, and one at the bottom. The greenish-black oxidation showed how much the metal had corroded but despite that, the handles retained their strength. Connor unlocked the door before grabbing two of the curved bars, bolted at either end. He heaved the door upwards as Ugoki quickly grabbed the third handle to help, although he could see that Connor was capable of lifting the door on his own.

There was a hissing noise as the locks released and the bronze hatch opened, bursts of whitish-grey steam ejecting from the once concealed edge of the foot-thick door. A damp, earthy smell was the first thing that Ugoki noticed as he peered down the crudely lit descending tunnel. A single electrical lamp was buzzing at the bottom of steep, steel ladders: an eerie invitation into a derelict looking dwelling. Connor balanced himself on the muddy ladder before he began his descent down the hastily manufactured steps, quickly disappearing into the flickering shadows. Ugoki climbed after him, steadying himself against the wall, feeling the coarse, crumbling texture. Fleeting light glistened against the moist cracks and pale, lime-green moss clung sparingly to the curved architecture. The sound of Connor's heavy footsteps echoed around them and small drips of moist mud periodically detached themselves from the sides and dropped into the depths. Ugoki pulled the heavy door downwards and it thundered shut above them, the whole tunnel shook, rattling the casing of the lonely lamp. The damp earth squelched under Ugoki's feet as he stepped off the ladder. In the dim light, he spotted an adjacent tunnel through which a path ran, terminating at another large, metal door, looming through the dull, yellowish light. Connor removed a second bulky key from his belt and inserted it into the lock; again, Ugoki heard a hiss as it opened outwards. Connor had to turn his head as warm steam gushed into the tunnel. Stepping through the arched doorway, Ugoki found himself in a warmly lit, maze-like entrance chamber, actually, he realized, it was more like a large, oblong room. Curved stone walls sloped upwards to a smooth, arched ceiling. Moulded into the damaged walls were protruding weight-bearing reinforcements, crusted with flaking metal. They held the arches in place, and they periodically partitioned the room.

Ugoki looked around in amazement. "Tunnels – like home, only better."

"This way, I'll show you to the barracks." Connor guided him through under the partitions, his shadow split into four from the overhanging lamps.

The barracks, a semi-circular chamber housing at least two hundred beds, had plastered walls and narrow, individual sleeping places where some men lay resting.

"We always have men on missions who come back exhausted," Connor told him. "These barracks are rarely vacant." He pointed towards one of the narrow cots. "You can have this bed. Please, rest. I'll fetch you some food from the mess hall."

"Thank you." Ugoki lowered himself down onto the thin mattress. The bed was a little small for him but he didn't mind; it was strangely soft when compared to the forest floor but he found it quite comfortable. Relaxing, he stretched out on his back. Abruptly, he was overwhelmed by loneliness. For the first time in his life there was no warm crowd of Rhajok'Don bodies to huddle up with. Worse still, his Kinoko was in some place he didn't dare to think about. Tears slipped from under his closed lids, chasing each other down his face. Ugoki ignored them, tonight, he thought, was going to be a long one. No sooner had he formed the thought than exhaustion pulled him into a deep, dreamless pit.

* * *

When he awoke, Ugoki saw a bowl of mushy green paste had been placed on the cabinet next to him. Glancing around himself, he saw Connor seated at the other side of the bed.

Connor smiled. "I trust you slept well?"

Levering himself into a sitting position, Ugoki swung his legs to the floor. "Thank you, yes." He nodded slowly. "These… beds are comfortable."

Ignoring the spoon, he reached for the porridge and set to work, spooning mush into his mouth with his fingers.

"That's been there all night," Connor told him. "Let me get you something fresh."

Ugoki shook his head, cold porridge was his daily sustenance. "Thank you, there's no need, this is good."

A young child stood, fiddling with his fingers, in the doorway to the barracks. About five years old, he wore loose-fitting, worn, beige clothing. He seemed to be waiting for something.

Connor looked over at him and smiled. "Someone wants to meet you, Ugoki. He's never met a Rhajok'Don before." He waved the boy to enter and the youngster quickly shuffled across the floor. "Xanoth and his sister are orphans; they're cared for by their aunt. Their parents died liberating a Rhajok'Don village."

Hearing that was like a blow to the stomach. Ugoki put down his bowl, his appetite suddenly fled. He stared at Connor, shaking his head. "Why?" he whispered. "Why do people whose battle this is not, sacrifice so much?"

"Ahh!" Connor smiled down at the sandy-haired, skinny youngster who was now standing shyly, round-eyed gaze fixed on Ugoki. "Come! Come." He placed his hand on the boy's shoulder, drawing him even closer. "Introduce yourself, he encouraged."

Xanoth beamed a gap-toothed smile at Ugoki. "Hello," he said. "I'm Xanoth."

"I am honoured, Xanoth." Ugoki bowed his head formally as he spoke.

The child tentatively reached out and touched Ugoki's grey, cracked skin.

"It's good to meet you," Ugoki added, holding out his hand. Xanoth took hold of his finger with his tiny hands and solemnly shook. "You look like a strong young man."

Xanoth looked to Connor, confusion plain on his face. "I don't understand."

Connor smiled. "Ugoki admires how strong you look."

Xanoth blushed and grinned, then jumped up onto the bed. He reached into his pocket and pulled out a sketching pad, swiftly drawing a picture of himself and then another figure, obviously meant to resemble Ugoki, he drew a curve capped with arrows at both ends, joining the figures.

"Yes." Ugoki smiled. "We will be friends." The boy touched his heart, and they had a shared connection of loss.

Xanoth drew another arrow, then two swords criss-crossing, then a final arrow, before carefully printing the word 'Zygeth'.

Ugoki softly put his large hand onto Xanoth's shoulder. "We'll fight the Zygeth together."

Xanoth didn't understand the words, but he was intelligent enough to know Ugoki agreed. He beamed up at the huge Rhajok'Don before lunging at Ugoki and throwing his arms around him.

Ugoki's joy at Xanoth's obvious acceptance was tinged with sorrow as he remembered the last hug he had received from his nephew. He ruffled the child's hair. "You remind me of someone very special," he murmured.

"Hmm?" Xanoth gazed up at him, a frown creasing his small forehead, his brown eyes puzzled.

"He said," Connor translated, "you remind him of someone special."

"Awww." Xanoth hugged Ugoki again.

Ugoki ruffled his wavy, sandy coloured hair again before looking to Connor. "How did you all find this place?"

Connor chuckled. "Now that's a story going back generations. Everyone you see here was born right here after the evacuation." He looked around the barracks. "This whole place was renovated by previous generations."

"What was it like when your ancestors found it?"

"This was all just a derelict network of tunnels, originally built by the banished, maybe a millennia ago," Connor explained. "When our ancestors evacuated from Kraag'Blitz, they brought with them some simple technology and worked with it here to develop these liveable dwellings."

"Banished? Kraag'Blitz?" Ugoki echoed, bewildered. So much new information, so much he had never heard of or even imagined existing.

"Hmm." Connor shot him an appraising look. "We'll save explanations about the banished for a later time, when you're a little more settled in. But, Kraag'Blitz is where the Zygeth come from."

"I see." Pictures rose up in his mind; kinfolk running, screaming, dying. He shook his head.

"Are you okay? Would you like more rest?" Connor asked, concerned.

"It's... so much to take in." Ugoki was dismayed to hear the way his voice shook. "I was so ignorant – we all were. We thought the world was simple. I had a perfect, humble life – and within a week, everything's gone." He glanced down, blinking back tears.

"I know," Connor said heavily, "and I'm sorry for your people." He sighed. "You need time to heal – take that time, take as long as you wish." He patted Ugoki's muscular arm before nudging Xanoth. "Come on, Xanoth."

The boy was still tucked against Ugoki. He did not stir. Ugoki realized he very much wanted him to stay. He met Connor's gaze. "I'll look after him," he promised.

Connor nodded. "Very well, in that case, I'll see you both later," he said, stroking the boy's hair.

* * *

Xanoth nudged the sleeping Rhajok'Don with the crown of his head and was rewarded by a grunt as Ugoki slowly woke. Lifting his arm, he allowed Xanoth to clamber underneath it. Although sorrow still weighed on him, the Rhajok'Don chuckled, happy for the momentary comfort being close to another warm body brought.

Xanoth giggled as he sat up. Pulling his notepad and pencil off the bedside cabinet, he passed them to Ugoki.

"Oh! You want me to draw?" Ugoki tapped the paper. The youngster nodded quickly.

Ugoki's hands were much too cumbersome for a child's pencil and as soon as he touched it to the paper it snapped in two. Xanoth chortled loudly. Taking the end half, he sharpened it with a knife.

"You have a knife?" Ugoki exclaimed, surprised. "You need to be careful with that... dangerous!" He pantomimed cutting himself.

This time he was careful to hold the pencil gently. Drawing a knife on the paper, he wrote the name in his own language, then drew a big cross with diagonal lines.

Xanoth grabbed the pad and drew himself with the knife and a criss-cross of swords, then the word, 'Zygeth' and wrote 'safety' next to it.

Although he couldn't read the word the child had written, Ugoki could easily discern its meaning. "I understand," he told him.

The small boy took hold of Ugoki's finger and tugged. "Come," he insisted, leading the Rhajok'Don out of the barracks.

* * *

Xanoth led Ugoki under one of the partition arches and into a small cubby room. Sat at a desk was Connor. He immediately looked up as they entered. "Hello, you two," he said, smiling.

"Show him what you teach me," Xanoth demanded.

Connor pushed to his feet. His grey eyes scrutinized Ugoki. "Your call," he said. "Are you ready to start training?"

Ugoki met his gaze unflinchingly. "I'm ready to learn all you can teach me."

Connor nodded, once, sharply. "All right, follow me. You can watch Xanoth go through his paces." He smiled grimly. "Maybe you can pick a few things up." Shuffling the papers he had been working on together, he threw them into a drawer. "Let's go," he said, ushering them out of the hideout.

* * *

The distinctive sideways slanting trees were Xanoth's playground and immediately they reached the forest, he ran straight to the closest tree and began to climb.

Impressive for one so young, Ugoki thought. The boy went up the tree like a hini; one of the small, native, tree reptiles. A scant few feet from the top he stopped, clinging to the swaying branches with one hand, he aimed his knife at a small target flag pinned to another tree, a fair distance from where he hung, before throwing the blade with as much force as he could muster. The knife sailed through the air and hit the target squarely, though it failed to embed deeply due to Xanoth's undeveloped muscles. Gradually peeling free, it dropped to the forest floor.

Ugoki's eyes widened in amazement. "He's good, very good, in fact."

"He's learning fast," Connor agreed. "I believe he'll be our best Resistance fighter yet. He seems to passionately want that, too," Connor said proudly.

Xanoth climbed quickly and agilely down the tree, using branches as swing ropes. He dropped off the bottom branch and ran over to Ugoki and Connor. Connor opened his arms and the young boy hugged him.

Releasing Xanoth, Connor stepped back and sized up Ugoki. "How about you?" he asked. "Shall we see what you know?" Connor took up a fighting stance.

Ugoki studied him silently, noting the spare, lean frame and muscle tone.

"Defend yourself."

Ugoki nodded.

Connor launched a forward punch at his head.

Ugoki blocked it by crossing his arms in front of his face. The force of the impact rocked him on his feet a little but he narrowly avoided losing his balance completely.

Connor nodded. "You could stand some work on your balance, but otherwise, very good." He picked up a nearby thick stick. "Now, try against a weapon." He quickly jabbed at Ugoki's torso.

Ugoki, grunting with effort, managed to repel the attack successfully.

"Very nice, I'm impressed." Connor tossed the stick a few times, then passed it to Ugoki. "Now you. Strike me."

The Rhajok'Don swung the stick from right to left. Connor

nimbly dodged it, grabbing Ugoki's wrist, he yanked it to his side, whilst quickly turning, effortlessly twisting the stick from Ugoki's tight grip.

Ugoki yelped sharply. "That... I need to know." He smiled at Connor.

Connor patted Ugoki's back. "I'll start your training tomorrow, for now, let's go back inside and get some warm food."

"Indeed," Ugoki agreed, grasping hold of a metal handle. They heaved the hatch door open and descended down the ladders, back into the safety of the hideout.

* * *

Over the years, Xanoth and Ugoki sparred for hours each night. They developed an unbreakable bond, like that of a father and his son. Both vowed their honour to fight for the freedom of the Rhajok'Don and to end the torment of the Zygeth.

3

Kraag'Blitz

Fifteen years later…

The flicker of a flaming torch danced against the ash-grey, uneven bricks. Wooden batons covered in wax soaked twigs were mounted in crude sconces, their illumination bathing the scene in an eerie glow.

Xanoth breathed in the bitter cold air as he hid behind a wall in the gloomy shadows of the L-shaped chamber, seeing it plume out in front of him as he exhaled. He could smell the dirty, fusty stench of the dungeon from where he crouched. He adjusted his dark, earthy coloured hood, pulling it down low over his perceptive hazel eyes; the rest of his face masked by a few days growth of stubble. A single wave of sandy hair dropped from under the cloth and hung just above his brow. Xanoth's almond-shaped eyes narrowed; he lifted his gloved hand, clenching it.

"Wait! Guard!" he mouthed to a second shadowy figure. Jaydaan squatted behind him, wearing similar attire, short knives attached to his pant legs. Xanoth tensed his square jaw as he waited.

Slowly, he inched forward, risking a quick glance around the corner. "There's just one." His whisper was barely audible. Snatching another covert glimpse around the corner, he surveyed the guard's movements. "Can't see his throat." He kept his voice low, his eyes fixed on the formidable sentry, who, wearing a black, ground length robe, patrolled the area. The slender watchman strolled in the opposite direction, looking briefly into the prison cell on his right. He turned around, making his way back towards them and Xanoth caught a quick glimpse of the man's intricate armour before hastily tucking himself behind the wall again. The armour plates were made from unusually thin, smooth, black metal. A strange, fluorescent aqua-blue glowed in between the plates.

Xanoth's gaze narrowed. "Enchant!" he mouthed. As the guard drew closer, the two men observed his shadow growing larger as the sound of the armour plates sliding across each other with a disconcerting rasping noise increased. From his position, the guard was just about visible to Xanoth. A foot appeared from behind the stone wall, closely followed by a second foot, and then by the rest of the Zygeth's armour-plated body. Xanoth signalled to his companion: time to attack. "Psst..." he hissed, baiting the guard. The Zygeth turned sharply, glaring down at them through two, diamond shaped, eyeholes, slashed horizontally into the anonymous helmet. Xanoth just had time to take in at close quarters the way the eyeholes glowed with the same oddly luminescent aqua brilliance that shone from between the plates before his companion notched and let fly a thin, wooden arrow. It arched diagonally upwards, its specialised metal tip accurately penetrated the vulnerable throat area, striking home between two elongated cheek guards. The bright-blue glow winked out immediately and the armoured body went limp, crashing to the hard stone floor like a sack of rocks. Xanoth and Jaydaan wasted no time in springing into action. Xanoth running straight over to the prison cell, while Jaydaan stood over the guard's body. "They'll know he's dead," Jaydaan said. "They always know when an enchant's killed. We need to hurry."

Xanoth grabbed the charcoal hued bars and rattled them. "Damn!" he swore. "What the hell are these things made from? Can't be metal, they don't make a sound." He peered into the darkness of the cell. Slumped on the floor lay a large, stocky figure, clearly unconscious.

"The hand... quick."

"On it." Jaydaan unhooked a small hatchet from the inside of his coat. The blade of the weapon was crafted from the same materials as the arrowhead. Swiftly locating an exposed area between two armour plates, he raised his arm above his head and took careful aim. Swinging the blade down, he precisely and cleanly amputated the lifeless guard's hand, the axe effortlessly slicing through the armour. Jaydaan scooped up the hand and threw it over to his Commander, who deftly caught it.

Xanoth pointed the fingers towards the locking mechanism, executing a series of movements. The lock made a quiet humming noise then clicked open and Xanoth, tossing the severed hand back to Jaydaan, hurried inside the cell. Hunkering down beside the figure, he ran a practiced eye over his still form. Dried blotches of bloody cloth stuck to the pale-grey skin and the ripped and dirty prison clothes revealed obvious signs of torture; bruised and bloodied needle-marks were visible at all the major arteries and veins. Xanoth grabbed one arm and shook it insistently. "Ugoki, we're here to get you out. C'mon, wake up."

Ugoki's head rolled slowly to the side, Xanoth watched him fighting to open his eyes.

"W… where… what?" he muttered, his words slurred. A dribble of saliva trickled from the corner of his mouth, dripping down and around his left jaw horn.

Xanoth glanced over to Jaydaan. "We'll need to lift him," he said, frowning." Easier said than done, Ugoki was twice the size of him or Jaydaan. "Here, grab his other arm," he instructed, pulling Ugoki's right arm over and around his neck and hoisting him upright. Jaydaan took Ugoki's other arm and together they heaved him onto his wobbly legs, dragging him along between them. They half dragged, half carried him into a long, dimly lit corridor with barred windows, behind which the panes had been thrown open to the outdoors.

A groan alerted them to the fact that he was beginning to rouse as the fresh air revived him. "Wh–wha?" Ugoki croaked, dazed, his blank eyes fixed on the dark, cloudless, starry sky beyond. The three of them staggered on toward the end of the corridor and the heavy metal door set there.

"I'm... I'm... " Ugoki stammered, struggling to find his feet. "I'm good," he finally managed, shrugging free of his friends and walking, a trifle unsteadily, but unaided.

Jaydaan reached the door first. Opening his cloak, he casually pulled out another dismembered hand. "Be a whole lot easier if one hand opened all the doors," he muttered, pointing the appendage at the lock, then carrying out a series of movements. The mechanism hummed quietly and clicked open. Pulling the door wide, the three men entered the next chamber, the torches flickering as colder air rushed in. Inside the square room lay two dead guards – the work of Xanoth and Jaydaan. One was slumped over a solid looking desk, his head inches from a candlelit lamp, papers scattered around him. Another lay on the floor, with empty eyes and an arrow in his face; his right hand was missing.

"This way," Xanoth hissed, darting down a short corridor on their left. Jaydaan took the third, and final, severed hand from within his cloak. As he was positioning it, an alarm began to wail, getting louder with each second.

"Enchants on their way... hurry up with that lock," Xanoth growled.

"Damn!" Jaydaan swore as he fumbled with and dropped the hand. Scooping it up quickly, he continued with the complicated sequence of movements that would unlock their escape route. A whooshing sound, signifying steam being forced through thin pipes to release the locking system, reached their ears and the last door slowly began to open. Substantially bigger than the others, constructed from the same metal but three times as thick, it was the heftiest door Xanoth had ever seen. Another body with its hand missing greeted them outside. It lay on an unnaturally flat mountain summit. The bitter air buffeted them as they stepped over the threshold and the dark, midnight-blue, almost black sky above them glowed with a slight amber sheen; the glow of a sun which never rose.

From further back down the corridor came the sound of running footsteps against the hard stone floor; Jaydaan raced ahead as they grew louder. Xanoth threw a hasty glance over his shoulder, relieved that the guards were not within sight yet. He and Ugoki stuck close to Jaydaan, hearing the steam powered door hiss closed behind them.

Xanoth's feet pounded against the rock, the whole plateau was a burnt-umber colour, dusted with powdery sand. Despite the polluted, steamy air, smelling of burnt coals, his breathing was steady as he ran. Behind him, he heard the steam door make its distinctive whooshing sound as it opened. Checking over his shoulder again, he saw two Zygeth enchants exit the prison in hot pursuit. Their swords were drawn and the aqua glow from their armour was stark against the dark skies. Jaydaan, the fastest of them, drew close to the edge of the cliff, the prison was located so high up it was only when he was within a meter from the edge that he could see the smog-ridden world below. Jaydaan stopped abruptly, the sheer drop almost upon him, as if the earth had simply fallen away and left a clean, vertical, ridge bridging upwards to the flat surface on which he stood. His feet dislodged an avalanche of small rocks which tumbled down over the edge. Jaydaan, helpless to resist, followed their path with large, terrified, bronze eyes, watching as the rocks fell out of sight through the thin layer of sooty steam. A single bead of sweat dripped from his dirty forehead to join the rocks in their seemingly endless drop. Jaydaan stretched his arm out towards the desolate, sunless sky and drawing in a lungful of the chilly atmosphere, he began to chant a summoning verse.

He waited... A moment passed, then two more. Jaydaan began his chant again. This time, barely had the last sound slipped from between his lips when two, huge, winged orpids, their elongated, lizard-like bodies glinting against the darkness, swooped up from below the smog. Their long, narrow tongues flickered as they gave voice to shrieks that carried across the plateau. Muscular, lengthy necks swayed with their aerial movement, allowing for their scaly heads to remain perfectly still and focused. Jaydaan gestured to them and they perched themselves, surprisingly gracefully, on the edge of the cliff, gripping onto it with their powerful hind legs. Once landed, the creatures lowered themselves, tucking their wings against their sides, their striking, spherical black eyes with contrasting orange pupils looking directly at Jaydaan. In a fluid, practiced motion, he mounted one of the orpids, feeling its cold, rough skin under his hands as he gripped its shoulders. Glancing back, he saw that Xanoth and Ugoki were within sprinting distance of their ride. Close behind them, in the dark, something flashed and Jaydaan saw a group of Zygeth running towards them, their swords gradually beginning to illuminate, gleaming with the same aqua light as poured forth from their eyeholes and from between the armoured plates.

"Oh no," Jaydaan whispered under his breath. "Run!" he shouted, tapping the orpid's neck, signalling it to launch. Immediately its colossal wings unfolded, revealing webbed, elongated fingers. The creature lifted upwards from the cliff edge, its webbed, fanned tail extending as it dropped fractionally, adapting to the weight it was carrying. It hovered in the air.

Jaydaan frantically beckoned to his companions to hurry. The second orpid could sense they were close; it shuffled its clawed feet and extended its elongated fin tail in preparation for flight. Xanoth was first to reach it, he jumped onto its back, offering his hand to Ugoki and pulling him up to sit behind him. He tapped the creature's neck and it lifted off the ground. For a long, terrible moment, it struggled to stay airborne with the added weight of Ugoki, but then it stabilized and the powerful wings rode the currents as it moved, painfully slowly, to put distance between the Zygeth and themselves.

The guards ceased their pursuit and Xanoth's gut tightened as one of them raised his sword, aiming it at the fleeing men. He and Ugoki watched in horror as the dreaded luminescent blue ooze began to pulse down the soldiers' raised arms, flowing in malign waves into their swords. Glowing bolts of fluorescent blue substance pulsed from the weapons, following a deadly course towards the escapees. The first shot flew harmlessly between them, but the second grazed Jaydaan's arm, burning straight through his leathers. The blue goo instantly attached itself to his skin where it began to bubble, slowly absorbing his lifeblood and, still glowing brightly, changing colour as it drew more and more of the scarlet liquid into itself. The contagion rapidly spread outwards from the wound as Jaydaan desperately attempted to get rid of the substance off his arm, instead infecting his hands. He shook his arm as panic overtook him but the stuff held strong, continuing to expand before his terrified eyes. He turned to Xanoth, his face signalling defeat.

"It's too late!" Jaydaan called, his voice flat, accepting his fate. "Get out of here – get home!"

Xanoth and Ugoki watched helplessly as he let go of his mount and was instantly blown off the orpid's back, his body tumbling downwards as the infection, unstoppable, took over more and more of his body, turning him into a glowing, mottled-blue human torch.

Stunned, Xanoth and Ugoki watched until there was nothing left to see, as Jaydaan's body disappeared into the polluted, grey cloud.

"Jaydaan!" Xanoth screamed, cords standing out on his neck. "No! He's not going to die," he spoke half to himself. He was about to signal his ride to turn when Ugoki interrupted.

"We can't help him now, Xanoth." Ugoki's voice was regretful. "What we can do is to make sure his sacrifice stands for something. But to do that, we have to get home."

Glancing over his shoulder, Xanoth looked back at the isolated prison atop the table top cliff. A sheer drop surrounded the keep on all sides, much like a castle with a moat, although, this 'moat' was not for keeping enemies out. He could see the Zygeth enchants charging up their weapons, ready to attack them again. He reacted almost automatically, urging his orpid into a steep descent, the second creature following instinctively. The deadly bolts could not keep up with the speed of their plunge, passing harmlessly overhead. Xanoth watched as the Zygeth rushed to the cliff edge as they descended through the sooty blanket of cloud.

Once under cover, they grimly headed for home.

* * *

The polluted industrial atmosphere choked Xanoth and the toxic chemical smell clogged his nostrils, the acrid taste of contamination drying up the inside of his mouth. He blinked hard as his irritated eyes filled with tears which quickly overflowed onto his cheeks. He swiped them away with his sleeve as they re-emerged from the lethal smog. Their orpid was still flying strong, even with the hulking Rhajok'don on its back. Below them lay a dark, dismal world, a city in the grip of a brutal yet chaotic authoritarianism. Pollution hung like a heavy pall and visibility was low, smoke obscured the horizon. Even so, looming through the haze, the silhouettes of tubes, towers and pipes belonging to the factories, spewing foul impurities, along with steam from towering chimneys could be seen. Every once in a while, a chemical explosion would send forth contaminated debris, together with bursts of dirty grey steam raining into the sky. Xanoth knew that, even though they were barely visible, the factory buildings themselves, as well as the fetid slums of the slaves, lay below him and he was mindful not to steer his orpid too low. Casting his gaze ahead, the horizon seemed so far away, the beauty of its glow destroyed by the products of industry. Xanoth set his course through the pollution, heading for a cleaner land that lay in front of them, letting their flight carry them away from the oppression of Kraag'Blitz.

4

A Soul Must be Seen

Isolated forested areas became visible as Xanoth and Ugoki approached the safety of the Resistance hideout. Even though they were still quite a distance away, they could see the familiar tai-qay trees, gradually increasing in size as they drew ever closer. There was very little life in the low-lit, cold, harsh climate, but each life form was perfectly evolved to habituate these lands. Xanoth could already smell the soothing herbaceous aroma of the leaves wrapping around him and the feeling of safety warmed his soul.

The two orpids flew towards the staggered woodland; nature had naturally curved the trees' wide, strong trunks to hold the leaves towards the limited sunlight. As the riderless orpid led them down through the smooth, leafy blanket, they prepared to land in a group of the tallest trees. Xanoth protected his face as the leaves whipped back as they followed the first orpid down. Heavy shade greeted them as they flew under the canopy; giant trunks were twisted towards them trying to leech the last bit of sunlight from the sky, reaching up over the tops of the younger, shorter trees in front; their greed for light forcing them to an almost unsustainable growth. Many of the huge trees had already met their fate; slumped trunks collapsed inwards, succumbing to their own mass, their fallen leaves scattered, a testament to the hostility of the land.

The crackle of dry leaves could be heard as the claws of Xanoth's orpid touched the ground and the animal rested its weight. Dismounting, they immediately began to plough their way through the old foliage that covered the entirety of the level undergrowth, heading for the concealed door. On reaching it, Xanoth quickly unlocked it with a bulky key. Ugoki pulled the hatch open and was the first to descend the rusted ladder. The dingy lamp wobbled as it always did as Xanoth pulled the strong metal door inwards, letting the steam gush out. Inside, there was a cleanly dressed man sat in a shaded side room on their left. Getting to his feet, he ducked his head under a low, stone, arched doorway and hurried over to them. His wizened face, illuminated by the dull, unsteady glow of the crude electrical lamps, revealed the features of an experienced veteran of war. Xanoth wiped his grimy hands on his trousers and offered his hand. The two men greeted each other with a firm handshake.

"Just the two of you?"

Xanoth lowered his head. "Jaydaan fell, General."

The older man's heavy eyelids closed momentarily, a gesture of respect to their fallen ally. He looked to Ugoki. "Were we compromised?"

"I... Ugoki's voice was uncertain, "don't know, sir. Regretfully, I've no memory of my time as a captive."

General Connor's leathery lips puckered whilst he contemplated his next sentence. "The soul-seer will help you remember."

"Soul-seer?" Xanoth echoed. In all his twenty years of life, he had never before heard of such a being. "Sorry, sir," he apologized immediately, "didn't mean to interrupt."

The General cleared his throat. "Very few know about her, and fewer still ever seek her knowledge. She resides in the lowest levels of this bunker." His mouth twisted into something vaguely resembling a smile. "She never leaves her dwelling," he told them. "She's locked in from the inside, hidden away from everyone."

Xanoth and Ugoki watched as he pulled a thin chain from under his top and over his head. There was a small ivory key attached to it. He handed the key over to Ugoki. "Take this, go as deep as the tunnels will carry you, there you'll find the soul-seer."

"Yes, sir." Ugoki dipped his head before turning away. Abruptly he swivelled back around. "This... soul-seer? Does she have a name?"

"Anamai – Her name's Anamai," Connor told him.

Ugoki walked away, leaving the sound of his footsteps ringing through the room.

Xanoth looked at his superior. "May I?"

General Connor's sharp grey eyes followed Ugoki as he crossed the room. He nodded. "Go!"

Xanoth jogged agilely under the arches, the patchy glow from the lamps lighting his way with a criss-cross of contrasting shadows.

He caught up with his friend just as he opened the door, revealing yet another wet, dingy tunnel. "Hey, hold up," he called. "I'm coming with you."

* * *

Finally, Xanoth and Ugoki made their way into the very deepest level of the underground hideout. The smell of stagnant water was all too familiar, although at these depths it was staler than usual.

A thick, burnished door awaited them; like the other bunker doors, this one was made with hefty metal plates, sturdily held together with heavy bolts. However, the door which faced them had an extra feature, a small ivory engraving, a perfect fit for the key. Ugoki removed the chain from his pocket; the key was too delicate for his bulky Rhajok'Don fingers to manipulate, so he passed the almost weightless object to Xanoth. Holding it gently, Xanoth inserted it into the keyhole and turned it carefully. They heard a soft click and then the edges of the door began to glow with a golden hue as steam gushed free, the door becoming incredibly lightweight, until Xanoth was easily able to pull it open with just the tips of his fingers.

An embossed, brass coloured, rectangle door stood at the end of the tube-shaped corridor. Brilliant, almost white light reflected of its glossy metal surface, forcing Xanoth to squint as he entered the walkway. The light radiated from evenly spaced lamps, embedded into the plaster above his head. A few bronze pipes ran over the immaculately smooth plastered walls, leading into whatever place was behind the door. There was no handle, instead, there was a smooth hand-wheel, positioned under a glazed, bulging, circular window. He ran his hand over the elegant metal door engravings, mimicking nature in design. The small window was not completely opaque; Xanoth could see a blurred image beyond it. He firmly held the hand-wheel with both hands and turned it. The wheel mechanism swivelled with ease, and the clanking of metal could be heard from inside. The door opened.

* * *

A musky floral aroma surrounded Xanoth and Ugoki as they stepped into the arched hallway, accompanied with an immediate feeling of tranquillity. The hallway resembled other, similar bunker areas, with plastered walls and alloy bolted shafts; however, the bunker in which they stood did differ markedly, the plaster was not cracked, but smooth and pristinely painted a rusty-sand colour. The metals were not oxidised, but highly polished and gleamed as if recently cleaned. The entire area looked newly built, although Xanoth surmised that it must be as old as the rest of the place. The glow from brown-tinted glass lamps, swaying gently from short chains attached to the ceiling, was mellow and peaceful. Nestled between three partitions were two side rooms, one to the far right and another to the middle left. A warm, sunlight-orange glow flickered from the room on the far right. The two men exchanged curious glances before making their way towards it, passing low chestnut tables glossed to a high shine and adorned with unusual metal gadgets. Similar items hung from the clean walls and one, larger device, at the end of the hallway caught Xanoth's attention. Crossing to stand in front of the wooden wall mount, covered in cogs and dials, he admired the skilled craftsmanship before his gaze was drawn back to the rest of the gadgetry. He frowned, confused. Where had all this stuff come from? Glancing at Ugoki, he saw he was busy examining the curious objects, his face filled with the same curiosity that burned within himself. Xanoth reached out towards the soft, pastel cream curtain, moving it aside and entering the beckoning, mysterious room.

Anamai, the soul-seer, sat on a chair carved from a rich, sepia coloured wood, marbled with knots; the cushions supporting her delicate frame were fashioned from a honey-gold fabric and the whole thing gave off a warm lustre. The small, octagonal shaped room was sparsely but tastefully decorated throughout, in a manner completely foreign to Xanoth. But, lovely as her surroundings were, they could not even begin to compete with the breath-taking beauty of the seer. She was staring in rapt attention at a wall-mounted painting, but as she became aware of him, her wide eyes, disconcertingly pigmented the hue of flame, fixed on him. A coral-tinted, silken veil covered her deep mahogany hair, revealing below it a flawless, milky-white complexion, fine cheekbones and a mouth that Xanoth might easily have sold his soul to kiss. But it was her strange, flame-touched eyes that mesmerized him; ageless and calm, yet speaking of sorrow. Her legs were crossed under the long, satin, embroidered gown and her hands lay elegantly on her lap, one cupping the other.

Xanoth tore his eyes from her, fixing them instead on the painting she had been examining so intently when he entered. He gazed at an enticing view of lush, green lands and straight, upward growing trees. Scattered in the grassy landscape were vividly colourful plants, and crowning the scene was a clear, brilliant-blue sky, lit with the purest of sunshine.

"May I help you?" Anamai's voice was like a dash of spring water.

Xanoth shrugged himself awake. He cleared his throat. "Err... Yes," he stuttered. "You're... err... the soul-seer?"

"I'm Anamai, yes," she said softly. "I know why you seek me." She gestured toward the curtain. "Please – tell your friend to enter."

Xanoth nodded, flicking back the curtain and inviting in the Rhajok'don.

Anamai slipped off her veil. Smiling, she directed them to deep, comfortable looking seats. "A pleasure to meet you both," she added. "Please... sit." She waited for them to be seated before turning to Ugoki. "Your path is hidden from you," she told him, her eyes wearing a faraway expression.

Ugoki watched her full lips as she spoke.

"I can help you remember." She rose, opening up a cabinet to her left and lifting out a bronze armillary sphere which she placed on the cabinet surface. The object and its meanings were unknown to the two comrades. They looked on in amazement as Anamai spun the spherical framework of rings and they began to rotate independently of each other. Each glistening ring caught the light as it turned, creating a dazzling aura of reflected light. Ugoki found himself helplessly fixated on the moving parts of the sphere as Anamai's low, soothing voice began to release him from his conscious self. "Relax and let go," she instructed. "Relax and let go." Anamai crossed the floor to Ugoki. She stroked the back of her soft hand down his rough, chunky skin. "This safety will not last... " she murmured. "... It will not last."

Abruptly, she knelt down, grasping Ugoki's arm and shaking it. "You sense danger!" she said, harshly.

"You were taken! Where was that – where were you when they came?"

Ugoki raised his head, his movements sluggish. "I... was...

foraging. The... the Zygeth... they ambushed me."

"Go on," the seer ordered. "Keep telling me."

"They... It must've been a scouting party. I... they attacked from the trees... I was taken by surprise." Ugoki's body twitched. "I didn't even see them."

"You're in your cell now," Anamai pressed. "You can hear the guards. What's happening?"

Ugoki suddenly stiffened. "There's a sword at my throat. I'm chained," he told her. "I'm on my back. There's flames and torches everywhere." His head turned right, then left. "More cells." He grunted, flexing his arms against invisible restraints, which, nevertheless, appeared completely real to him. "I'm... I'm strapped down in another cell." He paused, confusion plain on his face. Then he screamed, thrashing his head wildly from side to side. "Bright! They're so, so bright!"

"What's bright?" Anamai questioned.

"The lights. My face is covered with a mask – a see-through mask." The hypnotised man winced. "It hurts. There's tubes, red tubes everywhere." He winced again and grunted with pain. "It's all too bright! My eyes are burning! I can't see!"

Anamai saw a trickle of tears squeeze from beneath his bulging, closed, lids. "I see outlines. It's them!"

"Tell me what you can hear!" Anamai urged.

"Bubbles... " Ugoki answered, his voice ringing with certainty.

Anamai paused, frowning, as if at a sudden recollection.

"I can't hear them." He craned forward in his imagined restraints. "I can hear bubbles and the walls are red tubes. There are too many reflections. It's too bright." Suddenly agitated, he shouted, "No, they're hurting!"

Anamai saw that he was shaking like a leaf in the eye of the storm.

"Hurting me!" he whimpered.

Anamai's voice was soothing. "You feel no pain, warrior.

Relax. There is no pain."

The tension immediately poured out of Ugoki and he lay still.

Once she had the situation back under control, Anamai went straight to the heart of the matter. "Were we compromised?"

"No." Ugoki's answer was quick, short and without doubt.

"Vakim erg." *Wake up,* Anamai spoke in Ugoki's native tongue, using the back of her throat to 'cough' the words. The instruction, given in Rhajok'Don aided Ugoki to come out of his deep sleep state. His eyes blinked open and closed a few times as he came back to himself, his face clearing of confusion. He pushed himself upright, letting out a heavy groan.

Anamai looked at Xanoth. "You can tell the General that our position is safe," she told him.

An awed Xanoth nodded in return. "Thank you."

A small, fleeting smile touched the corners of Anamai's mouth, but her eyes remained shadowed and troubled. She lowered her head with a sombre nod. Her work complete, she once more pulled her veil over her burnished mahogany tresses and returned to her beautifully crafted chair. Crossing her legs and laying her hands on her lap as before, her flickering, orange eyes stared again into the painting on the wall, as if there had been no interruption and no one had visited her that day at all.

Watching her graceful movements, Xanoth could not help but feel pity for her, although, if pressed, he would not have known why. One thing he did know; he was completely captivated by the mysterious, melancholy maiden, and one day, he was certain, he would frequent her dwelling again.

5

Twisting Dreams

The gentle sound of water as it flowed, rippling over small rocks, gradually awakened Xanoth. He lay on his side, cushioned by sweet smelling grass. The fresh spray of unpolluted water misted his face and excited his senses. Around him, the air was filled with the exotic calls of jungle birds and the whirring of insect wings grew increasingly louder as sleep fell away from him completely. He shaded his eyes from the penetrating solar blaze that blinded his vision. Pushing himself to his feet, enjoying the feel of the mild warmth of the grass beneath his hands, he stopped, locked in place momentarily as a colourful fluttering insect flew past his nose. An insect he had never set eyes upon before. In a daze, he stared around himself in wonder, marvelling at the lush green trees, shooting, straight as an arrow, up to the sky, in stark contrast to the slopping growth he saw daily. Blue and pink birds flew from their upper branches and smooth fronds of verdant ferns sprouted between their strong trunks. Spying a stream, Xanoth made his way over to it and knelt down, gazing into the clear, translucent flow. Never in all his years had he seen water as pure as this. A longing for a life where trees grew tall and proud; where the sun rode high in a clear blue sky, and where brooks meandered crystal clear filled him. Please, he begged silently, let this be! The plea tore its way out of his being with such intensity he felt himself tremble with the need to make it so. A small splash brought his attention back to the brook and the shoals of brightly coloured fish. Below them he glimpsed turquoise coloured algae and pretty pebbles. Tracing the stream to its source, Xanoth saw a small, tiered waterfall, its froth pluming forth only to settle as it flowed.

Peering closely at his clean-shaven reflection, Xanoth

scrubbed a hand over his face before running it through his trimmed, recently washed, tidy hair. His attire was spruced and well kept, without any tears or patches and, as he dropped his hands to the water, he noticed how spotless they were, without even a hint of dirt under his nails. His bewildered gaze went back to the creek... and then a blissful smile washed over his face. He dipped his fingers into the tepid flow and hesitantly drank. The liquid slipped down his throat like the finest nectar; Xanoth tasted a hint of berries as well as an underlying mineral tang. A brisk, warm breeze carried the uplifting scent of blossoming sylvan and a sudden gust stirred the waters of the brook.

An image formed, coalescing out of the ripples – flame-touched eyes; eyes that not so long ago had turned him into a stuttering idiot in the face of utter beauty. The surface stilled, becoming clear again and Xanoth saw that the pebbles had disappeared and instead armillary spheres covered the stream bed. Drawn to one particular sphere, he lifted the palm-sized object from the slow current, inspecting it. Holding the base, he flicked the outer ring, activating the inner bands, watching as they spun rhythmically, bouncing glistening beams of light off the metal. An unnatural calm stole over Xanoth.

"Save my people." The voice of Anamai echoed in his skull. "Please! Save them!"

An abrupt change in pressure bolstered the wind, bringing it shrieking around him. The vivid blue sky darkened, shadowed with the polluted charcoal hue of a dense smog. Xanoth's sandy coloured hair was flung around wildly by the tempest and the heavy roll of thunder from deep within the smoke reached his ears. The acrid fumes of toxic chemicals filled his lungs and he spluttered, vainly attempting to dislodge the muck. He watched in horror as black, lumpy, sludge poured down onto the once crystalline stream, churning and bubbling as it flowed. Before his eyes, the stunning landscape of trees darkened and their trunks cracked and bent, disease twisting them over to a sideways position, their bark lost its healthy appearance, drying out and hardening and their leaves deepened in colour. A plague of bioluminescent mushrooms marched their way towards him, sprouting from the brown sheets of crisped, dead leaves where once there had been lush grass. Damaged, rusted pipes emerged from under the muddy sludge and traversed across the defiled creek. While Xanoth watched, the corrupted metal widened and cracked, grey smoke burst from the fractures causing him to cough heavily.

The smoke thickened around him and once more he heard the seer's voice. "Save... My... People... "

Her voice rang in his head as he spluttered himself awake. He shook his head, glancing down at himself and pulling in a deep lungful of air. His clothes were still grimy from his rescue mission and his hair, in need of a wash, lay limp and straggly over his temples. He surveyed the discoloured, torn sheets of the rudimentary bed. Sighing, he glanced around at the neighbouring cots. There were two rows, all vacant, all recently made. He was alone in the barracks. Hearing the door open, Xanoth let himself fall back against the pillows, his eyes tracking the smartly dressed man, in typical military attire, who was making his way down the aisle towards him, carrying a folded garment.

"Get up. It's morning," he growled, throwing Xanoth's hooded coat over to him; still dirty from the night before, the strong smell of sweat and steam was all too familiar.

Xanoth yawned, eyes clouded by sleep, he glowered at the officious individual, only to be jolted wide awake. There – brief but unmistakable, was a spark of flame glowing in the man's eyes.

Xanoth's first thought was of Anamai. Feeling around in the pockets of his leather jerkin, he pulled out the fine silver chain with the delicate ivory key on it. For a long moment, he stared at its dainty structure. His brow furrowed as he remembered the dream. He needed to see her, his inner voice insisted, and when his inner voice was that persistent, Xanoth knew better than to delay. He put the key back into his pocket, jumped up from the midway bed and hanging his coat over his shoulders, hastily jogged the length of the spacious, rectangular room, with its familiar architecture, decrepit walls and corroded metal pillars.

* * *

Arriving at the lower levels once more, Xanoth sniffed the stagnant air and he knew he had only one more ladder to climb down. Squelching through the grimy, muddy dirt, he made his way towards the door. Something was different! As he got closer, he could see flaking plaster and other signs of deterioration. The door was ajar and there was no keyhole, just a completely rust-crusted hole. Xanoth gasped in disbelief at what he saw. The door was so corroded that it could not close anymore. As he gripped the handle, he felt the rough metal crumble under his palm.

The corridor beyond was in much the same condition, eroded surfaces exposing the brickwork underneath. Continuing towards the next door, he noticed the lamps above him were hanging by their wires. The brass no longer shone, the exquisite door had lost its glamour and the engraved metal sheets had peeled away from its surface. He pulled at it and it jerked open.

Here too was more dereliction; the ravages of time had worked their lack lustre charms against the structure, roots protruded through gaps between the bricks searching for nutrition. The intricate gadgets that had so held his attention were gone, including the piece at the end of the hallway that he had been fascinated by. All around him was rot: old tables and burnt out oil lamps. The side room on his right was screened by a tattered, shredded curtain, weaved with cobwebs, mottled with mould and festooned with dust. Gingerly, Xanoth pulled aside the cloth. Anamai's elaborate armchair was withered and worn, water dripped onto the once rich fabric of the upholstery from roots hanging above it. Xanoth frowned: the cushions bore a faint scorch mark. The big, comfortable chair where Ugoki had sat was collapsed under the weight of a fallen chandelier; it, too, was water logged from the steady drip-drip of brackish moisture, leaking through the gaping hole left by the once pristine light fixture. There were only the two chairs, the one in which he had sat was gone. His eyes roved around the room. The painting that the seer had been so intent on, and which had drawn him deep into its vibrant landscape, lay blackened and scorched, propped up at an angle by a smashed oil lamp. Xanoth scrubbed his hand across his face, unable to believe what he was seeing. What the spirit was going on here? Remembering the cabinet, he glanced over at where it had stood, relieved to see it still there. Hurrying over, he knelt down, opening up the carved doors. Empty! There was no sign of the armillary sphere; it had vanished along with everything else.

Xanoth pulled in a shaky breath. Ugoki! Perhaps Ugoki could shed some light on all this?

* * *

Returning to the upper levels, Xanoth made his way to the residential living quarters. The bunker might not be the most homely of places, but the garrison had at least constructed somewhere clean, well-kept and self-sufficient, with all the amenities of a civilized society. The door steamed shut behind him, accompanied by the clank of the well-oiled pipe mechanism. In front of him was a basic, chromite stairway with a simple, soldered handrail, leading down to a spacious and airy social hub. The usual abundant smell of burnt wood and damp steam was less dense here and the architecture differed from the general bunker design – the resident miners who had first excavated and built the facility had creatively altered this part of the underground complex. The locals who now occupied it referred to the large, central area as 'Haven's Heart'.

As Xanoth made his way down the stairway, he noticed the generators were rattling more than was usual. Fortunately, that didn't seem to have impacted on the energy production; the low hanging light fixtures, encased in their circular, cage-like pendants, moulded from opaque, orange-tinted glass, were shedding their illumination as brightly as always.

Housed in the underground lofty ceilinged town centre were basic shops, together with domestic services. Cut into the stone walls, with wooden façades giving them a simple but smart appearance, they stretched away from him on either side. In between were narrow, arched passageways, chiselled deeper into the rock, leading to other rooms and facilities.

Xanoth scanned the faces of the crowd of around twenty to thirty people going about their business. He could not see Ugoki amongst them. Deciding to head to the mess hall, he ducked into the first walkway on the left. The well-lit corridor passed by more side rooms and a sudden acute smell of pure alcohol ambushed Xanoth's senses. He had almost passed the medical room when a familiar figure caught his eye. Backing up a little, he saw Ugoki sitting on a crude bed in the square room. A medic, wearing the clinical attire of loose trousers and simple tunic top, neat and almost white in colour, was busy washing his hands in a large glass bowl, preparing to re-dress Ugoki's injuries. Xanoth hurried across to his friend.

"Xanoth. What is it?" The injured Rhajok'Don stared at him curiously. "You seem agitated, youngling. Has something happened?"

Xanoth wasted no time. "The soul-seer, you and I... saw her? Yes?" Xanoth held his breath, waiting impatiently for Ugoki's answer.

"The... what?" Ugoki's expression said more than his words.

"Anamai... she helped you remember what happened when

you were captured. The sphere? You can't have forgotten."

Ugoki shook his head, his eyes, worried. "I remembered everything when I woke today," he said, slowly and carefully. "We weren't compromised. I've already informed the General."

Xanoth raked his hands through his hair. "What? But we saw her last night! The General himself ordered you – he sent us down to the lowest levels."

Ugoki gave him a searching look. "Xanoth... are you feeling okay? Last night, as soon as we got back, you went straight to the barracks and I came here."

"What? No!" Xanoth glared at Ugoki. He pulled out the chain with the key on it. "Then where did this come from? Huh? Tell me that. I sure as spirit didn't have it when I set out to bring you home."

"Xanoth," Ugoki said, his voice calm and reasonable, although his eyes, fixed on Xanoth, were still troubled. "I gave that to you... last night. I figured if I was lucky enough to still be alive, you might be able to make better use of a 'lucky charm'."

"What? This is crazy!" Xanoth wheeled away from the bed.

"Xanoth! Wait! Where are you going?"

"I need to see the General," Xanoth called back. "Something's going on here and I want answers."

* * *

Running through the bunker's entrance hall, Xanoth hurried into the side room. General Connor was in his usual spot, browsing through documents. Surprise widened his eyes as Xanoth, one palm on the desk, leaned forward, holding up the key.

"This key... you gave it to Ugoki."

"That's correct, soldier. Evidently he passed it on to you."

"You gave it to him when you sent him to the soul-seer, Anamai." Xanoth was convinced the General had the answers he needed and would be able to explain what was happening.

General Connor pushed away from the table, treating Xanoth to a long, appraising look. "Excuse me?

"Anamai – the seer, the woman you sent Ugoki to. Beautiful. Fire in her eyes."

The General got to his feet. "If I didn't know better, I'd say you've been here too long." He shook his head. "The only woman here with strange eyes is our Rhajok'Don weapons maker, and she's, let's say... " He twitched one eyebrow, "an acquired taste, if you know what I mean."

He walked around the table to Xanoth, clapping him on the shoulder. "Son, I've been fighting my whole life, and that key, that key, my friend, has kept me safe. That trinket brings good fortune." He smiled briefly. "I gave it to Ugoki as a symbol of his survival. Clearly it's destined to be in your hands. Treasure it, and I assure you, it will keep you free from harm."

Xanoth stared at the mysterious key in his hand, completely captivated by it for a few slow breaths. He was about to put it back into his pocket, changing his mind, he dangled the chain in front of him before looping it over his head and tucking it under his shirt, close to his chest... and... close to his heart.

6

Infiltration

The sound of a large bell chimed through the barracks as Connor marched down the corridor "Attention! Attention!" he called.

Most of the soldiers immediately awoke: a few covered their heads with their pillows, wanting to sleep on, but in vain. Xanoth had not been asleep; he lay, propped in a sitting position, reading a book. Laying it down on a side bench, he got to his feet and walked over to where the General was waiting.

"What is it, sir?"

"We've received a message from Johan."

Xanoth's ears pricked. "Where's he posted?"

"He's situated below Kraag-Blitz's eastern prison, the lower levels, assigned a smelting job. Excuse me." The General brushed Xanoth aside and continued on down the aisle, ringing the bell. "Attention! We have intel from Kraag-Blitz. There'll be a briefing in five minutes."

* * *

A slate chalkboard hung at the front of the briefing room. Xanoth chose the chair closest to the board and waited impatiently for the other nine chairs to fill up. It didn't take very long, and looking behind him, he could see a row of soldiers now lined the back wall. Ugoki was last to join them, slipping into the room just ahead of the General.

The single ceiling light dimmed as the chalkboard was illuminated.

Connor strode into the small room on Ugoki's heels. "Morning." He gazed around the assembly. "As we all know," he said solemnly," Lieutenant Jaydaan fell to the enemy yesterday.

It's fitting that we all honour his courage and take a moment to pay our respects to a great soldier and a good friend. He will be much missed by us all." He lowered his head, clasping his hands together in front of his waist.

Chairs scraped as the seated men rose, standing at loose attention. The silence was absolute; losing any man was a blow to the small unit, but Jaydaan had been not only a brave and skilled soldier, he had also been well liked.

Respects paid, the General turned to the business of the day.

He cleared his throat. "Unfortunately, Jaydaan had all the tech-hands when he fell so, for us, receiving this information from Johan has come at a good time. We've now got a run at getting hold of some replacements." Turning to the board, Connor started to draw a schematic of Kraag-Blitz. "From here." He stamped the chalk against the slate. "On the eastern side, is a chance for us to get one of our people inside. The plan is to scout these southern cliffs," he told them, circling around the area with his chalk, "for a good vantage point of the prison base."

Out of the corner of his eye, Xanoth saw a soldier get to his feet. "Sir, would it not be best to move in from the north."

"No, the intel from Johan informs us of an increase in defences to the north. It's too dangerous," Connor said, dismissing the man's objection.

"We'll scan the prison area. We're informed there's a way in about here, with no enchants." He put a cross on the map. "We don't know specifics; our man will need to establish the facts."

Another man stood. "How many guards, sir?"

"We don't know," the General admitted reluctantly, "but even ten loyalist guards would be easier to take down than one enchant." He nodded, signalling the soldier to sit down. "We'll have our most experienced warrior in the field."

Xanoth absently rubbed at his stubble.

"So, to cut to the chase, we all know who's best qualified for this." Connor pointed at Xanoth, who immediately got to his feet.

"Yes, sir."

"Once inside," the General spoke over his shoulder as he cleaned the board, "Johan will be waiting at the hatch. He'll guide you after that, and the rest is up to you."

A hand raised. "Sir, do we know if Johan will be alone."

"No, we don't. But I trust him to do his best." Connor paused, glancing around at the assembled men. "Any more questions?"

Xanoth raised his hand. "May I read Johan's file. I want to know who's got my back."

"Certainly." The General nodded. His piercing grey eyes swept over them all one last time. "Okay. If there's nothing else – you're all dismissed."

The soldiers hastened to follow orders and the room quickly emptied. Connor gave Xanoth a searching look. "I know Jaydaan's death must've hit you hard," he said.

Xanoth stiffened. "Yes, sir."

"Are you ready for this, son?" he asked. "There's a lot riding on it."

"Yes, sir, General, sir." Xanoth squarely held the other man's gaze. "They're going to pay for what they did," he ground out.

Connor clapped him on the shoulder. "Meet me in my office and I'll get you that file.

* * *

Xanoth dropped onto a chair standing next to the General's desk and opened the thin file. On the first page was Johan's photo. Staring back at him was the type of guy Xanoth knew would draw the attention of any hot-blooded female. He turned to the next page. "Okay, my good looking friend," he muttered, "let's see who you are."

The dossier told Xanoth little more than the basics. Johan had lived in the lower levels of Kraag'Blitz with his family. He had first come to their attention as a member of a sympathiser group with connections to the Resistance. Imprisoned by the Zygeth for surface infringement, he was now forced to live as a loyalist.

"Be loyal or be killed, more like," Xanoth mumbled, before continuing.

Johan had become useful as an informant for the Resistance, sending his messages by carrier-corr. Xanoth paused a moment, reflecting on the small, easily trained, featherless flying creatures so vital to the Resistance communication network. The Zygeth currently had Johan working in the lower smelting pits, meaning he had been forced to leave his family behind.

From what Xanoth could work out, reading between the lines, most of his motivation was fired by a desperate need to be reunited with them. Nothing in the records suggested he was anything other than a trusted informant.

Xanoth raked his fingers through his unruly, sandy coloured hair. It all looked fine but there was always an element of risk when you were working with someone new. It wouldn't be the first time the Resistance had been betrayed by someone they had trusted. He put the file back onto Connor's desk. Well, as the old saying went – the only way to tell if the stew was good was to taste it.

* * *

Xanoth left the forest hideout on his orpid, heading for the dark haze that signalled industry a few miles ahead of him.

The orpid flew down through the smog and nestled on the southern mountainside behind soot-covered boulders. Xanoth dismounted. Taking care to stay under cover, he took out his compass and checked his bearings. Happy that he was where he should be, he dug into his pack and found his binoculars, eagerly scanning the complex below.

A dilapidated mass of factories with tall, blackened, smoking, evil smelling chimneys desecrated the land. Periodically the gas produced as a by-product would explode into blue and orange gouts of flame, a sudden crackle would follow. Electrical wires, connected by pylons, steamed as the smoke drifted by. Pipes linked the high concrete blocks: cracked and rusted, they dripped molten metal onto an unremittingly grey, derelict surface.

Xanoth's attention was caught by a pile of half-cooling solder in the debris. Widening his focus, he scanned across the tops of the highest buildings. Those, he knew, housed the prisons, similar to the one he had rescued Ugoki from. One of those ugly, jutting towers was what he was searching for. Running his gaze closer to the ground, he spotted two figures in charcoal grey armour with jet-black under-plates – no sign of the tell-tale blue illumination. These were Zygeth loyalists; regular soldiers, quite often prisoners themselves, who had been manipulated to fight for the Zygeth, through fear of death for themselves or their loved ones. Very few loyalists had consciously made a choice to fight for Zygeth beliefs. Loyalists were an easier target altogether than the enchants and generally thought of as disposable by the Zygeth.

The guards were monitoring a chained Rhajok'Don slave who was pushing an overloaded cart along predesignated rails that weaved in and out of arches under the factories.

"Save my people!" The words burst into his head, haunting him and he found himself wondering what they really meant – who exactly were her people? Were they the Rhajok'Don?

Staying low, under cover of the smog, he ran across the crumbling, pock-eaten rocks of the mountainside and tucked himself behind another rock formation. He scratched his beard; a few weeks growth, and refocused his binoculars.

In the far distance, he could see the camps, with their sludgy ground and massive, steel bunkers; this was where the slaves lived out their brutal existence, and where they died. The Rhajok'Don were bred like animals, straight into slavery. Xanoth

could just make out a few figures; these would be the unfortu-
nates who had displeased their masters and were now paying for
their mistakes by being humiliated and collared to the impris-
oning bars, lying naked in the sooty scum. There were four
enchants guarding the gates.

Off to his right, something moved. Quickly Xanoth refocused
the binoculars, just in time to witness a Rhajok'Don defiantly
shove an enchant back, away from him. Without hesitation, the
Zygeth guard struck down the Rhajok'Don, killing him outright.
Xanoth's hazel eyes blazed. His inner need to help these people
was overwhelming.

Sensing movement above him, he glanced up as, on the
horizon, something streaked across the sky like a meteor. Xanoth
stared at the strange sight as the glowing object slowed
fractionally before smashing into the ground with a noise like a
bomb blast, tearing up great chunks of blackened earth. Looking
at the crash site, he could see a half-buried, pod-like object. His
eyes widened as he saw what appeared to be a door open, and
out of which, to Xanoth's complete disbelief, climbed a solitary,
male figure. From his hiding place, Xanoth watched as the man
stared around himself before collapsing onto a nearby rock. Even
from a distance, Xanoth could see his confusion. Lowering his
head into his hands, clearly upset, he made no move to seek
cover, seemingly oblivious to the danger he was in.

Abruptly, another craft hove into view. As it sped closer,
Xanoth could see that this was a roofless vehicle, approaching at
speed, heading towards where the stranger still sat. Xanoth
followed the vehicle with his eyes as it set down. Again, the
metallic skin of the strange craft cracked open to reveal another
male figure, who waved urgently at the stranger, urging him
aboard. Xanoth saw the first man hesitate, staring around
himself again, before slowly walking towards the vehicle and
stepping up into it. No sooner had the opening the stranger had
disappeared into closed behind him than the craft turned and

sped across the murky landscape once more, heading back the way it had come.

Xanoth stared after it until it dropped out of sight behind one of the tall buildings. "What the spirit —" he muttered. The mystifying vehicle – whatever it was, demanded investigation. But, he had other priorities first.

Determinedly, Xanoth resumed scouting for the location of the prison. Finally, after what felt like an age, as his eyes crawled slowly over every inch of the tallest towers, he located the area he was looking for to his right. His eyebrows twitched in surprise. "Well, well!" He grinned mirthlessly; this was turning into a day packed with surprises. Two loyalists were escorting a Rhajok'Don who was pushing a leather covered mining crate. The Rhajok'Don effortlessly hauled it off the track before dragging it across the filthy street and into a refuse cluttered alley between two, old, disused buildings, concealing it from view. Xanoth chewed his lip. Time to make his move, he decided. Checking the vicinity for any onlookers, he quickly descended the mountainside. Uncoiling the grappling hook looped over his shoulder, he expertly scaled one of the cranes that stood, like so many skeletal mammoths, dotted across the ravaged landscape. Arriving at his new vantage point, he once more focused his binoculars.

One guard held the Rhajok'Don's chain, while the other busied himself preparing the crate. Finished, he inserted his hand into a square hole in the wall; a panel flopped down. As Xanoth watched, the Zygeth tapped in a code and moments later blue, rectangular edges appeared under the crate and the mud began to shift as an elevator slowly moved downwards, taking the leather covered box down with it.

Xanoth knew he would need to move quickly if he didn't want to miss his chance. Seconds crawled by as he crouched on top of the crane, scanning the scene below. Then his opportunity came; the guard stationed by the crate looked away, out across the soiled, gloomy streets. The other Zygeth had retreated further into the alleyway. Xanoth swung into action, abseiling down the rust pitted metal carcass of the crane. As he lowered himself into the stench-ridden pits of Kraag'Blitz, the stomach churning smell of burnt sewage and nearby silos filled his lungs. He pulled up his half-face mask and hastily ran for cover behind the crumbling remains of a wall. Removing his reinforced double-string bow from his back, Xanoth notched an arrow and moved towards the crate. He had to hitch a lift on that thing before it left him behind. Carefully judging the drop, he leapt.

His jump landed him on the top of the box as it jerked its unsteady way down the shaft. Xanoth fought to keep his balance, his eyes on the guard at the top of the elevator. He had barely succeeded in getting his feet squarely under him when the Zygeth glanced down, to see him perched precariously on the container. His arm went to his weapon but, before he even unsheathed the deadly sword, Xanoth's arrow found its mark and the guard went down. Another armour covered face appeared at the edge of the shaft; the second Zygeth had come to investigate what had befallen his comrade. The arrow took him in his left eye-slit and the body tumbled past Xanoth, to the floor of the lift shaft. Luckily, any sound the body might have made was muffled by the electronic whir of equipment. Tucking himself under the heavy leather sheet, next to the crate of blue crystalline lazulic metals, Xanoth settled down for the ride.

* * *

The descent was shorter than expected; Xanoth prepared himself as the lift rumbled to a halt. Lifting a corner of the leather cover, the dim illumination of the crystals revealed a long, dark, single-track tunnel ahead, sloping gently downwards towards a soot encrusted, round hatch.

A loud hiss heralded the activation of an automated, steam-powered device, pushing the crate onto the track and then retracting immediately. As the box slowly clunked along its way, a door at the end of the passageway inched open and torchlight flooded the tunnel. Adrenaline coursed through Xanoth's system; he was trapped and headed for certain capture. Instinctively, he threw aside the cover and crawled to the rear of the crate. Jumping down, he made his way back up the track as far as he could. Huddled against the wall, Xanoth concealed himself with his cloak. There was no sign of Johan and, having come this far, Xanoth had no idea how to proceed. All he could do now was wait… and hope.

After what seemed like far too long, the hatchway opened and Xanoth's eyes, by now so adjusted to the dark that even torchlight made him squint, teared up immediately.

The crate stopped at the edge of the opening, before juddering over onto the next track, the hatch slamming shut behind it.

Once more he was alone in the lift-shaft tunnel, with only the smell of greasy mud and the sound of dripping water from the slimy walls. Muffled voices reached him from beyond the door. Then there was silence.

* * *

"We need you." Her gentle voice was insistent.

Xanoth opened his eyes; sitting motionless in the dark, he must have drifted off. The sound of the tunnel door opening jerked him back to full consciousness.

"This way! This way, quick!" Someone hissed.

"Johan?" he whispered.

"Yes, come on!"

Xanoth crawled quickly through the tunnel and Johan's young, careworn and anxious face came into view. Hopping into a stone-bricked room, lit by torches fastened to every wall, he spied three tracks leading through other circular doors. There were more, regular, doors next to the hatches. He nodded at the slim young man standing to one side of the entrance way.

Johan barely acknowledged him. "We need to get you out of here fast." He was already on the move. "I'll show you where to go," he mumbled over his shoulder. "You'll need to eliminate an enchant in the next room," he told Xanoth nervously, pointing to the door on the far left. "I only have access to that room. There are steps leading upwards, giving you a clear view of the sorting room. An enchant patrols the area, but there's a spot behind the conveyor machine where he'll be hidden from sight." He looked at Xanoth. "Your mission is to take him down – get the hand, and I get you out again."

"Got it." Xanoth nodded.

Johan pulled opened the door. "Go! Now!"

Briskly, Xanoth made his way inside the room and ascended the steel stairway, crouching down behind a barrier. Peering through the gaps between struts, he watched as crate after crate poured its contents onto sectioned metal belts. The smell of burnt coals, steam and mineral dust hung in the air. The belt rolled through the first machine and a dull blue filth burst out of it as the metallic crystal chunks were crushed before the conveyor carried them on to the second machine. This one shot high pressure water over the pulverized lazulic so that it rolled out the other end gleaming, to continue on through a further hatch and into another room beyond.

Three prisoners were manning the machines, dressed in shabby, grey overalls. A single Zygeth enchant patrolled the area, keeping a close eye on the prisoners. These workers, considered too weak to be loyalists, were also slaves but were treated with a little more dignity than the Rhajok'Don. Xanoth took careful stock of the route as the guard patrolled behind the men, looking over their shoulders. Glancing up he could see the steel girders in the ceiling.

He waited for the guard to disappear behind the conveyor

machine before producing a rope from an inside pocket of his coat and looping it over one of the beams. Hoisting himself up, he replaced the cord and proceeded slowly, and in a crouch, along the joist. Reaching the spot where the guard would be hidden from the rest of the room, he waited for his moment.

The enchant was slowly making his way down the room towards Xanoth. Removing a small, curved knife from under his belt, he readied himself. As the guard stepped underneath him, Xanoth jumped. He landed on top of the Zygeth, his weight bearing the enchant to the ground and pinning him there. Before the guard had even collected himself, Xanoth struck, burying his knife in the enchant's skull. The cold blue glare emanating from the eye-slits of the faceplate winked out. Xanoth pulled out his blade, watching as blue goo oozed from the hole left by his weapon. Wiping his blade clean, he returned it under his belt and took out his hatchet. Without hesitation, he swung, cleanly amputating the hand with one practiced blow. Pushing himself to his feet, he opened up his backpack, hastily thrusting his grizzly prize inside. His eye was caught by the glistening lazulic and grabbing a few of the blue stones, he pocketed them. Looping his rope around the joist, he quickly hauled himself back up, ears pricked for the wail of a siren, knowing it wouldn't be long before the alarm was given. A frown creased his forehead as he watched the conveyor belt disappear through the next hatch. His gut was nagging at him, telling him to find out where those shiny pretties were headed and what they were being used for.

Hurriedly scanning the area as he crawled along the dirty girder, he saw steam billowing into the air; there had to be a vent somewhere close. Following the wispy clouds of steam, he crawled through a labyrinth of rafters, finally reaching a small opening in the top corner of the roof. A cold breeze flowed through a vent positioned above his head. It smelled of cinders and sulphur and it irritated his face as he pried the grate free. Pulling himself into the freezing, dingy, ducting behind the vent, he replaced the grate before proceeding.

* * *

Johan paced the elevator room. It was all taking too long – something must have gone wrong. Hurrying over to the sorting room, all appeared normal; the three prisoners were working at their machines as usual but the guard was nowhere to be seen. One of the workers spotted him and glanced over. Johan nodded back. He scanned the room, the workers obviously hadn't noticed the absence of the Zygeth enchant yet. He wondered what they would do when they did.

More worrying was the fact that there was no sign of Xanoth either. Anxious though he was, there was nothing more he could do. To get into the next room required a pass – and he neither had one, nor any way of getting hold of one. All he could do now was to go back to his room and wait for something to happen.

* * *

Negotiating the lumps of dirt that coated the floor, Xanoth could see other vents up ahead. Pressing on to the next panel, he pulled it aside and crawled down into another tunnel. Through the grid, although the light was dim, he could see the blue dust dropping off the conveyor belt into a smelting oven, manned by a single prisoner, 'supervised' by another enchant. There was nothing much more than that to see, so Xanoth advanced down the smog-filled pipe. Shortly, he came to a junction, one way was lit by the familiar glow of a torch, the other way lay darkness. It was from that direction that the cold air came, and that was the way he needed to go. Turning right, he crawled towards the venting point. He applied pressure to the grating but it wouldn't budge. Finally, he had to resort to kicking at it, only to watch it tumble down into a huge fan situated at the bottom of the cylindrical chimney. The force of the spinning blades made short work of the flimsy grate, smashing it into jagged pieces. A metal ladder was fastened on the opposite wall, leading up to the chimney opening. Xanoth jumped, hearing the ladder rattle under his boots. His coat billowed upwards in the draft created by the fan and it was all he could do to hang onto the stuff crammed into his pockets. The foul smelling steam congested his lungs and burned his sinuses. Covering his nose and mouth with his facemask, he grimly continued up the rusty ladder. Ahead was nothing but blackness, not even a star shed its light to guide him on his way. Xanoth wondered what the spirit he was heading into.

* * *

Back in his quarters, Johan was growing increasingly concerned. He rubbed at his clammy face, absently smearing coal dust on his cheeks as he moved restlessly around the sparsely furnished box of a room. Again and again his attention was drawn to a single picture of his family, standing on the bedside table. Johan paused in his aimless pacing. They were always in his thoughts, together with the desperate hope that one day they would be reunited. Abruptly, he was overcome with despair: would that day ever come? Would he ever be anything more than a puppet for the Zygeth: a loyalist with no loyalty? He pulled in a ragged breath, he was taking great risks in aiding the Resistance, but that way lay the best chance he had of seeing his family again. The Zygeth had, of course, made him promises to keep him loyal and slaving away for them, but he was not fool enough to think they would keep to their word. His gaze wandered back to the picture and he stared at it for a long moment, drawing strength from the brief escape from his current situation.

He couldn't just sit here, he realized. He had to go back to the elevator. Just as he reached the lift, he heard the crash of another mining crate touching bottom. In his heightened state the noise reverberated through his nervous system, his heart lurched and his breathing speeded up. Pulling himself together, he took a deep, steadying breath. Any minute now someone would come to help him with the crate and he was going to have to behave as normal when that happened. Especially when the heart monitor from the enchant activated and everything became complicated.

* * *

Midway up the chimney, Xanoth clung tightly to the metal ladder, light-headed from the venting fumes. He squeezed his eyes open and closed, fighting to clear his blurred vision and trying to ignore the nausea that churned his stomach, doggedly forcing himself on up the ladder.

A loud clanging pierced his eardrums. Xanoth lowered his head, a grimace of pain stretching his features. Even when, after a few seconds, it cut off, it went on ringing in his ears. Xanoth hung there, dazed and confused. The sound came a second time, ripping through his ears and into his head.

Xanoth recognized the sound, it was the alarm signalling the death of an enchant. Soon there would be an army of the monsters, crawling all over the building. A moment of clarity washed his senses. He had to keep going, he had to reach the exit.

* * *

Sweat beads stood out clearly visible on Johan's forehead; even though he had been expecting the alarm, it had still startled him when it came. He forced a surprised expression onto his face as he and the man who had arrived to help him with the crate stared at each other. Xanoth had to be dead, he thought despairingly, turning back to the job at hand. The alarm might be sounding, but Johan knew better than to stop work. It was for the

Zygeth to deal with any 'intruders'.

* * *

Finally, he'd reached the top. Gripping the edge of the chimney, Xanoth hauled himself up and gazed around. He was looking at four other identical, huge, ventilation shafts, venting into what seemed to be a large cave. The architecture confused him. Where was the pollution going? He assumed there was ventilation somewhere. Was there something else hidden here? Something that needed to be concealed by a cave.

Up here the contaminated air was warmer, clammier, it pressed in on him, restricting his breathing and clouding his mind. Below him was a rocky surface into which the chimney was embedded. To his relief, Xanoth found another ladder fastened to the outside brickwork. Wearily, he set his feet on the rungs and started his descent. The alarm sounded again, echoing against the cave walls below him, bouncing back and crashing around in his head with all the intensity of a mad man gleefully smashing pan lids together. He blinked hard, trying to clear his vision, his legs shook from the constant effort demanded of them. Below him, he heard voices, spurring him into action once more. Abruptly, his vision dimmed, his foot miss the next rung and he slid. For an instant he hung, like some huge bat, scrabbling frantically for a sure grip on the ladder and then he was falling.

* * *

He awoke lying on his back. Forcing his eyes open, he saw a beautiful, straight growing tree towering above him. Groaning, he pushed himself to his feet and ignoring the protest from every inch of his body, he glanced around. This was the creek from his dreams, except there were only five trees and just one bearing fruit. Anamai was sat under it, wearing the same coral gown she had worn in his other dreams. Like a moth drawn irresistibly to the flame, he walked towards her. She held out her hand and Xanoth gently took hold, his fingers touching her soft skin. He tightened his grip.

There was a flash... and he was holding a different ladder leading up and into yet another chimney. Xanoth realized it was the only chimney without any smoke rising. He could hear the alarm again but now the sound was just a delicate tinkling, pleasing to the ear.

Xanoth drew in a deep lungful of the pure, cool air, clearing his head. As with the previous chimney, he could see a ladder fastened to the brickwork; he began to climb. Reaching the top, he stared down into the enormous shaft. The mild breeze ruffled his hair, carrying with it the fresh scent of blossom. The inside of the chimney was pristine, as was the ladder leading down into it. Climbing into the sparkling clean chimney, he approached a smooth, shiny vent. The smell of blossom was stronger here; removing the grate, he entered the duct and began to walk. Rounding the next corner, he stopped short, awed by a brilliant white light pouring through another grid. This was the purest light Xanoth had ever seen. He slid his hands over the gleaming metal, peering into the duct to determine the source giving rise to such clear, brilliant white light. He was not prepared for what he would see.

"Anamai, I need to wake up now," he whispered.

7

The Void

Xanoth awoke in the familiar barracks of the hideout. "Whu?" he mumbled, raising himself on one elbow and gazing around. His last memories were of radiant, blazing white light. What he had seen within that light had amazed him; Botanical gardens framed within a perfectly pure-white enclosure, huge windows opening out on a beautiful vista, similar to the world from his dreams. Golden sunlight beyond his wildest imagination poured vitality onto the exquisite scene. Soft, fluffy clouds moved slowly by the windows and vivid potted plants raised their heads to the sky. Everywhere he turned, his eyes had feasted on tree shrubs, vegetables and fruit of all varieties. His final memory was of a lustrous feathered animal, in colours he hadn't previously known existed. Was it all a dream?

His thoughts were interrupted by the General. "You had us worried, son."

Xanoth turned his head to see Connor sat by his bed, fiddling with his watch. Xanoth was shocked by the General's appearance. Overnight, it seemed, the man had aged ten years; his lined face was tired and drawn.

"You were unconscious when your orpid brought you home. It's a miracle you stayed in the saddle." Reaching over, he clasped Xanoth's hand briefly in his. "Your mission was a success, soldier," he said softly. "We have the Zygeth tech-hand."

Xanoth breathed a sigh of relief. They had desperate need of that hand. Losing it would've necessitated another dangerous mission and slowed down the work of the Resistance.

"Rest now," Connor said gruffly. When you're ready, we need you in the lab."

"I'm ready now," Xanoth insisted, getting groggily to his feet.

Nodding once at Connor, he walked towards the exit.

"Oh, Xanoth," General Connor called after him, his white, greying hair glinting under the spotlights. "Good job."

* * *

Haven's Heart, was quiet at this hour, the steady hum of the generators the only sound to be heard. Descending the stairway, Xanoth took the first right, down a narrow alley, towards the science lab; located in the same area as the medical lab, except on the opposite side of the underground town.

The stale smell of recycled air warmed his nostrils as he entered the lab and the acute taste of soldered metal was all too apparent as it rushed his senses. A young, fair-skinned scientist, wearing the same distinctive white attire that medical personnel wore, greeted him .

"Xanoth! Well done! That tech-hand's going to make a big difference to us!" He pointed towards the transparent, rubber-strip curtains dividing the two rooms. "Through there, Doctor Kaelan's examining it."

Xanoth grinned. "Thanks, Quinn. I just hope it was worth it. We need every advantage we can get.

Pushing aside the curtain, Xanoth saw a wizened man with sagging eyes bending over the central table, peering through a magnifying glass into a dish containing what looked like blood. The tech-hand lay to the side of him on a clean, ceramic bench. Examples of technological devices littered the desks arranged around the room and diagrams hung neatly on the walls.

"Doctor."

An expression of frustration flashed across the thin, intelligent face at the interruption to his work. "Oh!" he said, glancing up. "You must be Xanoth. Well, young man, we all owe you a debt of gratitude." His voice was dry and to the point. "Come," he added, beckoning Xanoth forward.

An intensely bright light shone down onto the table, reflecting back up off its white surface, further enhancing the illumination in the lab. Xanoth noticed a ceramic sink embedded into the table and a thin, metal tray containing laboratory equipment. The doctor had just begun washing his hands, when another young assistant pushed through the rubber strips and entered the room. A few years younger than Xanoth, and decidedly pretty, with ear length, caramel coloured hair, her attention was on the papers she carried, so she didn't immediately see him.

"Xanoth!" she shrieked delightedly. "You're back!"

Xanoth pushed back his hood and opened his arms as she rushed him, tucking her head just under his chin. "Hey, sis," he said, wrapping her into a bear hug.

Rosia snuggled against him contentedly. "I know you always come back, but I worry *so* much when you're on those missions."

"I got the hand, Rosie." He grimaced. "For Jaydaan – so he didn't die for nothing." He planted a kiss on her forehead.

Rosia pulled her head back and looked up at Xanoth, her tawny eyes sparkling with excitement. "We got one?" Gently nudging her brother to the side, she stared at the tech-hand.

"A bit of help here?" Doctor Kaelan said impatiently, moving across to where the tech-hand lay, awaiting examination.

Rosia walked around to the end of the table and pulled the magnifying glass down, so that the doctor had a clear view. Picking up the hand, Kaelan turned it slowly around, noting that the armour plates were not stable.

"No material to hold them together," he mumbled, studying the blue substance that seemingly powered the armour. Twisting the hand onto its end, he considered the amputation site. The clean cut had gone straight through the tissue; there were no bones, just veins and a heavy neural network. He grunted. "The armour acts as an exoskeleton."

Taking hold of some sturdy tweezers, he grabbed a piece of the flesh, tugging the hand firmly out of the glove. It peeled out, making a sticky, sucking sound as it came. Clear mucus covered the smooth, red, skinless meat, perfectly moulded to the shape of the glove. "This... what is this?" he muttered. The thing looked almost as if it had grown inside or had been somehow 'poured' into the armour.

Rosia drew in a sharp breath, her hand going to her mouth, disgusted, yet, excited at the same time. Xanoth just watched unemotionally.

Turning to the tray, Kaelan chose a scalpel and sliced down the centre of the open palm. The gelatinous texture cut easily, revealing a mishmash of fibrous flesh. Deepening the incision, the scalpel disclosed a small, dull blue capsule, entangled in a knot of vine-like nerves. Exchanging the scalpel for tweezers, the doctor pulled at the strange object, trying to twist it loose. "Hah!" I'll have to cut the nerves further," he said. "It's jammed in there as solid as a rock!"

Eventually, he managed to pull the item free, holding it up at eye height, dangling it in front of them – streaked with thin blood, a few nerves still attached, before dropping it into a Petri dish. Moving the magnifying glass across to the dish, he squinted down at the small device. "Rather non-descript, isn't it?" he said, glancing at Xanoth.

Indeed, Xanoth had to agree; deep blue, with smooth edges, about an inch in length and half an inch in width, it didn't presently look as if it was worth dying for. He shook his head to dislodge the memory of Jaydaan's last moments; seeing again the blue plague as it consumed his friend, and the courage it had taken for Jaydaan to let go and fall. He turned away, blinking back the tears pricking at his eyes.

Without much idea of what they might be hoping for, there was nevertheless a sense of disappointment as the seconds ticked by and the lozenge lay there and did nothing.

"Hmm." Kaelan scratched his balding pate.

Rosia found a syringe and filled it with alcohol. "May I

clean it?"

"Yes, of course," Kaelan said, nodding assent. "Go ahead."

Rosia squirted the clear liquid over the capsule, and as they watched, the blood diluted, the nerves loosened, sliding into the dish, revealing a shiny surface.

The doctor picked it up with tweezers again, examining it closely on all sides. "No sign of an opening." Grabbing a serrated scalpel, he sawed at the smooth surface. "Not even a scratch," he said irritably, throwing the scalpel aside.

"Fetch me the clamp stand please," he asked, holding out his hand without raising his eyes from the magnifying glass.

Rosia hurried to do as she was told.

Doctor Kaelan clamped the object to the stand and picked up a lamp with a shade designed specifically to force the beam of light in one direction, positioning it to shine through the blue capsule. He shook his head. "Unreflective! It seems to swallow the light! Hmm."

Xanoth had had enough of the frustration. He decided to leave the two scientists to it and excused himself. "I'll be back later," he told them as he headed for the door.

* * *

A few hours later and well rested, Xanoth returned to the lab. Ducking through the rubber strips, he overheard the doctor chuntering to himself.

"Any luck?" he asked.

"Nothing so far," Kaelan grated. "And I'm just about out of ideas."

"We could try force?" Rosia butted in.

"That is a last resort, Rosia." Kaelan sighed. "But I guess we've tried everything else." He passed a shaky, gnarled hand across his faded blue eyes. "Yes, okay!" He nodded. "Pass me the burner please."

Rosia quickly slid it across and turned the gas valve on. Lowering his safety glasses, the doctor played the flame over the surface of the capsule. Nothing. No change in colour or to the surface at all. The strange object remained as flawless as before.

Kaelan glanced from one to the other of them. "All right, that leaves acid."

Rosia didn't need telling twice, hurrying over to one of the cupboards on the wall, she took out a jug of acidic fluids, placing it on the table next to the capsule. Pulling on protective gloves, the doctor carefully poured some of the liquid into the dish containing the Zygeth object. They all watched as he lifted it out with the tweezers. Again, the thing showed absolutely no change, remaining undamaged.

Kaelan sighed. "Nothing!" His eyes hunted around the lab, searching for something, anything that he might have missed. He shook his head, slamming both of his hands onto the desk. "I've tried everything," he said, defeated. "The best chance we've ever had to steal a march on our enemy and I can't even dent the surface, never mind anything productive." He faced Xanoth. "I'm sorry, son. I wish there was something more... something else... but—" He scrubbed at his wrinkled forehead. "I think I'm just getting too old to be useful anymore."

"Doctor Kaelan, you've done more to advance our cause than anybody else except for the General!" Rosia protested as Kaelan, shoulders slumped, disappeared into the next room.

"No! Rosia—" Xanoth shouted, as, against protocol, she picked up the capsule with her bare hand, his warning dying away as, between her fingers, the lozenge shaped object ignited, a crystalline glow growing rapidly inside the casing. Rosia hesitantly placed it into her palm and its glow developed into an intense aqua-shimmer... then it pulsed. Gripping it tightly, she ran for the other room.

"What is it?" Xanoth held out his hand but his sister rushed past.

"Wait!" he called, following.

The doctor was sitting at his office desk, tiredness and dejection stamped on his features.

"Look at it... Look!" Rosia laughed delightedly as she ran to him and opened her hand to show him the glowing cylinder. "It's amazing."

"Oh my, let me see." Kaelan reached out, pulling the object, which now looked like nothing more than a large bead, free. Immediately, the glow ceased and it returned to its dull blue, 'lifeless' state. "Hmm." He passed it back to her and immediately it activated again, attaching itself to her as if magnetised.

"Only you," he mused, shooting Rosia a sharp look. "Why? Come." He pushed himself to his feet, heading back to the lab. "Put it down in the dish please," he instructed.

Rosia obeyed, pulling at it with her other hand, only to have it jump into the centre of her other palm. She looked up, surprised. "I can't!"

Doctor Kaelan took hold of it and again it deactivated. He dropped it into the dish, his forehead creasing into a frown. "I was afraid of this," he murmured. Meeting Rosia's curious gaze, he carried on, "I think this... contraption." He tapped his fingers on the bench. "It would seem this... 'thing' has a genetic element to it. It came from inside the body... and I think it's looking for a new host. My hypothesis is, it'll respond and activate if we implant it into a genetically viable candidate." He rubbed absently at his cleft chin. "There must be more people than you who can activate it," he mused.

Rosia stuck out her chin, her mind already made up. "And how long will it take to find someone willing to be implanted? No... you have to let me do this!"

"Wait! We don't know anything about it! We've no idea what it might do!" Xanoth cut in.

"Don't you see? That's all the more reason to let me do it," Rosia argued. "Look, Xanoth!" Taking hold of the lifeless lozenge she opened up her fingers to reveal a glowing bead.

Xanoth shook his head, unconvinced.

"It only seems to respond to your sister," Kaelan said. "I suspect there are others who might be a genetic match, but—"

"I want to do this," Rosia interrupted determinedly.

"Do... Oh no! No, no you don't. I've seen what this goo does. It's too dangerous." Xanoth glared at the doctor. "Find someone else!" He made to snatch the capsule. "I won't let you—" He broke off as the blue bead rolled down Rosia's hand and into his palm, immediately attaching itself strongly.

The doctor's eyes widened. "Brother and sister," he said slowly. "Two blood relatives... and it responds to you both." His eyes narrowed. "This has to be linked to your bloodline, your DNA! But that's impossible!"

"I'm sorry, sis." Xanoth grabbed the closest scalpel, plunging it into his palm just beneath the capsule. Instantly, the glowing device sank under his skin.

"Xanoth!" Rosia grabbed his wrist but it was too late to stop him. "No! I can't lose you."

Even as they watched, the capsule burrowed its way between the muscles in Xanoth's flesh; veins wrapped around it; fresh nerves began to grow from the pod as his hand blossomed with blue light. Xanoth gripped his wrist in pain. The blue illumination pushed upward; he could feel growing nerves forcing their way through his arm, up into his shoulder, thrusting into his spinal cord, before locking onto his brainstem. The blue glow pulsed, following the growth. As they stared, transfixed, Xanoth's eyes flashed blue and letting out a heavy groan, he stumbled forward. Rosia grabbed him, but she did not have the strength to steady him and he slipped through her arms, to the floor, where he lay motionless, face down, eyes wide, glowing with strange blue light.

"No!" Rosia screamed. "No... no... Xanoth!" Tears streamed down her cheeks as she knelt beside her brother. She stared, anguished, at Doctor Kaelan, busily checking Xanoth's vital signs.

Pale and visibly shaken, Kaelan met her eyes. "He's alive," he said tersely.

* * *

Endless aqua. A seamless void of empty space, tranquil and encapsulating. The glow surrounded Xanoth as he stood, turning... turning... seeking some landmark, some beacon in this desolate place. There was nothing but shimmering blue.

Silhouettes, shadowed images of humanoid people began to blink in and out of his vision. An image would appear and almost immediately disappear, only to reappear elsewhere. More shadows spawned within the void, gradually becoming more stable as they multiplied. More and more identical figures came into focus, all clones of each other: featureless beings, seemingly with no joints. As he looked on, their bodies became saturated by the colour red. Small blue points appeared in their heads, their hands and their feet. A neural network of blue liquid spread, linking the points together. Xanoth tasted fear, something he had not felt for a long time. Before him, the beings multiplied ever faster, the motionless bodies floating on the same level as Xanoth. *Blue everywhere!* All around, above and below.

More figures spawned, in every direction and as far as he could see. Xanoth screamed, overwhelmed with an inexplicable fear. Turning frantically, he could see no escape. He was surrounded by thousands of beings. Each time he turned or blinked, they came closer. He didn't see them move, they just flashed closer and closer. His heart pounded, the echo of his scream reverberated through his skull. Dizziness struck him; he couldn't get his breath! A black curtain descended... And in his mind, spoken as if it were from his own consciousness, her voice followed him down into oblivion – *The blood machines are many... Save us.*

8

Finding the secret

"Anamai!" Xanoth screamed himself awake. Craning his neck, he blinked hard trying to clear his vision, and a blurry, watery view of a bright room, with a strong smell of cleaning agents, assailed his senses. The gentle pressure of a hand on his shoulder brought him jerking upright and he found himself pulled into an embrace.

"What did you do?" A voice whispered brokenly against his shoulder.

Xanoth gazed into his sister's oval, tawny eyes. "Anamai?"

"No, it's Rosia, who's Anamai?" she asked, letting go of him and quickly brushing away a stray tear.

Xanoth's focus cleared and he realized they were in one of the back rooms of the medical lab. He glanced down at his clothing, loose and very thin, night attire, yet clinging to him. A single white bed sheet covered him and as he shifted under it, he became aware of the sour reek of stale sweat. Glancing around he noted five other beds, all empty. He stiffened as memories crowded in on him. Groaning, he locked bleak eyes on Rosia. "Get me the General," he grated.

* * *

Xanoth had changed out of his sweaty clothing and was sat up on the bed by the time Rosia returned with the General.

"Sir, we can't win this war," he said the moment Connor came close enough.

"What?" General Connor's brow wrinkled, worry and confusion chasing each other in rapid succession across his face.

"We wanted intel on the Zygeth." Xanoth's hands balled into

fists. "Well, I have it, and I'm sorry, sir, but... our cause is lost." He shook his head. "Don't ask me how I know." Closing his eyes, he let out his breath slowly. "But, it's true." He showed the General the glow under the bloody bandage on his palm. "This... connected me to them in some way," he said, unable to look at the General any longer; unwilling to see the expression of utter loss and discouragement that had replaced his usual high morale. It was as if all his vitality had just drained away and he sank down onto the metal chair next to the bed like someone who had received a fatal blow.

"We can't free them, sir." Xanoth's head dropped forward. "We–we have to think of our families now. He glanced around himself as if seeing everything for the first time. This 'home' we have. We're safe here, we're still hidden. But, this fight can't be won."

Rosia sat on the edge of the bed. "She told you this? Anamai?"

"What?" The General stared at him incredulously. "You want me to retreat our men based on the word of a woman you imagined?"

"Please! Sir... " Xanoth clutched at the General's arm. "Believe me. The Zygeth are thousands, maybe tens of thousands. We–we're a small bunch of, what? A few hundred? I hate it as much as you. But, our priorities must change. After everything I've done, trust me when I say, I've seen their army."

Rosia laid her head on his shoulder. "I know you," she told him. "I've never heard you speak anything other than the truth, but I need more proof, Xanoth."

"We don't know why the Zygeth have amassed such an army, but they certainly don't need it to simply enslave the Rhajok'Don." Xanoth glanced desperately from one to the other. "You have to believe me – something else is going on here." He looked at the General. "And I'd like your permission to continue to investigate," he said. "It's not over, sir. There's more to this."

For a long moment Connor said nothing, then, "All right,

needless to say, I know you'll keep us safe."

Some of the tension eased out of Xanoth's frame. "Thank you, sir. I won't let you down."

The General sighed, scrubbing a weary hand across his face. "When we know the extent of this threat. What then? What do I tell the people? Our people." He shot Xanoth a hard, almost angry glance. "Do we need to evacuate?"

"No, sir. We're safe here, they don't know about Haven's Heart. We could live out our lives, build ourselves something from this." He stared around him at the walls and ceiling. "Evacuating will only bring us too much attention."

The General nodded. Getting to his feet, he straightened his jacket. "I'll arrange what's necessary. There'll be a committee meeting later today." He nodded once more and turning, back ramrod straight, walked out of the medical lab.

Rosia silently slipped her small hand into his. Glancing down, Xanoth saw the blue glow through his bandage. Mustering a smile, he said, "I'm still hoping for a life above ground, sis. I want you to keep hoping too."

Before Rosia could answer they were interrupted by a nurse coming to check on Xanoth's hand. Unravelling the dirty bandage, she examined his stitches and gently cleaned the wound before wrapping a fresh dressing over it.

"Thank you," Xanoth said. He was beginning to feel much better and his clarity of thought had fully returned. "I'm going back to see the doctor," he told Rosia as he dropped one leg out of the bed, ready to stand.

"I'll get you some outdoor clothes then, unless you want to wander about in your night suit," she said, giving him a small, sad smile.

Xanoth didn't care so long as he wasn't stark naked but the fear shadowing his sister's expression stopped him in his tracks and he struggled to curb his urgent need for action and schooled himself to wait patiently for her to return.

* * *

Checking his bandage, Xanoth headed down the aisle leading to the town centre. The street was relatively busy and he had to gently shoulder his way through the crowd. It was morning and Haven's Heart was about one-third full of local people going about their business. The delicious smell of fresh baked goods wafted out to him from the baker's opposite. His stomach growled loudly and Xanoth realised just how hungry he was. Entering the little shop, he scanned its one shelf and cramped counter. His stomach growled again as the aroma, intensified within the confined space, assailed his nostrils. Before him, standing at the counter were a mother and her child. Xanoth didn't really know them, although he did recognise them from around town. The young boy pointed at a sweet bun and his mother shook her head. "We only have enough ration tickets for the bread this week."

The youngster, maybe four years old, looked very disappointed.

"Yes, please?" The shopkeeper asked Xanoth. "They're waiting for the bread to come out of the oven," he explained in response to Xanoth's enquiring glance at the mother.

Xanoth pulled a ticket out of his pocket and handed it over. "One sweet bun please, and one cheese bun."

The shopkeeper wrapped the two buns in crispy, thin paper. Xanoth thanked him, then passed the sweet bun to the boy. "There you go."

"Fankooo," the youngster all but shouted, his voice high and sweet, bouncing up and down with excitement as he held out his hand to accept his gift.

Xanoth's own hand tugged slightly towards the child's, beginning to glow dimly. The boy took his bun and Xanoth quickly retracted his hand, hoping no one had noticed. He hastily tucked his bread in his pocket and walked out of the shop.

Forgetting his hunger, he continued toward the science lab, turning into the next stuffy, narrow aisle, the lack of width, as always, adding to the sense of busyness.

Gently pushing through the constant stream of people, he noticed his palm glowing dimly again as he walked past certain individuals. As discreetly as he could, he tried to monitor those who activated it: one middle-aged woman, an adolescent boy and a slightly older man. Xanoth's gaze swept the crowd, estimating the amount of people in the aisle. He frowned – around twenty-five, and three of them activated the glow. Reaching the science lab, he turned right through the door. The first room was empty, so he carried on to the adjoining room. The doctor was at his desk, he glanced up from his paperwork wearing his perpetual frown.

Xanoth got straight to the point. "Doctor Kaelan, I wanted to ask you what happened yesterday, and... I noticed something else strange on my way here." He held out his hand. "This glowed as I passed some people in the street, four in total."

"I see." The doctor placed his pen carefully on top of his writing pad. "It would seem you've more relatives than you thought." He stared at Xanoth for a long moment before adding, "I'm guessing the glow was dim?"

"Yes."

"Distant relatives then."

"What's going on, Doc?"

"I heard you saw an army?" Doctor Kaelan said, ignoring him and narrowing his watery, brown eyes.

"I did... But... it was like a dream. Then I heard Anamai before I woke." He shrugged. "I know what you all think, but she's real and... I trust her."

"What did she say?"

"She said, 'The blood machines are many... Save us.' I believe she was warning me about the army."

The doctor stood up slowly, hands behind his back he walked

towards Xanoth. "My opinion of this is speculative, but there are technologies we don't fully understand. That capsule embedded in your palm is evident enough." He turned and paced the other way. "It's most definitely connected to your bloodline and Anamai's cryptic words lead me to believe you're also blood related to the Zygeth enchants in some way. I don't know how. I don't have all the answers."

Xanoth's jaw dropped. "I'm related to the Zygeth? No. That's impossible!"

The doctor half turned, looking over his shoulder at Xanoth. "Not impossible," he stated. "I'll find out what's going on here. Let me take a sample of your blood."

Xanoth raised his finger to allow the doctor to prick it and dribble a little blood into a test tube.

"We need more information. Maybe another scouting mission?" Doctor Kaelan continued.

"Or maybe another talk with Anamai?" Xanoth murmured, posing a rhetorical question aimed at himself, and an idea he preferred. "Sedate me, I'll get us our answers."

"I can't just sedate you, Xanoth." Kaelan protested.

Xanoth was in no mood to argue. "As your commanding officer, I order you to sedate me."

* * *

The ivory key clicked in the metal door and Xanoth opened it slowly. As he entered Anamai's dwelling, he recognised the tranquillity of the illumination and the delicate scents. The sunlit hue once again lured him to the room on the far right. Walking past the mounted device, he noticed something different from last time, a ticking clock was embedded in the very centre, unusually, the second hand moved backwards. Lifting the curtain, he re-entered the octagonal room with the glittering chandelier. The beautiful Anamai sat, as before, crossed legged in her chair, staring at the wall-mounted painting.

"Anamai. I seek your help." Xanoth kept his voice soft, the last thing he wanted was to alarm her.

"I know you do." She turned her head toward him and stood, her embroidered silk veil dropping away. She walked slowly towards Xanoth, her steps so graceful it was as if she glided across the floor. Reaching him, she gently took his hand. Xanoth caught his breath as the blue capsule beneath his skin flared into fierce life.

"This is your fate," she husked, the flames in her eyes flickering as she gazed up at him. "What you saw were the blood machines."

"The Zygeth enchants?"

"As you call them, yes."

The soul seer joined her palm with his, slowly lifting his hand and Xanoth followed her lead. "Your community needn't worry. This army isn't for them." The iridescent blue glow brightened and spilled into her hand before flowing down her nerves. "That doesn't mean you don't have a purpose. Your purpose is more important than you could ever imagine."

"The army isn't for us? What? Are we just a pest to them?" Xanoth was both relieved and angry. So many lives sacrificed – and now he was finding out it had all been pointless – for nothing!

Anamai's gaze drew him in. "Maybe," she said quietly. "Maybe that is what you are, but you'll prove a more formidable pest than they expect." She paused. "The magic growing inside you will aid you. You're my people's only hope."

"What? What do you mean? Who are your people?"

Slowly she twisted her palm so that it lay under his, then slid it gently away. The blue glow dimmed and broke between them as she turned towards the painting. "Look," she ordered.

Xanoth stared at the painting as it began to move and change before his eyes. The grasses blew gently, leaves rustled, and white fluffy clouds started a slow journey across a sky dominated by the beautiful bloom of rich sunlight shining through. Two graceful young women danced into view, with much the same elegance as Anamai herself, dressed in long, silken, coral gowns: fair skinned with blonde strands of luxuriant hair flowing over their faces in the light breeze. Small, colourful birds flew past, the animation developing sound so that the room filled with their song, as well as the sound of giggling from the women.

"It's magical… " Xanoth found himself unable to tear his gaze away. "A dream," he murmured. Finally pulling his eyes away, he fixed his attention on Anamai. "Where is that?" He shook his head. "I have to know!"

Anamai smiled. "It's closer than you think, Xanoth." She drew nearer to him, until only a finger width separated them. "And *you* can save them from the Zygeth."

"How? Xanoth reigned in his growing frustration. "How can I save them when I don't even know where that is." He thrust his glowing hand in front of her." I don't know what this is!"

Anamai continued staring at the painting. "You don't need to know," she told him calmly. I'll guide you." She moved towards the painting. "You need to send a message, but, first you need the means." She took hold of the frame, lifting the painting off the wall. Behind it, embedded into the wall, Xanoth could see a safe. She sketched a gesture in the air with her long, delicate fingers and it steamed open, revealing an oblong palette, obsidian in colour and smooth edged. This she gently took from the safe. Turning, she carried it back to him, placing it in his hands with the utmost care. "Send this north," she told him, "across the seas."

Xanoth stared at it bemused. "There's nothing on it," he said, turning the tablet around on all sides, peering at it intently and cautiously rubbing his hand over the smooth surface. Giving up, he looked at Anamai, puzzled. As far as he was concerned, it was a meaningless slab.

Once more he found himself lost in the twin flames of her eyes. He heard her voice. "You know this is a dream," she told him. "Make it real." She moved closer to him once again, sliding her velvet skinned cheek against his rough one, whispering in his ear. "Now wake."

* * *

Xanoth awoke dazed, but the dream was crystal clear in his mind.

Kaelan hovered nervously by the bed. "Welcome back," he said.

"I need to make it real," Xanoth muttered. He stared wildly around himself. "I know what to do." He struggled to launch himself out of bed, but found himself foiled by his unsteady limbs.

The doctor grabbed him. "Careful, maybe wait."

"No! I need to do this now! I'm fine," he insisted. Pulling himself to his feet, he paused a moment to regain his balance before exiting the science room.

* * *

Inside the crumbling walls and rusted metal, he made his way through the shredded curtain and approached the burnt out painting. The moment he touched it, the scorched canvas crumbled in front of him. Behind it was the safe, deteriorated beyond recognition, with holes in the door. Xanoth poked his fingers through the holes and gently pulled it open. Detaching from its top hinge, it hung for a moment before crashing to the floor. Inside, as he had expected, was the faceless, oblong tablet. Xanoth knew exactly how it would feel when he took it into his hands. He stared at it for a moment, as he had done in his dream, felt its smooth edges and turned it around fully. Abruptly, the tablet came to life. A golden glimmer from deep inside pulsed upwards like liquid, filling what looked like moulds just under the glassy surface. There were marks he recognized as some kind of writing on one side and a map of a country completely foreign to him on the underside.

As he stood gazing down at it, Xanoth was certain he had found the message that Anamai had spoken of.

9

Ugoki's Destiny

The heavy pounding of thick-soled boots thumped against the concrete passage floor. The thuds reverberated off the hollow walls as Xanoth tore towards the exit door. His fingers tracing over the now lifeless surface of the oblong tablet as he ran. Only one thought occupied his mind; he had to get to General Connor and show him what he had found.

* * *

Bursting unannounced into the General's humble quarters, filled largely with flimsy metal filing cabinets, a rusty lamp shedding a yellowish light on some old schematic displays, Xanoth slammed the tablet down.

"This! This is the answer."

Connor stared at him uncomprehendingly. "W–what?"

"She visited me again," Xanoth said, "and told me where to find it. She keeps telling me to 'save her people'."

The General studied the object before picking it up and running his fingers over it. "There's nothing here, Xanoth. You're asking me to listen to something you've dreamt up," he said impatiently.

"Please, sir," Xanoth said desperately. "She helps me, she keeps me alive. I know how important this is. This... thing... the power in it... will help our future. I'm sure of it."

Connor dry washed his face, then, "Against my better judgement," he ground out, "I'm going to let you run with this." He sighed. "I take comfort from the fact that you haven't been wrong yet. So... " He ran his fingers across the tablet once more. "What do we do with it?"

"It has to go north, over the ocean… to another land."

The General laughed quietly. "And, how do you propose we do that?"

"I'll talk to Ugoki. I think he knows of a Rhajok'Don tribe northeast of here. A small fishing colony that've managed to stay off the Zygeth maps." Xanoth picked up the tablet. "We can sail from there."

The General nodded. "Well, get to it, soldier. Go and make some plans."

"Yes, sir." Xanoth shook the General's hand and tucked the tablet under his shirt before leaving the room.

* * *

As Xanoth headed to the barracks he passed a young recruit, who took a double take of him.

"Wow. You're him."

"Yes, I'm me," Xanoth said, grinning, not really understanding what was going on.

His confusion must have showed because the soldier added, "The one who rescued Ugoki and infiltrated the smoulder pits." He patted Xanoth's upper arm. "Could you please sign my cap?" He took off the voluminous, lovat-green cap, flattened at one side, and handed it to him. As Xanoth reached to take it, he felt the device buried inside his palm give a tug. The soldier provided him with a pen, and Xanoth proceeded to sign the inside hem.

As he handed the cap back, he said. "This may seem out of place. But, who was your mother? You, err, look familiar." He smiled disarmingly.

"My mother was Dion, she passed away. My father's Tobias. We used to live over in the western quarters."

Xanoth didn't recognise the names. "Oh," he said slowly, "I'm sorry for your loss."

The young man shrugged. "It's fine, we weren't close."

"I do have family in the western quarters, but I don't know those names. You remind me of someone though," Xanoth pursued.

"Not sure from where, I've not been frequenting Haven's Heart much, I heard all the stories about you in the barracks and I've seen you a few times. You were never alone though, so I could pester you." The soldier winked at him, then saluted. "Good day to you, sir."

"And to you," Xanoth replied, continuing on his way.

* * *

Xanoth arrived at the mess hall, a long, half-cylindrical room, with cracked plaster walls and a row of heavy, metal pots, large enough to hold a body. Big, wooden soup spoons hung on the wall above the pots. The tables were arranged in rows; Ugoki was sat on the second row. Xanoth walked over to him and sat opposite. He waited for Ugoki to stop stirring his grey, watery, porridge; overcooked to a sticky dough.

Ugoki paused with his spoon halfway to his mouth. He sighed. "I know that look, Xanoth," he said. "And every time I've seen it, I've ended up in a bad situation."

Xanoth leaned across and clapped his hand on his old friend's shoulder. He grinned. "Don't tell me you'd have it any other way."

For a second Ugoki's expression remained unchanged, then a huge, crooked smile split his face. "Well, give me the details."

"Ana – I've got something new, and I'm pretty sure it's going to help us in our fight with the Zygeth, and I need you to help me." Xanoth laid the tablet on the table.

Ugoki glanced at it. "What's that?"

"All I know is that I need to go across the oceans with it."

"Excuse me?"

"I need to know where your kin settled after the invasion." He passed Ugoki the tablet. "Here take a look. I think this thing's going to save us all." He paused, running his fingers through his hair. " Only… don't ask me how, least not yet."

The Rhajok'Don briefly examined the tablet. "I'm in." He placed it back down on the table. "My remaining kin evacuated to the north coast, we can fly there in a day."

"They have boats?" Xanoth asked hopefully.

"Yes, crude little things," Ugoki told him, putting his spoon down.

"It's settled then, I'll meet you above the hatch in three hours. Enjoy your food." Xanoth launched to his feet, excitement lighting his eyes and trotted out of the mess hall.

Ugoki watched him leave. He stirred his porridge for a moment then gulped down another large spoonful.

* * *

The orpids responded immediately to their chants, landing obediently next to the two travellers. Swiftly mounting, they flew north, leaving behind the Stygian forest.

Before long the edge of Stygia's landmass came into view, a coastline that had trapped them for so long. Small bumps could be seen on the horizon and as they got closer, they emerged as mud houses, domed in shape, built in a circular shaped village around a communal house from which white steam puffed out of a central chimney.

They guided their orpids lower, flying them towards the outskirts of the village and landing gently on the sandstone.

Ugoki's armour rattled as he jumped off his mount, as three Rhajok'Don kinsmen pounded towards him.

"Ugoki, my friend, it's good to see you." The first Rhajok'Don called.

Xanoth leaned over and whispered in Ugoki's ear. "How well do you know them?"

"They're my kinsmen. After the invasion they met another lost tribe and settled here. We've been in contact via carrier-corr ever since. They're the last remaining free Rhajok'Don," Ugoki replied before embracing his kin.

A second Rhajok'Don ran back towards the village shouting. "Ugoki! He's returned to us!"

It only took a few moments for other Rhajok'Don to look out of their doorways and stop what they were doing to stare at Ugoki and Xanoth as they approached. Food was being prepared by the time they arrived at the communal house.

Inside, his kin were already gathered and as Ugoki and Xanoth entered, everyone got to their feet and knelt on one knee until Ugoki took his seat.

The acting chieftain, the eldest, Moksana, greeted him with the utmost respect. His elaborate horns were adorned with leather and feathers. "We welcome you back, our chief," he said, bowing his head as a mark of respect.

"Thank you." Ugoki's manner was equally respectful.

"Who's your friend?" The elder asked.

"I'm Xanoth," he volunteered, holding out his hand to shake the chieftain's. Moksana, however, stood up and touched horns with Ugoki, then tried to do the same with a bewildered Xanoth.

After sitting back down, he asked. "Why are you here, my friend? It must be important after so many years without a visit."

"We are in need of a boat," Ugoki told him. Thinking about his words, he decided to nominate himself as the one to travel. A human would never survive the oceans. "I'm to travel over the sea, to the north."

"What?" Xanoth stared at him in disbelief.

"Please be calm," Ugoki said, locking eyes with him. He turned again to the chief.

"I see." The elder nodded his head.

"Any boat will do."

Moksana gave a signal to his tribe and they trudged out of the communal mud house in a line. "Why are you set on this, my brother?"

Xanoth was the one to answer. "We may be able to end our struggle with the Zygeth." He scratched his head. "It could be our last and only hope."

"We may even get our families back," Ugoki pitched in.

Moksana shook his head, his face grave. "We don't know what lies over those oceans, you're aware of that," he said. Glancing away from them, he added. "It's unlikely you'll surviv—

"I should be going," Xanoth interrupted.

The chieftain looked at him. "You have one heart, you lack our tenacious strength. If you go, you are guaranteed to die."

Xanoth couldn't meet his eyes; the elder spoke truly and he knew it.

"We'll also need some strong bindings, the strongest you have," Ugoki added.

Catching sight of a passing Rhajok'Don, Moksana made his request and obediently, the Rhajok'Don went to fetch what was asked for.

Xanoth stood up. "I need to show you something," he said, hurrying over to his orpid. The animal, perhaps thinking it was time to leave, fidgeted as he approached. Xanoth removed the tablet from its carry satchel and retraced his steps, handing it over to Moksana. "This is why we're here."

The chieftain glanced at the strange object, seemingly without interest. "It looks like Zygeth technology."

"I believe it is. A… trusted friend of mine, she insisted we take it north. To save her people, who I'm sure will then save us."

The elder gave Xanoth a long, searching look. "Very well. I hope you're correct."

A Rhajok'Don approached the doorway. "The boat is ready."

"Thank you," Moksana replied, nodding his head.

"First we need to secure this to Ugoki. If it falls into the depths and we lose it – we'll have failed before we even start," Xanoth said, helping Ugoki remove his heavy cloak, revealing the armour underneath, a sword sheathed at his side.

Removing the chest piece, Ugoki wrapped the tablet in a thick cloth, tying it to his chest with the bindings. He replaced the chest piece, holding his hand firmly on the insignia. *Kinoko.*

He secured the rest of his armour with the robust straps.

"Are you ready?" Xanoth asked, trying his best to ignore the feeling of loss already eating at his heart and focusing instead on the success heralded by the mission.

Ugoki nodded. "Let's go," he said, striding towards the entranceway of the domed house, followed by Xanoth and Moksana.

A couple of Rhajok'Don waved them over to a small fishing boat. They handed Ugoki a satchel of supplies for his journey.

"Thank you," Ugoki said gratefully.

The little boat wobbled on the gentle tide. Oblong in shape, with a rounded front and a single sail, Xanoth didn't think it looked very sturdy.

Ugoki stepped off the dock, setting the boat pitching and rocking more than either he or Xanoth would have expected.

"Don't worry, it's a sturdy boat, our finest," Moksana tried to reassure him.

Ugoki trimmed the sail and picked up the oars. "Goodbye, my friends. May the spirit grant me favour." He sharply raised his fist. "For freedom!" Pushing off from the dock, he made one final salute before he picked up the oars and rowed out into the endless, desolate ocean, towards the sun that had fallen as a casualty to the horizon.

* * *

Xanoth watched him sail into the empty distance, a dot on the skyline, until finally consumed by it. Reluctantly, he turned away, his face bleak. Ugoki would not be coming back and the hard ball of unshed tears threatened to choke him.

10

Modifications

The gleaming tiles were flushed with a translucent blue gel. It splashed over the floor and slopped down the wall like congealed jelly.

Unconscious, Anamai lay in the ebbing, glutinous tide. Splintered glass was scattered everywhere. Some of it had penetrated her milky-white gown, leaving it blotted with small bloodstains. An indistinct gurgling noise echoed eerily around the spacious genetics laboratory with its ceiling high, cylindrical test tubes, attached to the walls by translucent pipes.

Anamai slowly regained her senses, dazedly wiping the gel and glass off her as best she could. A distinctive smell of formaldehyde mixed with ammonia emanated from the blue slop. Balancing herself with the compromised test tube, she noticed a jagged hole; it had been forcefully smashed from the inside. Composing herself, she made her way over to the curved lab table. She pressed a couple of symbols and virtual screens appeared in front of her, one of them showing an image of an unusual, mutated animal, with two legs and three arms, all different in size and width. Its proportionately small head was atop the middle arm, which acted as a neck.

The repeated boom of the alarm reverberated off the walls, as two Amunisarian guards hastily entered the area. Armed with sleek staffs, they aimed their weapons around the expanse of the lab. There was no sign of whatever was making the low gurgling cries. The guards cautiously moved down the wide room with the large test tubes either side: perfect for hiding behind.

Suddenly an adolescent sized 'boy' skipped – it couldn't move any other way, across the room from one hiding place to another. The gap it chose was broad and the creature had limited speed.

One of the guards aimed his staff at the mutant. He fired and blue liquid shot from the barrel, encapsulating the young deformity before rapidly solidifying. In seconds it had completely encased the creature which froze and fell to the ground.

* * *

The mutant was carried to a laboratory table, lit from below and with a virtual screen above it. The encapsulated child was laid onto his back and the overhead screen pushed down close to him. There was the sound of gentle clinking and then one of Anamai's assistants passed her a small cylinder, white in colour, with a gauge on its side.

Anamai rested the device onto the surface of the blue shell covering the boy and squeezed. The gauge filled up with pale-pink fluid, which she injected into an extraction point on the virtual terminal. Symbols flashed in front of her eyes and then a likeness of the mutant appeared. The pink fluid flowed through all of the blood vessels, lighting up the image. Anamai drained some light-blue fluid from the mutant and injected that into the terminal point. Almost immediately, all the nerve connections lit up in blue. She pressed a few symbols and the device started to analyse the results.

"The mutation isn't in the blood," she murmured, "but I do see a discrepancy in the cerebrospinal fluid."

Her assistant studied the screen over Anamai's shoulder. "It may be a defect in the brain."

"Yes." Anamai pushed another symbol and a beam focused on the brain, projecting a 3D picture at eye level. Anamai studied the different sections as they presented themselves. "I see a lump attached to the hypothalamus."

"Dissect?" The assistant asked.

"Yes, please."

The girl gestured at a terminal on the wall and a horizontal laser sliced down, dissecting the top of the mutant's skull, revealing the brain and leaving it intact.

Anamai took the strange device from the casing and slide her finger up the gauge. A translucent blade appeared and started to energise. First, she cut away the outer membrane, to facilitate better access to the fleshy brain tissue, carefully inserting her fingers into the cavity, she pulled the brain forward before cutting away the spinal cord and optic nerves. She nodded at her assistant who quickly prepared a counter for her.

The brain made a sticky sound as it was gently placed on the solid counter top and Anamai pulled another screen across, over the brain, and began removing each segment in turn until she arrived at the centre to find a semi-transparent chunk of brain tissue, mottled by deep-blue, pulsing nerves.

"Hmm!" Anamai frowned. "It's similar to what we saw with the last specimen," she said, dissecting the anomaly and dropping it into a Petri dish. "I can't seem to adjust the serum to stop it from happening."

"It's only with the spliced candidates?"

"Yes. I think we should leave this research alone for now and concentrate on the cloning technology," Anamai said reluctantly, crossing her arms.

Her assistant gasped. "We can't do that! Ceolm wants the splicing done."

"I don't care what Ceolm wants," Anamai hissed. "This research won't advance our race at its current stage, yet we're close to solving cloning."

The girl stepped away from her, shaking her head. "I'm sorry, Anamai, you'll need to find a new assistant. I won't go against Ceolm."

Anamai looked at her evenly. "He needs me," she said. "I'll take the risk."

* * *

Xanoth awoke from another dream about Anamai. He was having them more regularly now, since Ugoki had left. He had been allocated his own quarters and promoted to sergeant. Although he was a distinguished member of the military, he mostly pursued his own agenda, and, obsessed with Anamai, he would follow her guidance.

Levering himself out of the hard bed, he pulled on his typical 'in the field' attire; leather trousers went on over an array of small knives attached to his calves. After fastening his reinforced leather, hooded shirt, he buckled two sturdy straps diagonally over his chest. Donning his powerful, compact bow, he lifted his hood over his head. Just before he left his small room, he picked up his sword and sheathed it onto his belt.

Arriving at General Connor's office, he shut the door behind him and sat in a robust, wooden chair, across the table, opposite the General.

"I had another one," he said calmly.

"What did she show you this time?"

"She was working for someone called Ceolm, on splicing and cloning. Very hi-tech."

"So are these the Zygeth she's showing you?" Connor asked curiously, sliding his chair closer.

"I think so, what else could it be?"

"I don't know." Connor tapped his rough fingers on the desk, searching for the right way to phrase his words. "I need you to assemble a small group of men for an ambush mission. We have intel of a medical shipment in transport."

"But, sir, I need to find out more about Anamai, maybe I can go back to the gardens I found," Xanoth insisted, edging his arms over the desk.

"You heard me, soldier." Connor's voice had taken on a hard edge. "You still have your duties. Now assemble your men and expect heavy resistance." He pushed back his chair and got to his feet, holding out his hand.

Xanoth reluctantly stood and shook the proffered hand. "Indeed, sir."

* * *

It was lunchtime and the mess hall was crowded with soldiers, Xanoth could see only a few spare seats. He wasn't there for food though, he was there to look for possible candidates for his newest mission. He held a clipboard in his hands, searching faces as he narrowed down his choices. One man crammed bread into his mouth whilst looking for a chair, finding one, he sat down.

"Okay if I sit here, Aiden?" Xanoth asked politely.

The young man, in his twenties, with short, neat hair, shaved at the back and sides, saluted before replying. "Of course, sir." Aiden, born into the Resistance, had a strong military background. Both his parents had fought for the liberation of Elon'Ki, the same Rhajok'Don village that Xanoth's parents had died defending.

Xanoth sat opposite him.

"So," Aiden said, "what can I do for you?" He cracked a smile. "Other than my good company, that is."

Xanoth didn't mince his words. "I'm looking for strong soldiers to accompany me on a mission, to the north of Kraag'Blitz. Our data's out of date and there's news of a medical shipment."

"Sir, is there a point to collecting data anymore?"

Xanoth shook his head. "Just because their army's beyond our capabilities doesn't mean we shouldn't keep collecting intel. You never know when it might be needed."

"I understand, sergeant, which of my men would you like?"

"The best ones," Xanoth said flatly. "Report back to me at sixteen hundred, in the briefing room." Xanoth passed him the clipboard for his signature. He got to his feet as Aiden executed a crisp salute before Xanoth walked away.

* * *

At sixteen hundred, the briefing room began to bustle with activity. Xanoth watched the seats fill up with dedicated young soldiers.

As Aiden closed the door once they were all in, a small piece of plaster fractured and crumbled off the wall. "This place is getting worse each day," he said before finding his seat.

There was a few minutes of settling, as the chatter and shuffling quietened down, then the hum of the little lamp above the chalkboard broke through the silence. Xanoth scanned the gathering.

"All right, I'm glad you're all here." He clasped his hands in front of him. "I've assembled you here in order to brief you to assist me with a covert mission." He turned the board over, exposing a map of Kraag'Blitz on the other side. "We'll land here." He drew a cross. "It's a secluded and unused factory to the east of Kraag'Blitz." He drew another two crosses. "We'll split into two small units on the ground, eight men in each. Aiden will command the second group and infiltrate the southeast. My unit will stay northeast." He folded his arms. "The objective of the mission is to update our information on Kraag'Blitz and to retrieve much needed medical supplies.

"That is all. I'll let Aiden sort your units out." Xanoth saluted smartly. "We leave in two hours."

"Yes, sir." The men spoke in unison, rising and saluting before leaving the room in an orderly manner.

* * *

Two hours later and the squad were flying south on their orpids.

They landed behind a derelict chemical factory. Its chimneys looked like they hadn't fired in years. The blackened windows were broken and the crumbling walls were caked with soot.

Xanoth called his men to formation. "Aiden, take your men south." Just as he finished speaking, his palm began to vibrate: he knew, under his glove, it would be glowing.

Aiden and his men, staying low to the ground, made their way over to the southern building. Xanoth watched as four of Aiden's men began to scale the walls to establish a better vantage point.

Xanoth quickly ordered four of his group to do the same. Hugging the cover of the structure, he pulled out his binoculars, keeping an eye out for any uninvited guests. Suddenly his hand tugged hard, pulling him forward. Gesturing to his men to stay, he allowed his hand to lead him, taking cover behind support beams and old crates as he went. He reached the next building down and peered to his left. There were ten Zygeth enchants patrolling the streets. His hand was vibrating so much it hurt. Removing his strengthened hide glove, Xanoth clenched his fist – his entire hand glowed, the nerves pulsating upwards through his wrist. He grabbed hold, hoping to numb the pain but it didn't help.

Suddenly, as one, the Zygeth enchants looked directly at him. In the next second, they were marching in his direction. A wave of panic obliterated all thought and Xanoth sprang from his position, running back towards the derelict factory, jumping over any obstacles in his way. Behind him, the marching had quickened pace; his heart raced.

"On guard!" he shouted, "Zygeth incoming!"

Aiden's unit were already on their way back to join them. Forming a line with Xanoth's men, they ranged themselves across the alleyway and prepared for the Zygeth guards. Xanoth signalled for them to withdraw their bows and aim at the oncoming enemy.

"Wait until they close in and then aim for the throat and fire!" Xanoth waited as the distance between them and the guards narrowed, panic had been washed away by a surge of adrenaline and he was once more completely in command. "Now!" he called, sweeping his arm down in a chopping motion. The soldiers fired their first round, bows thrumming almost in unison. Most of the arrows deflected off the enchants' armour, clinking as they did so. But one did hit the target and the Zygeth flopped to the ground in a heap. The rest quickly reformed.

Xanoth's soldiers reloaded, ready to fire another round. "Fire!" he commanded.

Their targets were almost upon them now and the second round managed two more hits. The enemy stopped in their paths and raised their double swords.

"Take cover!" Xanoth yelled as men scrambled for safety. The Zygeth fired and three men went down: the pestilent blue gel instantly beginning to dissolve their leather armour, spreading onto two more men as they took shelter. Aiden watched helplessly as all five dissolved into the muddy ground.

The Zygeth relentlessly kept up the attack, hitting the buildings they were concealed behind and sending gouts of rubble covered in blue gel into Xanoth's troop, infecting another man.

"We need to retreat!" Aiden shouted hoarsely across the alley.

Xanoth nodded tersely, giving the signal to retreat to the orpids. At the sound of heavy steps, he spun around, shock robbing him of his senses for an instant as he stared at the massed Zygeth. Fear gripped him as he realized his squad were sitting ducks. The guards raised their swords.

"Run!" Aiden screamed.

Xanoth watched, frozen, as his squad scattered, running in the opposite direction, sloshing through the muddy, dirt-filled streets. Bolts of blue burned through the stale air landing on target. Xanoth was hit but, incredibly, he absorbed the corrosive gel, as if his body had sucked it in.

Two of his men dived into the muck, only narrowly avoiding enemy fire. Aiden was one of them, his many hours of training paying off. The rest of the troop were disintegrated in seconds. Xanoth stared in disbelief, all the power seemed to run out of him and he dropped to his knees, sinking into the muck, exhaling sharply as he looked at the piles of congealed slop through a haze of numbness and grief. He spat bile, shaking his head in an effort to clear it as he exhaled deeply again. Suddenly he was furious, whirling around, his first arrow notched even before he finished the turn, he fired repeatedly, his arrows finding the vulnerable throat area and penetrating with a satisfying clunk. Letting fly his last arrow, he eyed his remaining four opponents. Before he could unsheathe his daggers, the enchants aimed their weapons once more. Xanoth raised his hand in an impotent warding off gesture. Immediately, his hand began to vibrate rapidly, pulsing aqua blue. To his amazement, the Zygeth powered down, their heads flopping uselessly to one side.

Gingerly, Xanoth approached them, prodding the nearest one to him. Receiving no response, he pushed the thing, only to see it crash to the ground in an unresponsive heap. Testing out the other three, he found the same response, or lack of. For some reason beyond his understanding, the monsters remained completely harmless.

"What did you do?" Aiden had crept up behind him.

Xanoth kept his eyes on the enemy. "I don't know." He did know that the technology in his hand had somehow just saved them both. Above their heads, the sky filled with the flapping of orpid wings as the only other survivor of their group approached with their rides.

Aiden's eyes widened as he stared at Xanoth's hand, still pulsing with a cold, blue light, his own hand going instinctively to the dagger hanging at his side. "What the…" He cleared his throat and said a little more calmly. "Mind telling me what's going on?"

Xanoth gave the young man a long, measuring look, finally he said, "I was implanted, Aiden. It's a confidential experiment with Zygeth technology." He blew out a breath, "but I think it just saved our lives."

Aiden nodded. "It'll go no further, you can trust me." He saluted Xanoth. "Now, let's get out of here."

11

Mind Control

An elegant, elliptical room surrounded Anamai as she slept. There was an archway leading to the bathing area, and an exotic fish tank embedded into one complete wall.

She was woken by the small communicator device on her bedside table.

"We need you in splicing, we've a new specimen," a female voice announced.

"I'm on my way," Anamai answered, wearily getting out of bed. She walked to the wall on her right and gestured at it. A wardrobe opened and she pulled out her laboratory clothes: white trousers with side pockets and an airy top. Tying her glossy, mahogany hair away from her face, she walked over to a curved information terminal.

"Xatine."

The machine fizzled for a moment, then a screen appeared and Anamai reached through the screen to pick up a cup of Amunisari's most stimulating warm drink.

Carrying the drink with her, she made her way into the bathing area, where warm air blew over her blemish-free face and refreshed her whilst she finished her drink.

Taking the cup over to the terminal, she placed it back through the screen and exited the room.

* * *

Pure, bright light beamed from between angular, aesthetic blocks. The splicing room was of an interesting design, large and rectangular in shape, with a high ceiling. There were numerous textured-marble terminals embedded into the straight walls and curved tables in the middle of the room, all with a big virtual screen.

A pretty, young assistant approached her. "Here are the samples." She passed Anamai the two pen-like containers.

"Thank you." Anamai strolled to the middle desk and pushed a few pressure pads on the screen. A virtual test tube filled with fluid projected itself from the flat screen to make a fully formed 3D image. She focused to the molecular level and manipulated the fluids. The machine then dripped the genetic material from the samples into the test tube, allowing it to mix. Once done, the mixture dribbled through a small pipe and she collected it into a new injection container.

"Is the host ready in genetics?" she asked.

Her assistant nodded agreement. "Yes."

* * *

The two scientists arrived at the genetics laboratory, crossing immediately to a helpless man floating in blue liquid. He had many pipes and tubes connected to him.

"Where's this one from?" Anamai asked, injecting the spliced RNA into one of the tubes and watching as it flowed quickly into the subject.

"Somewhere called Alkoryn. I don't know where that is," the assistant replied.

"I've not heard of them."

"Indigenous to this planet, I believe."

Anamai shot a look directly at her assistant, her tied back, mahogany ponytail whipping to the side. "We're experimenting on the indigenous people now? You know I only work with volunteers and basic clones," she said, anger sharp in her voice. "I'll speak to Ceolm about this. But, it's too late for this poor man."

She handed the injector to her assistant and shaking her head in dismay, hurried from the room.

Storming down a series of white passageways, she stopped at Ceolm's office door.

"I need to see you, sire." Anamai aimed her words at the comm device next to the door.

"Enter." Ceolm's voice, slightly tinny through the device, reached her ears as the door slid open allowing her admittance. Anamai faced the mature man with pitted skin and the darkest black hair she had ever seen on anyone, ensconced behind a large, smooth, white desk.

"Sire, I wasn't told we were experimenting on the local people." She placed both her hands on Ceolm's desk. "This isn't what I agreed to."

Ceolm eyed her silently, taking in her outraged expression and the frown etched on her forehead. He sighed. "Anamai, we needed new blood, our splicing and cloning technology is behind schedule." He folded his arms and sat back in his chair. "I'm sorry, but we can't elevate our race if we don't go further afield to do our research." He pinned her with a look from his stern, crystal-blue eyes.

Anamai refused to be cowed. "I'm not happy with this," she told him evenly. "I won't work on splicing anymore." She stood up straight, drawing herself up to her full height. "I request a transfer... full-time... to cloning."

"Very well." Ceolm shrugged, undeterred. "I'll get Ethen to continue your work."

"I'll visit him, make sure he's up-to-date."

"As you wish."

Ceolm glanced back to his holo-screen and Anamai realized she had been dismissed. She turned and walked away from her superior.

* * *

Xanoth roused himself from another dream of Anamai. Swinging his legs out of bed, he sat up, savouring how good he felt, as if all was right with his world. His eyes lit up with humour as he took in his surroundings: hardly paradise, but he had the growing idea that anywhere would be just fine if only Anamai was there too. Then reality came crashing in and he scrubbed his hands through his hair, mocking himself for a fool. Sighing, he squared his shoulders and pulled on his beige shirt, steeling himself for the coming meeting. Once dressed, he ambled across to the equipment locker. Opening it, he took out his bow and daggers before reluctantly reaching for the sheaf of papers at the back. His next stop was the mess hall. After a quick breakfast, he made his way to General Connor's office.

The General had not yet arrived. Xanoth glanced down at the papers clutched in his right hand and let out a long, pent-up breath. The sooner this was over, the better, it was not a meeting he was looking forward to. He tried to focus his attention on a small group of photos hanging on one wall. Family portraits, he presumed, he stepped closer, scanning them for any resemblance to the General but could find none. Military schematics covered another wall; this morning, he could find nothing of interest in those either. The dim lamp crackled and buzzed as it hung low over Connor's messy desk.

Who *are* the Alkoryns, he found himself wondering. His thoughts were interrupted as the door opened and his superior entered the room. Xanoth snapped to attention, holding out the mission report.

The General met Xanoth's gaze, his own eyes expressionless. "Xanoth." He gave a brief nod. You're here, good," he said, crossing to his filing cabinet and slamming closed an open drawer. He flicked through the report, then, sitting down, he gave it his full attention. Silence stretched whilst the General read through the report. Suddenly his eyebrows shot up almost into his hairline and he skewered Xanoth with a disbelieving stare. "Nearly the whole squad – wiped out?"

Xanoth put his head in his hands, sighing. "Yes, sir."

Connor thumped his fist down onto the report, jumping up from his chair he strode around the room.

Xanoth said nothing. He knew exactly how the grief ate at you, twisting your guts until you had to move, walk, run, do something to try to contain it in some small corner of your mind before it drove you crazy.

Finally, the General stopped pacing and looked at him. "Yet you found out, by accident, that the technology inside you can control the enchants?"

Xanoth had to clear his throat before he could speak. "T... they... all just stopped at my command, yes."

Connor grunted. "Well, soldier, we payed a heavy price, but this discovery may yet save many more lives."

Xanoth nodded slowly, that was the one thought that offered him any comfort. "We should tell the colony, sir, about this, I mean." He held out his hand, palm up. He could feel it, an alien entity, burying its way into his nerve pathways, into his neural network. He swallowed hard; how far would it go? How much of him would it devour? Xanoth forced himself to let the fear go. Done was done, and no undoing it now.

General Connor was speaking, "Absolutely not, man! It could cause widespread panic in the civilian population. And soldiers will all be wanting it, which we can't provide." He clenched his lips together.

"You're right, of course, sir." Xanoth was just about to stand up when he paused. "I had another vision of Anamai's life," he said, avoiding the General's eyes. "Whoever those people were or are, they experimented on a race known as the Alkoryns."

"And yet you say these are the good guys." Uncertainty coloured Connor's tone.

"We don't know the full story yet. Anamai insists we save them, despite their shortcomings," Xanoth persisted.

"And what use is this information to us?"

Xanoth kept his gaze on the floor. "It isn't – yet."

"Hmmph! Well, moving on." The General sat back down in his chair and put his elbows on the desk. "We need to utilise this power you have—"

"I want to go back to the gardens, sir," Xanoth interrupted.

"The gardens from the infiltration mission?"

"Yes, sir. I'll be able to test this ability I seem to have to control the enchants; should make it easy to get inside."

"What about the Loyalist guards? It won't work on them."

Xanoth shrugged, anxious to put his new found skill to use. "I can dispose of them in the usual way, and sneak in from the high plateau at the top of the prison."

Connor rubbed his chin, considering. Finally, he nodded. "All right. Go and get some rest for now. Your mission can wait till tomorrow."

Xanoth saluted smartly and hurried out before the General had time to change his mind.

* * *

The bulky, rusty hatch opened out into Stygia and Xanoth climbed out. There was a smell of musty leaves and decomposing wood as he chanted to his orpid. A few minutes later, a shadow fell over him as the animal circled prior to landing. Once on the ground, it settled immediately and patiently waited for him to mount.

Keeping a high altitude in order to stay above the smog, Xanoth flew south, heading once more for Kraag'Blitz. He directed his orpid towards the plateau and as if the creature recognized the need for stealth, it landed in a discreet location above the entrance chamber.

Two Zygeth Loyalists were standing shoulder to shoulder, guarding the doorway. Xanoth quickly dismounted and pounced, taking them both down with him. He landed heavily on top of one of the Loyalists, hearing the air whoosh out of him, swiftly stabbing the other in the throat as he rushed towards him.

Before the first guard could react, Xanoth had turned, pressing his knife point home just below the man's lower jaw. The guard's expression turned to terror as he felt blood begin to ooze down his neck.

"Open it," Xanoth ordered, dragging him to his feet.

The armoured Loyalist complied and the steam driven components hissed as the door swung open. A slight increase of pressure on the knife herded the guard inside, where Xanoth smoothly severed his carotid arteries and jugular, watching impassively as the Loyalist sank to his knees before keeling over as his life drained from him in a warm, red flow.

When he was satisfied that the man was dead, Xanoth propped him in a corner and headed deeper into the building. Although he knew the route he must take, he didn't know the combinations to enable him to access the doors. He needed to find an exhaust shaft, and fast.

The next room was square with brick walls lit by torchlight. There was only one exit and the Zygeth enchant protecting it had already spotted him. He ran at Xanoth drawing his swords.

Xanoth lifted his hand, open palm towards the enchant. "Stop!"

The power seemed to instantly drain from the figure as the eerie blue glow escaping between the segmented armour faded and it came to an immediate halt, ceasing all movement, head dropping forward onto its chest.

"Open the door," Xanoth barked.

Blue fluid spilled back into the gaps between its sheathing plates and it turned around and gestured at the door to unlock.

Before crossing the doorway, Xanoth once more told the thing to stop, still experiencing a mild shock of surprise as the enchant immediately complied.

* * *

Inside what was the watchman's quarters, a venting shaft cover beckoned to him. Too high to reach, Xanoth silently breathed a sigh of relief for the sturdy table, one end of which was close enough to allow him some purchase. He wasted no time in climbing onto it. Pulling his grappling hook from a deep pocket on the inside of his loose fitting coat, he threw... and missed. The second attempt found its mark, and quickly Xanoth began to climb.

Clinging to the rope, he pulled the covering off and held onto it as he hauled himself into the shaft, replacing the cover from the inside.

The dark passageway ahead was strung with dusty cobwebs and the gritty taste of ancient grime tickled his throat, making him cough. In the polluted atmosphere his eyes prickled and watered.

Before moving on, he unhooked his compass to check his bearing. He needed to go down, then west, through the tunnels.

Still he lingered. What if the gardens were just a dream, a figment of his overwrought brain? He pushed the unwelcome thought away, real or not, he was here; he had this strange new ability to control the enemy. Whatever else he might accomplish, finding out more about that was worth the risk of the journey.

As he traversed through the many tunnels, Xanoth experienced a sudden flash of heat. *Keep going.* The thought was his own but it appeared in his mind involuntarily. He guessed it was Anamai communicating with him in a different fashion. His doubts falling away, he quickened his crawl.

Hours passed, taking a gruelling toll of his body; cobwebs, dirt and sweat covered him like a second skin, his knees, hands, elbows and shoulders threatened to give out and his back begged to be free of strain. Just when he thought he couldn't do it anymore, that he would have to lie down where he was, in all the filth and darkness, and rest, Xanoth finally glimpsed a dim light shining from around the next corner. Easing his aching body into the opening of an adjoining tunnel, running vertically, he saw a stream of light split horizontally by the gaps in the cover. Beyond the vent, he could see the five exhaust chambers which he had found during his last visit.

Urging his tired legs once more into action, he kicked the vent cover loose, letting it tumble down to the rocky ground below and abseiled down, allowing himself to come to rest in a heap on the cold, uneven floor. He remained like that for a long moment, massaging his knees and calves and working his shoulders and back before unhooking his rope and hobbling toward the chamber where he had fallen unconscious on his previous visit.

The layout was familiar and he recognised the correct chamber as soon as he reached it; he could feel the fresh floral breeze blowing from the huge vent embedded into the stone floor.

Cautiously, he climbed the outer ladder, then descended down the internal ladder. His coat blew up with the airflow from the massive, spinning fan blades and Xanoth gritted his teeth and hoped that he would lose nothing from his pockets.

Eventually he reached the pristine vent he had found on his last visit. Pulling it open, he entered the first of the final few shafts. He could see a bright light ahead and he followed that and the floral smell all the way to his final obstacle. A vivid memory of the absolutely stunning gardens arose in his mind, giving him the strength to battle with the remaining shaft covering. This one was more sophisticated than the others. A fine, semi-transparent film lay across the opening and he could see nowhere to get a grip. Xanoth set his shoulder to it, pushing as hard as he could. Nothing! He kicked at it, but it wouldn't budge.

Softer. Another involuntary thought. He obeyed without hesitation, softly touching the covering with the palm of his hand, gliding it to the right. Suddenly the vent skimmed open, revealing the gardens beyond in all their magnificent glory. From where he was, Xanoth could see an oblong room with terraces of plants and colourful flowers. There were windows with a view to the outside world he had previously only visited in dreams, where he walked with Anamai. He suspected the windows revealed nothing more than illusion, as he was underground.

Climbing down into the blissfully refreshing room and positioning himself behind one of the terrace aisles, he waited.

12

Hunted turned Hunter

A crude dagger flew between the trees of the dense Stygian forest before accurately striking a pecora, a skittish creature with scaly skin and fur poking between the scales. The dagger had struck it in the head, killing it instantly. From the undergrowth, a large, brutish looking Rhajok'Don, wearing animal hides, charged towards the dead beast.

Nis'Ka knelt down on one knee and pulled out the dagger before retrieving his kill and flinging it over his shoulder. The solitary survivor carried the dead animal back to his campfire settlement, where he lowered his prize onto the forest floor.

Dropping onto his haunches beside it, he began cutting a series of staggered incisions into the animal's underbelly, making easy work of skinning the carcass. Finished, he flung the skin to the side before gutting the animal and storing its innards in his large satchel.

He sliced off a piece of leg meat, chopping it finely before mashing it with a hand sized stone and mixing in a large quantity of bark. Rhajok'Don were herbivores; Nis'Ka, in hunting, was displaying a unique behaviour.

Slapping the mash onto a metal slab, he held it over the fire. As it cooked, he let his mind slip back in time to his early childhood, foraging for berries and brambles with his tribe. He hadn't understood what real hunger was back then. The small smile slipped from his face as a picture of the last time he saw his village arose unbidden. He had awoken to the harsh sounds of battle. His head pounded and his eye shot agony through him such as he had never before experienced in his short life. Terrified, in pain, he ran: as fast and as far as he could. Finally, when he could take not one more step, he sank down onto the sweet, loamy earth and let the horror and grief take him over.

That night, alone for the very first time, he cried until he had no more tears left. The next morning he returned, creeping stealthily to the edge of the tree line and then, trembling, into the village itself. Everything was gone! The safe and happy home he had grown up in had been raised to the ground. Bodies lay where they had fallen and the large scavenger birds who served spirt as a clean-up crew were already about their task. He had believed himself to be the sole survivor. "Nothing left," he whispered to himself.

Nis'Ka sighed, nothing but death, he thought as he looked around himself at the dying trees and sparse vegetation. The forest was at the end of its life cycle; food was scarce. He had been forced to adapt to eating meat in order to exist; interestingly, he also felt ingesting flesh made him stronger.

Grimacing, he took his first bite; digesting meat wasn't easy, and he was particularly vulnerable after every meal. As he ate, he recalled the men who had destroyed his home and killed his kinsmen. He might have been just a boy at the time, but the wound had dug deep, fostering in him a lust for killing and leaving only cruel vengeance in his heart. He stared at his makeshift armour. Over the years he had ambushed a number of solitary Zygeth patrols, looting their armour and weapons. Using sinew and tree sap, he had painstakingly joined the plates together, attaching them to a leather under-suit. He had yet to test it against an actual attack from an enchant, but he felt confident it would protect him at least somewhat from the bolts of infectious gel.

Having eaten the mushy patty he had cooked, Nis'Ka stamped out the fire and rested against a fallen log.

* * *

A few short hours later, Nis'Ka was up, packed and ready to

move. For the last few years, ever since he had found out that she was alive, he had been preparing himself for what had become his ultimate goal: to rescue his mother from slavery. He had been surveying Kraag'Blitz for weeks and now felt he was strong and fit enough to make his move.

Hiking through the forest and over the mountainous ridge overlooking Kraag'Blitz, he sought out a large boulder and settled himself behind the cover it provided. Cautiously, he peered over the top of his shelter, his right eye tracking movement in the camp below. All that remained of his left eye was a hollowed out hole, puckered with old scars. But he had long since ceased to be concerned by that.

Days passed and Nis'Ka patiently watched the camp where his mother slaved, monitoring activity and learning the movements of the Zygeth. Finally, eight days after first arriving, he was ready.

Descending the ridge, he closed rapidly on two Loyalist guards, normal men dressed in Zygeth armour, patrolling the parameter. As big as Nis'Ka was, he had practised the art of a stealthy approach. Once he was close enough, he launched himself at them, a dagger in each hand. The vicious blades penetrated the back of the guard's necks as easily as a spoon sinking into porridge, killing them both outright.

Dragging the bodies out of sight, he concealed himself behind a large outside chimney, built with segmented plates of metal circling around the shaft. There he waited until he was convinced the coast was clear.

He was only a few hundred feet away from the slave quarters when an enchant came into view. Nis'Ka stopped dead, hugging the shadows he patiently observed from a distance.

Suddenly a cry went up. "Intruder! Over here!" Swivelling around, Nis'Ka saw a Zygeth Loyalist running towards him.

Dropping to all fours, he charged at the man, knocking him aside like a youngling throws a rag-doll into the air, but he was too late, the enchant had spied him. Nis'Ka let fly his daggers, grabbing up the body of the Loyalist just as the Zygeth enchant raised his swords and fired. The flesh-eating gel shot home but was absorbed by the armour of the dead Loyalist. The enchant quickly realized his mistake and was now running full pelt at Nis'Ka. As the distance between them narrowed, Nis'Ka threw the body at his attacker, dodging a blow from the enchant's sword. Before Nis'Ka had time to draw breath, another stroke from the weapon whistled past his ear, narrowly missing his head. The Zygeth swung again and the Rhajok'don crouched and dodged as the sword slashed overhead. Seeing an opening, Nis'Ka rammed the enchant with the side of his body, the momentum carrying the enchant off balance and enabling him to roll it over his back, to land heavily on the ground at his feet. As the thing lay helpless, Nis'Ka stomped on the head, killing it instantly.

Nisk'Ka groaned quietly in frustration, he was so close, a few more moments and he would have reached the slave quarters, instead he found his way barred by a small platoon of guards closing in on him; luckily they had not yet detected him.

Quickly pulling the dead enchant into an alleyway between two factories, Nis'Ka looted some of its armour, tying it onto his current array of plating with his many leather bindings.

He waited for the Zygeth to pass before sprinting towards the slave enclosure. Abruptly, a figure materialized out of the dark: another enchant! The guard spotted him immediately and prepared to fire. There was nowhere to hide and no time to think, all he could do was put his faith in the Zygeth armour. The layered chest plate easily absorbed the first shot and he managed to block the second with his arm-guard. Before the young Rhajok'Don could tackle him, the Zygeth enchant let out a high-pitched screech. Daring a swift glance behind him, Nis'Ka saw the band of Loyalists that had recently passed him heading back at the run to block his only escape.

His heart beat quickened as he swung back and forth between the blockade and the enchant; outnumbered, with nowhere to go, he had to fight, the only question was – who. He chose the enchant, outrunning the incoming Loyalist patrol unit and charging at the Zygeth. The enchant raised his sword and then stabbed it into the ground at his feet; a blue deflector field appeared. Nis'Ka kept going, raising his protected arms and crossing them in front of his face as he struck the shield. There was an almighty thud as the Zygeth was knocked off his feet with the force, but he was soon up on his feet again and springing into action. Nis'Ka agilely blocked the enchant's side swipe, unaffected, so far, by the poisonous goo. He was desperate, fighting for his life, sensing the Loyalists advancing ever closer.

As he barged forward with a powerful upper cut aimed at the enchant, he was pulled to the ground and onto his back. Five Loyalists pinned him down, the other five circling warily as their comrades struggled to hold onto his arms and legs. Nis'Ka couldn't believe that, at the last hurdle, after all his patient planning, he was going to fail. Rage added him extra strength and he managed to throw one of the Loyalists off his arm, but another immediately took his place. Moments later he was pinned down by all of them, swarming over him like a pack of roaches. Gathering his strength one more time, he pushed to his feet, despite the weight levered against him. Grabbing one of the pack viciously by the throat, he lifted him into his arms and above his head, twirling around and around before throwing him into the others. The whole group went down; confusion reigned as they slipped on the muddy earth and tripped over each other. Nis'Ka pounded his feet on the ground and smashed his hands down on two of the guards. Unsheathing his sword, he buried the point into another Loyalist; the blade slicing through armour with deadly ease. Staring wildly about himself, Nis'Ka saw that the rest were once more on their feet and that the enchant was readying his weapon. Nis'Ka knew he was overpowered: that he was going to die here without ever setting eyes on his mother, but his hatred for the Zygeth kept him going.

As three more Loyalists approached, he threw his sword, like a dart, and had the grim satisfaction of seeing a guard drop to the ground. Two bounds carried him to the limp body and he pulled his sword free and charged the other two. At his back, the enchant fired in his direction. Nis'Ka ignored the killing bolts and continued battling the remaining Loyalists. From a corner of his eye, he glimpsed movement from the roof of a nearby building. Glancing up he saw a shadowy figure. *Another?* Well, he too would die, along with the rest.

The hooded man stood. He wore tight fitting black armour. His face was tattooed with many strange black symbols and his stare pierced through the shadows with all the deadly, unemotional precision of a hunting bird with its prey in its sights.

Nis'Ka's blood ran cold. Never before had he set eyes on an adept assassin but that didn't prevent him from recognizing what he was dealing with. The sect were infamous, their reputations spreading the length and breadth of Stygia.

He watched helplessly as the adept raised his arm, seeing something materialize from out of his hand: small and cylindrical, it pointed straight at him. A small metallic stalk shot through the air at great speed, embedding itself in Nis'Ka's neck. He stumbled, still feebly trying to attack, but the sword tumbled from his hand and he slumped forward into the churned up mud. The remaining Loyalists quickly and tightly bound his legs and arms.

The enchant walked over to Nis'Ka's weakened body and examined the restraints briefly.

Seconds later the adept stood beside him. "This one is strong, take him to Viktor," he ordered. He walked away without a further look.

The guards glanced at themselves, noticeably relieved at his departure. Taking hold of Nis'Ka's arms, they dragged him unceremoniously through the muck.

* * *

Nis'Ka, stripped down to his loincloth, was chained and thrown into a stone built dungeon. A wooden slab attached to one wall served as a bed. It was much too small for him but that didn't seem to trouble his captors. Under the slab, he spied a flimsy bucket. One of the guards placed a neck collar on him, attaching it to a chain above the bed. Another slammed a bowl of green mush down on the slab for him to eat. Retreating, they clanked the door shut, making a set of strange gestures at it. Nis'Ka heard the lock click into place.

* * *

Viktor, Chief Commander of the Zygeth, a young adult with a roughcast face and grey hair with a blue undertone, was sat at his desk when an officer entered the room.

"Sire, we've captured a Rhajok'Don, he was trying to compromise the slave quarters. He killed an enchant single-handed. It took an adept to bring him down."

"Oh! I see." Viktor paused thoughtfully. "Did the adept tell you to bring him here?"

"Yes, sire."

"All right, let me take a look at him. Oh, and get me a trans-lator."

"You don't speak Rhaj—

Viktor interrupted, "No, I never deemed it necessary to learn the language of animals."

The man nodded and left the room.

* * *

Nis'Ka's looked up tiredly at the sound of the cell door opening. Two guards entered and unchaining his neck, they quickly chained his limbs instead. Pulling him to his feet, they dragged him outside. Nis'Ka could smell their fear, he growled at them threateningly, tugging at the chains with all his great strength. Overpowering them easily, he wrapped the chain on his wrists around one guard's neck but before he could do any more, the second guard darted him with a sedative. Severely weakened, Nis'Ka found himself tugged along between the two men.

* * *

Nis'Ka was bundled into Viktor's office still chained and guarded. He snorted in disgust.

Viktor turned to his translator and nodded.

"Hello," he said pleasantly. "I'm Viktor, I command this sector. I do apologise for the chains," he added, the translator rapidly interpreting his words to Nis'Ka. "I hear you performed exceptionally against my elite guards." Viktor waited for the translator to finish. "I have a proposition for you." He walked around to the front of the desk. "This whole realm is threatened by a people known as the Amunisari. They intend to obliterate everything here, including the Rhajok'Don and the Resistance."

Nis'Ka stared at him silently.

"I'd like to train and enhance you, to fight for a greater cause." A tight smile lifted the corners of Viktor's thin mouth.

Nis'Ka snarled. "Never!"

"There's something else," Viktor continued smoothly. "I can arrange for your family and tribe to be released."

This caused Nis'Ka to look directly into his oppressor's dark, russet coloured eyes. His enemy was offering him the one thing he wanted more than his own life. No! He would not join them!

"No!" he growled. He looked away from the man in front of him, concealing the hunger he knew must show in his eyes.

"Think of your family," the Commander urged. They can go back to the village and I'll allow them to live in peace."

Nis'Ka could feel the fight going out of him. Was it worth the sacrifice? And to live as the hated and feared enemy? He closed his eyes, remembering his mother's loving touch; the sound of her laughter echoed in his mind.

"I want a simple trade. You... for them," Viktor pressed his advantage. "I'm offering you the chance of vengeance on the real enemy. The Amunisari of the Golden lands."

Nis'Ka blinked hard, slowly he brought his eyes back to Viktor's. "I want to see them released."

"We can arrange that." Viktor nodded.

Slowly, Nis'Ka lowered himself to kneel on one knee. He spoke only two words.

The translator turned to Viktor. "The Rhajok'Don accepts the terms," he informed him.

Viktor nodded at his guards. "Release his kin, then take him to engineering and begin the processing work immediately."

* * *

Led in chains to the outside pits of Kraag'Blitz, Nis'Ka waited as the guards opened the gates to the slave quarters, they then directed him north. Still suffering the effects of the sedative dart, he wearily trudged along with his captors. His mind, befuddled by drugs, refused to operate and he could not be sure if the Rhajok'Don now being singled out for release were truly his tribe or not; he just had to trust the Zygeth. Whatever tribe they were, they were of his race and he needed to see them further away from Kraag'Blitz. To that end, he summoned the strength for action. His arms lashed out and he tightened his grip around the guard's necks, lifting them off the ground. "I want to see them completely safe and free, well away from here," he growled. One of the guard, eyes bulging, nodded. Nis'Ka slowly put them both down, showing his obedience, continuing to watch as the tribe walked away into the distance. As he watched them disappear, a single tear dropped from his eye. This was the last time he would see them and everything in him flinched from the destiny he had chosen, yet he did not regret his sacrifice.

When he could no longer see the Rhajok'Don, he turned to his captors. "I'm ready," he told them.

The guards escorted him back inside where he was taken to a small room with mechanised walls and an upright chamber moulded to the shape of a Rhajok'Don.

The technicians were standing by. "We'll take it from here," one of them told his escort. He took Nis'Ka by his arm and guided him inside the chamber before injecting him with a sedating fluid.

Nis'Ka closed his eyes and surrendered to the drug, and to whatever his future was.

The technician walked to a virtual control panel and touched a few buttons. Black, mechanical tubes unravelled out of the wall and wrapped themselves around Nis'Ka, embedding themselves inside of him. One of the pipes had a panel attached to it, which was placed in front of the Rhajok'Don's hollow eye socket. The tech wasted no time in forcing it into the hole, where translucent tools secured it in place. Next, a circular device with a large ring around it was attached to the socket and panels were implanted into his skull. Nis'Ka's face tensed, as did all of his muscles as the procedure continued and the implants started to connect to his brain.

As he was being turned into part machine and part Rhajok'Don, a second technician tapped a symbol and blue gel filled a translucent tube intravenously connected to Nis'Ka's arm, causing his muscles to bulge as each vein and artery glowed with an unnatural, electric-blue colour.

"The procedure's nearly over," the technician standing closest to the chamber announced.

A comm buzzed. "Sire, it's done," another team member informed Viktor.

A short while later, Viktor entered the blue-hued laboratory and slowly approached Nis'Ka.

"Very good," he said, examining the transformation thoroughly. "Once he's healed, we'll test him."

"The arena?" the head technician asked.

"Yes."

* * *

A few days later…

Nis'Ka stood in absolute darkness, with only the blue-neon liquid glowing from between his black armour plates, each one elongated to a deadly, skewering spike. A door was in front of him as he waited for his cue. As the door skimmed open, bright, almost white light beamed down onto the large arena floor. The smell of stale air rushed into the small booth, it had the faint aroma of blood and sweat. Nis'Ka stepped forward into the oval fighting area, standing on a floor consisting of a gritty, crystalline surface, similar to sand, but shiny and ebony in colour. Doors were set all the way around the arena; above him, to his right, there was a small seating area, no more than a few rows deep, where Viktor sat, together with five of his associates.

Viktor leaned over to the man next to him. "We have him under control?"

"Yes, sire." The man nodded confidently. "The influence chip's installed and activated."

"Good! Now, let's see what he can do."

In the middle of the floor, Nis'Ka slowly circled, carefully surveying each door, his gloved fists were clenched, his arms tensed, positioning the spikes on his armour outwards.

Abruptly, all the doors opened at once. There was silence as the air chilled around him.

Regular Zygeth Loyalist soldiers uniformly stepped out of the booths and readied their weapons. Nis'Ka aimed his clenched fists towards the soldiers.

The Zygeth began their march forward. Nis'Ka scanned the area, awaiting his opportunity, his mechanical eye pinpointing the Loyalists' location with precision. His augmented sight showing them outlined in red. As they took another step toward him, these outlines changed to green. Nis'Ka's gloves began to glow a bright blue and small funnels raised at his wrists. Seconds later, a barrage of barbed darts shot from the funnels and swerved apart, a few hitting each target and hooking onto their armour. A moment later and the darts exploded, blowing massive, bloody holes in Nis'Ka's adversaries. The Loyalists' bodies flopped to the ground almost in unison. They didn't stand a chance.

Viktor laughed loudly, clapping his hands. "Wonderful. Bring in the enchants."

Again, all the doors skimmed open at once, revealing an enchant standing at every booth. Randomly, without formation, they entered the arena Nis'Ka retracted his fist weapons and they melded with his gloved hands. He touched his thigh and a new weapon surfaced from the inside of his leg: a small, hand-sized scythe with two blades, one either end. Gripping it tightly, he waited as aqua-blue sparks danced over the weapon and then covered the blades completely. This was not the same substance the Zygeth enchants used, this was something far more lethal. An enchant rushed Nis'Ka from behind, but his augmented hearing made it easy for him to pinpoint the exact position of his opponent. Almost lazily, Nis'Ka turned, lifting his arm. A segmented, tough shield grew from his glove, effortlessly deflecting the enchant's sword thrust. Nis'Ka slashed down with the scythe, slicing through the soldier's neck. Blue stuff flew sideways from the wound, followed by pumping blood. Just as the enchant fell, two more attacked, hacking at his armour with their fearsome weapons. Nis'Ka barrelled into them sideways, skewering them both on his armour, watching with grim satisfaction as the blue light in their eyes blinked out as they slid off the spikes. Another enchant raced at him, Nis'Ka threw his double-bladed scythe, seeing it spin through the air, decapitating the enemy in one clean swipe. The body dropped away from the rotating head as the spinning blades chewed their way through five other enchants, costing one his arm and badly wounding the others before returning. Nis'Ka caught it easily. He scoured the area, focusing on the injured Zygeth, his enhanced sight informing him who was weakest. He charged, unsheathing a curved sword from his back. He delivered his blow with all the might of his supercharged strength behind it, savagely cleaving his enemy in half, the two halves slumping to the ground. A few enchants still lived but it was all too easy for Nis'Ka to record their positions and identify their exact movements in real time. Turning swiftly, a barrel advancing from his forearm, Nis'Ka aimed in the general direction, letting fly several bolts. Suddenly, bodies littered the ground like leaves in a heavy storm.

Only one opponent remained. Dressed in black, with a tattooed face, the figure hung from the arena balcony by one hand, its bright-blue gaze piercing the space between them. An adept!

Abruptly the assassin leapt from his position and flew over Nis'Ka's head, his cloak hardening for flight, his armour, consisting of small, flexible plates for increased agility, fully visible. As the adept sped from one balcony to another, he threw sharp little darts at the Rhajok'Don, which his armour deflected effortlessly. Nis'Ka dropped his arms and segmented whips slithered their way down through the contours of both arms. They sparked with an electric-blue glow as they collected onto the ground. He began to swing both whips around in front of him, slicing through air with a whistling sound; allowing them to grow in length before suddenly whipping one towards the adept, who leapt easily away, firing off two of his bolts. Once more, Nis'Ka's armour deflected them. The figure leapt again, a little lower, grabbing at Nis'Ka's helmet, yanking it free, tearing through the blue substance welding it to the Rhajok'Don's skull. The adept hit the ground and rolled a few times before jumping gracefully to his feet, executing a perfect landing.

Nis'Ka roared, charging toward his enemy, who leapt upwards, throwing more darts at the Rhajok'Don, aiming for his unprotected head. Nis'Ka felt their impact as they stabbed into him, yet, almost instantly, they dissolved. Whatever had been done to him had given him a unique defence system.

The Rhajok'Don retaliated by unclipping a hand-sized circular device from his hip and throwing it at the slayer. The device flew across the arena, expanding open into a wide metal net; sparks crackled along the webbing. The adept attempted a jump, but the net was too wide and he found himself trapped and pinned to the wall. Completely immobilised, unable to move his arms, the assassin screeched as he squirmed trying to free himself, but it was in vain. Fear embraced him for the first time as he stared towards Nis'Ka. The Rhajok'Don swung his whip, letting it build momentum, until he propelled it towards the restrained Zygeth. The pointed end skewered the adept square between his eyes, for a moment he stopped squirming and his eyes deadened. Then, as if given a second life, the assassin awoke. Nis'Ka frowned, pounding towards the trapped adept. Once within reach, he ripped the slayer from the net and closed his fist around its head. He squeezed. The assassin thrashed desperately, screaming with agony as bones snapped and ground together. Abruptly, the head popped, splashing blood and brains over Nis'Ka, the body slumped to the ground, blood gushing from the neck. Satisfied, the Rhajok'Don let go of what remained of the skull.

Loud clapping erupted from the balcony as Nis'Ka slowly

raised his eyes. All six men were on their feet applauding the performance. Viktor was laughing heartily. "You're perfect!" he called.

Then, turning to his associates. "Our most advanced soldier yet. I'd say the project was a success."

The other men nodded in agreement.

Perfect.

13

Meeting the Amunisari... again

The door skimmed open and Xanoth quickly ducked behind one of the larger trees as a slim woman walked into the garden.

Peering cautiously around the trunk, he saw a girl, in her early twenties, dressed in lilac utility trousers, with a tight-fitting vest to match. Her hair was a pale lilac, too, tied back into a ponytail with a few shorter hairs framing her face.

Intrigued, Xanoth stayed where he was, quietly observing her. His interest was particularly caught by her colours. He had never seen such beautifully hued colours before. In one hand she held a small pad. She walked briskly over to a patch of vegetation where some kind of red fruit, approximately the size of a small plantae, a potato of sorts, hung from thin, spikey branches and plucked one free before taking a small nibble. Xanoth watched her tap the pad she carried and his eyes widened in surprise as it instantly enlarged. Her fingers darted across the surface. Moments later, it had gone back to its original size and the young woman attached it back onto her belt. Turning around, she headed for the door, and, stealthy as a tygrisa, Xanoth stole after her. Surreptitiously, he crept along, mindful to keep the rows of plants between them. He waited until she was out of sight before crossing to the door and risking a glance out into a white panelled corridor. Xanoth frowned, there was a black tint visible from in between the irregular sized panels. Doors stretched away from him on either side. Moving silently, Xanoth followed after the young woman. Pushing open a door on the left, she disappeared into another room, leaving a cloud of steam and the earthy smell of loamy soil trailing in her wake. Xanoth quickened his pace. Carefully, he cracked the door a little wider. What met his gaze was a steamy, close climate. He stared up at trees that were a dark, sodden umber; their barks were coarse and a deep-brown moss clung to the fissures, nooks and crannies of the trunks. Ahead of him, the woman pulled out her pad once more. Flattening himself against the wall, he took a deep breath and prepared to follow. Taking a tentative step into the room, he abruptly found himself face to face with the young woman.

She regarded him with honest, pale-violet eyes. "You can stop tailing me now," she said calmly.

Xanoth stared at her in utter bemusement. The last time he had felt this discomforted was when General Connor had caught him on his way to bunk off school so he could make out with his girlfriend. He was ten years old at the time. Then, just like now, he had had no clue what his next move should be. Snapping his mouth closed, he took a moment to ponder. "Er," he managed as he slowly raised his hands, palms outwards.

"I knew you were here the whole time." She turned her pad around to show him and there was a radar pulsing revealing exactly where Xanoth was. "I guess you're part of the Resistance?" she asked pleasantly.

"Er." Xanoth slowly and carefully lowered his hands. He was stumped. This wasn't going as he might have imagined an encounter would. He gave an open armed shrug. "Correct. Ten out of ten. So... how did you know I wasn't going to hurt you?"

"I didn't, but I never let you get close enough." She smirked. "And even if you'd tried, I can take you."

"Oh, really." Xanoth wasn't sure if that was an attempt at humour or if she was needling him. Given his situation, he decided to treat it as the first.

"You can relax," she told him. You're in no danger here." Throwing common sense to the orpids, he said, "Aren't you the Zygeth?"

"Good gracious no! I'd never join the Zygeth!"

The girl seemed almost offended by the question, and Xanoth

was growing more confused by the second. He scrubbed his hand through his hair. What the...? He pointed at the ceiling. "They're just above you, committing atrocities," he ground out.

"We don't interfere with them and they leave us in peace," she explained solemnly.

Despite his best efforts, Xanoth could feel the anger starting a slow burn in his gut. "So you just ignore it, huh, the enslavement of the Rhajok'Don?"

For the first time, the young woman in front of him couldn't meet his gaze. "We... don't like what they do, but we can't interfere! They're an authority over us and won't allow us to go above ground." She fiddled with her pad. "But they do also offer us protection. If we want to survive, we just have to be ignorant of the evil they commit. And we have a common goal – to return to our homelands."

"And what, may I ask, do you offer them in return – in order for them to leave you unharmed?" Xanoth's voice was harsh, cold.

"Our research."

"What? You make them stronger, harder to kill? Are you and your people the ones responsible for the pestilent blue muck?" This time Xanoth made no effort to hide his anger. Too many good men, brave soldiers and friends, had died in torment, eaten away by the terrible stuff.

"Please be calm," she urged. We... have no choice. We're not warriors, we're scientists."

Xanoth exhaled deeply, head lowered, giving in to a dull feeling of defeat. He was silent for a moment before raising his head to look directly at her. "If you're not Zygeth, then who are you?" He watched a triangular leaf fall from the tree behind her.

"We... are the Amunisari."

The words fell on him like rubble, burying his hopes. "I see," he said, glaring into violet eyes swimming with specks of pink. He scarcely dared ask, but he had to. He had come too far, risked too much to fail now. Pulling in a long, despairing breath, he said, "I need to know about someone called Anamai."

"Now that's a name I've not heard in a while." She stared at him, openly curious. "She wrote 'The Revolution Prophecy', you know. She has many followers, even now, years after she was taken by the Zygeth."

"Where can I find her?"

"You can't. I don't know where the Zygeth keep her." Her expression was apologetic. "You can try to reach the Collectors, they're a group of people she formed into a resistance against the Zygeth. I, too, believe in their teachings, but I must keep that to myself around here."

"Where can I find them?"

"The far side of the compound – take this locator." She tapped something into it before handing him a small pad, similar to hers. "I've marked on where the Collectors reside." She walked swiftly across to a sliding cupboard under a tray of plants and retrieved some clothes. "You may want to change. You won't need weapons here. You can return when you find a way to go above ground."

Xanoth's hazel eyes narrowed. "How do I know I can trust you?"

"You don't. But believe me, I trust you, I have faith in your cause. I'm happy here, the Zygeth fight for something which will destroy all our lives. The rest of the Amunisari are blind to it."

Xanoth was silent, then, abruptly, he came to his decision. Trust her or not, he was at her mercy. He nodded. "All right." Taking the bundle of clothing, he began to strip off his khaki uniform, hiding a smile as he saw his new benefactor's flushed face before she spun around, hastily placing her back to him. The fresh attire was very comfortable and Xanoth quite liked his new look, white vest with utility trousers. Having done up his boots, he straightened up. "I'm ready," he said. "Thank you." He grinned. "I'm Xanoth, pleased to meet you...?"

"Oh, Lilah, my name's Lilah, and I'm pleased to meet you,

too." She smiled a little nervously. "Just follow the directions on the screen, see?" She pointed at the pad.

Xanoth winked. I'll see you soon," he said, clasping her fingers in a brief handshake. "And thank you again."

* * *

Examining the map on the pad in more detail, it was fairly obvious to Xanoth that the location currently flashing green, to the east of his position, was his destination point. More puzzling was the strange symbol in the bottom corner. Xanoth gave a mental shrug, and set off down the corridor. He had taken no more than two steps when, suddenly, the flashing green beacon materialised from the pad and bobbed off down the corridor. When he took his eyes off the little machine, the symbol became invisible and he had to use the pad to track it.

He was already heading in the right direction. The corridors were brightly lit and the spotlights caused Xanoth to scrunch his eyes up against the pain the lighting caused. As he passed the other clear, doors, he stole a quick look into each one. To his amazement, behind them were gardens.

One was a desert, a sandy oasis, another revealed a frozen landscape where white flakes drifted lazily to the earth, another consisted of marshy ground with purple water; each area was unique and completely different from another. At the end of the corridor, ahead of him, lay another door. Further investigation revealed what looked like a small connecting room, leading to another room which was comfortably furnished with cushioned, segmented seats that curved around tables. Two people were sat conversing in one corner. As Xanoth hesitated, he saw them wave over a domed device. Astonished, he watched it open sideways, displaying an array of drinks and food.

Well, nothing for it – his map was insisting he go through there. Gingerly pushing open the door, Xanoth entered. The two men momentarily paused in their conversation, glancing at him. Xanoth gave a brief nod in their direction and almost sighed with relief when they went back to discussing whatever he had interrupted.

The trail led him to the right, where he entered another corridor similar to the one he had just left, with the same tiled walls slanting upwards to a point. There were another ten doors either side of him; a glance was all he needed to tell him that behind them were yet more climate controlled botanical gardens. Coming to the end of this hallway, he was faced by an elevator, the technology of which was like nothing he had experience of. The triangular door vanished as he approached, allowing him to walk inside unimpeded, before reappearing as the elevator whirred upwards.

* * *

The ride came to a smooth stop. Once more the door disappeared and Xanoth entered an area he recognized as lower Kraag'Blitz.

He was greeted by a huge, circular, communal hub. Groups of people stood around talking, mingling and eating. Every visible wall had machines and terminals dispensing all manner of food and drink. Everywhere he looked, translucent screens hovered just above head height. The technology was far beyond anything he had ever seen previously. In the middle of the room was another unusual sight. A glowing see through image of a nondescript woman stood on a pedestal. She was conversing with a few people gathered in front of her. More people joined as they got refreshments from the machines.

Xanoth grabbed a surreptitious glance at his map. According to the green do-hicky, he had to go left out of the hub, then immediately right.

That took him into a maintenance room. Unlike the rest of the city, there were signs here of neglect; dust covered once clean surfaces and hung in dirty, tattered ribbons from the walls. The place housed the city's ventilation and utility pipes. Xanoth noted that they ran in the same direction as his obliging little guide as it headed towards a gap between two machines. To Xanoth they were nothing more than just tall boxes attached to the wall, with flashing symbols and no obvious purpose. The glowing trail he was following disappeared through the wall. Xanoth frowned. "Now what," he muttered, perplexed. "Here goes nothing," he muttered again, rapping at the wall with his knuckles. He paused, waiting, but nothing happened. Rapidly running out of patience, he glanced down at the pad, his eyes drawn to the strange little mark on the screen. He jabbed at it with his finger a few times – nothing changed. "Great!" he said softly. "What now?" Frustrated, he ran his gaze over the machines on the wall before going back to staring blankly at the pad. Suddenly it hit him; the symbol on the pad matched one of the symbols on the machine closest to him. Reaching up he touched his hand to the corresponding symbol on the machine, relief coursing through him as the wall opened to reveal what looked like either a dingy room or a lobby. Glancing around, he saw the rock walls seemed to have been carved from the sediment. Xanoth took a cautious step inside and the temperature immediately dropped. There was a simple ladder attached to the internal wall, following the maintenance shafts. It stretched up too high for Xanoth to see where it finished.

Positioning himself, he began to climb.

* * *

The glowing trail passed through a hatch door which opened into a crawl-size tunnel. Xanoth hauled himself through and continued to the next hatch. This hissed open onto a small, low-ceiling room with rusted walls, coated in an olive coloured slime. Xanoth found himself looking at three wall sized monitors, all displaying different images of the outside of Kraag'Blitz. A dilap-idated old table stood in the middle of the space and a small electrical lamp cast its feeble illumination on the papers scattered around it. Two men, wearing dirty casual clothes, deep green in colour, stopped what they were doing and stared at him. Xanoth barely held back a groan as he slowly raised his arms and slapped what he hoped would be interpreted as a friendly smile onto his face. "Hello," he said. "Are you the Collectors?"

The two men looked at each other, then one said, "and just who's asking?"

Xanoth's gut told him honesty was called for. He cleared his throat. "I'm Xanoth, I'm part of the Resistance. I believe I was guided to this place. To the Resistance?"

The two men exchanged surprised looks. Then the second man, middle-aged, with a rugged face, who had remained silent to this point, offered his hand.

"I'm Elias," he said, shaking hands warmly, "and he's Alijah. And in answer to your question, yes we are."

Alijah, shorter and younger, grasped Xanoth's hand, pumping it up and down. "We didn't expect your movement to still be active," he said, grinning widely.

"Active?"

"I mean, after all this time"

"I see." Xanoth was not sure himself exactly how long the Resistance had been around. He had been born into it and it was all he knew, he didn't question it. He relaxed a little. "I'm hoping you can tell me how I can find someone called Anamai," he said.

"Well of course." Elias had stopped smiling. "She founded the Collectors," he said slowly.

Xanoth nodded. "I've heard that, but I need to know where she is now," he persisted.

Elias scratched at his chin. "She's up there, somewhere," he said, jerking his head towards the ceiling, "with the Zygeth." He sighed. "Tell you the truth – I don't even know if she's still alive."

He shook his head. "You can get up there. But it's dangerous."

"I'll take the ris—" Xanoth was interrupted by a loud beeping and the flashing of red lamps.

"We've one incoming, landing in five minutes," Alijah announced.

"Another one – so soon?" Elias murmured. "Signal the men to get the drifter ready."

He was rapidly pressing buttons on the nearby terminal and, as Xanoth watched, on one of the screens a shaft was opening on the outside of Kraag'Blitz. "What's happening?"

"We have a pod incoming," Elias told him, "with another banished." He hastily moved to the third screen, which panned out across the barren surface of Stygia.

"That's why we're the Collectors," Alijah said, "we collect the banished before the Zygeth do."

Xanoth shot him an astounded look. "How can you possibly get to them before the Zygeth?"

Alijah bared his teeth in a mirthless grin, his wide, golden-brown eyes fixed on the screen. "Their surveillance is limited, and we have a precise targeting system. We're able to decipher a minuscule frequency released when a pod is launched. We can track its exact destination."

As he finished his sentence, on the second screen, a smoke stream appeared far off in the dark sky. It was closing at an immense speed before levelling out and hitting the surface. It skimmed over the rocky ground, rolling and bumping, before finally coming to rest in a sludgy mud pool.

The comm buzzed. Xanoth heard static and then a voice. "Drifter's good to go."

On the first screen, a buggy slowly became visible as the lift shaft elevated it onto the surface of Stygia. On board was a Collector.

"You're good to go," Elias said.

The vehicle burst from its starting position, moving at sonic speed, hovering effortlessly over the uneven terrain.

Xanoth gave a low, admiring whistle.

Alijah laughed. "Cute baby isn't it?

The third screen crackled back into life, showing the view from the drifter's on-board camera. The only thing currently visible was the dust cloud kicked up by the high speed passage of the vehicle. As they watched, the screen turned purple and all objects were highlighted. About five hundred metres ahead of the drifter lay the half-submerged capsule. As the camera zoomed, the door opened and a slender man stumbled out and fell to the ground. From the way he lay, Xanoth guessed he was injured.

He made no attempt to move as the hover vehicle came to a halt beside him and the Collector dismounted and approached. The two conversed for a few minutes before boarding the drifter.

Moments later, the comm buzzed again. "He says his name is Daimeh and he knows Isak, a disembodied voice told them."

"Come, let's go meet our new guest," Elias said, leading the way out of the surveillance room and back to the ladder Xanoth had climbed. This time their climbing brought them to a hatch which was higher up.

Inside was a large, domed room with a triage area, and a small food dispenser; beds lined the edges and terminals hung on the walls.

"Is this all you have?" Xanoth asked. "But you've so much technology downstairs," he said glancing around.

Elias slapped him heartily on the back. "We're a little rough around the edges," he admitted. "Operating outside the walls has its limitations. But, overall, our technology's just as advanced as anything you'll find on Stygia."

Xanoth noticed a stout man, dressed in white robes, sat behind a thin drape in the triage area, seemingly deep in thought.

"Who's he?"

Alijah glanced toward the isolated man. "That's Isak," he said. "He arrived a few days ago."

Xanoth was silent for a moment. This must be the lonely man he had seen arrive in the capsule. Right at that moment, the hatch door opened once more. In came the Collector, followed by Daimeh, who was so tall he had to crouch down to enter.

"Come," the Collector said, leading Daimeh over to a tattered triage bed, "rest, my friend, you're safe here. Daimeh sank down gratefully.

"Daimeh, it's good to see you, my friend," Isak said, clasping his hand tightly.

"It's good to see you alive." Daimeh shook his head, relief plain in his voice. "I feared the worst." He sighed wearily. "Is this Kraag'Blitz?" His oval, peridot-green eyes were shadowed with worry.

Isak offered a tight smile. "Yes it is." He patted Daimeh's hand consolingly. "I only arrived a few days ago. It's still all a bit of a blur." He paused, forcing another small smile. "This place is very different to home – I've yet to settle."

Daimeh eyed the other man's unkempt stubble and weary face. "It's so dark... and cold."

"Yes it is," Isak's voice was wistful, "but we must get used to it. This is our life now, we'll never see the Golden Lands again."

Daimeh's shoulders drooped as he fought back tears. "I'll never see them again, will I?" he asked lethargically.

Isak sighed. "It's doubtful."

Alijah had found a wet flannel, he dabbed at Daimeh's nose and mouth, clearing away the blood that was drying on his skin. "You took a nasty knock there," he said.

"Who are you people?" Daimeh asked.

"We're the Amunisari," Alijah told him quietly.

Elias piped up. "The Collectors, to be precise."

Alijah nodded. "Yes – a small movement within the Amunisari."

Isak gave Elias a curious glance. "What exactly do the Collectors do?"

Elias shrugged. "We collect the banished before the Zygeth can."

"Who are the Zygeth?" Daimeh asked, his attention piqued.

Xanoth nostrils flared. "They're a vicious, authoritarian organisation with a single goal – to return to the lands they were banished from. They'll destroy everything that gets in their way of achieving that," he said flatly.

What... what would they've done if they'd reached me first? Daimeh asked nervously.

Alijah answered. "They would've either imprisoned you or offered you a life as a Loyalist to their cause or, of course, they may just have killed you."

Isak dry washed his face. "Do you know why they're the way they are?"

Alijah grunted. "They started out as a military movement, led by an activist who wrote 'Banished No More.' His name was Zygeth. He believed he could take back the Golden Lands and he gained support from many scientists and ex-Amunisari security people. Eventually they went above ground and amassed huge numbers, building everything on the surface. There, all cleaned up," he said.

Daimeh stared at Isak despairingly. "What do we do now?" All he really wanted was a way to take revenge on Ceolm but the idea seemed hopeless. He brushed his hand through his ear length, dark-auburn hair.

"You can stay with us," Elias told him gently.

"I don't belong here."

Isak leaned forward. "This is the only place you belong now."

Daimeh shook his head. "Ceolm has to pay for what he's done! That won't be possible if I stay here"

"You must let it go, Daimeh," Isak insisted. "These people are good people."

"Maybe the Zygeth will help me?"

"The Zygeth won't help you," Isak growled. "They'll use you

for their own ends. They want one thing only – war with the Amunisari in the Golden Lands." Isak shook his head. "Stay here with us, you can make a new home."

"If the Zygeth want war, I can go with them, and go back to Alkoryn."

"How do you even know there'll be an Alkoryn left?" Isak asked.

"If I were you," Xanoth interjected, "I'd seek out Anamai, she may have the answers you need."

"Who is she?" Daimeh grasped at Xanoth's suggestion like a drowning man clutches at a plank of wood.

"It was her who started the Collectors," Isak said slowly. Now she's a prisoner of the Zygeth." He looked squarely at Daimeh. "I won't be going with you."

Daimeh let out a breath he hadn't been aware he was holding. Fear rippled up his spine but he met Isak's gaze unwaveringly. "I understand, Isak." Laying himself down on the narrow cot, he closed his eyes. "I need rest now."

Isak nodded. "Yes, of course. We'll speak again later."

Abruptly, Xanoth felt the weight of his own exhaustion. He yawned. "That," he said, "is the best idea I've heard since I got here." He smiled at the two men. "I'm pleased to have met you both. And now, I'm going to find somewhere to get some shuteye."

"Over here," Isak said, leading Xanoth to another cot before disappearing back behind the covering curtain.

14

A Lesser of Two Evils

Ethen was busy when Anamai invited herself into his area. Marching straight over to him, she wasted no time coming to the point. "Ethen," she spoke crisply, still angry and disgusted at what she had discovered, "you'll be taking over my splicing research."

"I will?" He stopped what he was doing and studied her, his pale eyebrows crawling towards his scalp in surprise.

"Yes." Anamai frowned. "Did you know we were experimenting on a race of people called the Alkoryns?"

Ethan hesitated, then, "I did know."

Anamai wasn't sure what she had expected in answer to her question, but his bland admission made her want to scream in frustration. Instead, she gritted her teeth and waited, her eyes boring into him.

"Here," he said, "let me show you."

Ethen pushed a few buttons and panels on the wall slid aside to reveal a virtual screen. The monitor showed a bird's eye view of a group of islands: Alkoryn, she presumed.

"We've been observing them for millennia; taking one every three hundred years."

"What!" Anamai shook her head in disbelief. "Ceolm led me to believe this was the first time we'd done anything like this!" She slid her fingers over the map, tapping the screen to focus in on particular villages, staring silently as she watched the Alkoryn people going about their lives in peace. Her gaze once more fastened on Ethan. "You know this is wrong?" She waited, but if she had been hoping for some kind of reply, she was left disappointed.

* * *

The lighting in the corridors was dim, as always during sleep time. Luckily, the observation room was close to her quarters. She carefully cracked the door open and stepped inside, closing the door quietly behind her. The lighting was low here, too, but it didn't matter. Anamai stared at the screens covering the walls, seeking out the ones focused on various sites in Alkoryn. The names of the places were tagged onto the images. One said Aelston, another was Aedolyn's Promise. The buildings here were impressive and, even during sleep hours, here and there, people moved through the streets. Anamai guessed this was the capital. A third screen showed the view over somewhere called Ridgemead. It was volcanic.

She narrowed her attention onto Aedolyn's Promise. One particular building stood out. Anamai frowned as she swept the surveillance equipment around to the front of the building. There was no doubt; the building, in a foreign land, was just too similar to the Citadel to have been built by anyone but the Amunisari. She swept her hand over the monitor, moving it on to a different terrain. Everything that surrounded that one familiar looking building was completely different in style; the Alkoryns must have erected the rest of the structures. Were these people truly indigenous? She was beginning to suspect that all was not how it seemed.

Retrieving the complete map of Alkoryn, including all its borders and even Amunisari, she zoomed in. She needed a copy of this.

Pressing an on-screen touchpad, she stood silently, unmoving as the maps flashed over her vision and burrowed into her memories.

She was not going to stand by and watch these atrocities being committed. She was going to fight Ceolm and his cronies all the way.

* * *

Xanoth awoke with a jolt. For a moment he lay where he was, letting the events of the previous day replay themselves in his head. Then he forced himself to get up and get going; he needed his things.

Daimeh was already up and standing beside his own bed, checking through his belongings. Xanoth watched him lay out four items he had never seen the like of before. "What are those?" he asked, curiosity piqued.

Daimeh shook his head, hurriedly cramming them back into his bag before picking up his sword and backpack from the table. "I–I'm not really sure," he said. "A woman, Eleanor, gave them to me in the Golden Lands."

Xanoth stretched, yawning, then ambled over to the other man. "Are you leaving?"

Daimeh nodded curtly. "I don't belong here." He tucked the sword under his belt.

Xanoth eyed him silently for a moment. "I'm not from here either," he observed.

Daimeh straightened his tunic, giving Xanoth, a look full of curiosity. "No – you don't look Amunisari."

"Guess not," Xanoth said. An awkward silence followed.

Daimeh shot him another curious glance. "I see," he said, his voice conveying the exact opposite.

Xanoth hid a smile. "Where are you headed?"

"I'm… not sure exactly. I just know I need to get to the upper levels… somehow."

"That's where I'm headed," Xanoth replied abruptly.

"To look for Anamai?"

"Yes, she's… someone I have to find."

"I can help you," Daimeh volunteered eagerly, "if you let me join you. I'm looking for her, too."

Xanoth rubbed his chin, contemplating. "Have any combat

training? You'll need it."

Daimeh stared at his feet. His only experience with knives was to open shells. "Not exactly," he admitted reluctantly.

"Well, how do you expect to help me? I suppose at least that's a start." Xanoth pointed to the sword at Daimeh's hip.

Daimeh squared his shoulders, meeting Xanoth's gaze. "Look, I really need to get out of here, and into the upper levels. Can I just tag along?"

"Why were you banished?" Xanoth asked bluntly, his hazel eyes boring into Daimeh.

"It was my choice – and the only way to save my life." Daimeh shuffled his feet, thoughts of his home flooded his mind. He shrugged them off. "The Amunisari council are corrupt. They experimented on my people, tortured me and murdered the woman I love."

Xanoth froze. "The Amunisari? But they're here; they're *good* people." He had a sudden flash of realization; Anamai must have been banished, too.

"They're also far north, in the Golden Lands, where the sun never sets," Daimeh added, resting his back against the wall.

"Never sets?" Xanoth echoed. "And you're from there, too?"

Daimeh shook his head. "I'm from Alkoryn, a peaceful community just south of the Golden Lands."

Xanoth struggled to keep the surprise off his face. Alkoryn, from his dreams! "If you're Alkoryn, how did you meet the Amunisari?"

Daimeh sighed. "It all started when a body washed ashore. There was this strange tablet, at first it had nothing on it, than it lit up and showed me a map to the Golden Lands, there was a message with it too."

Xanoth's stomach churned. He was almost afraid to ask, but he had to. "When... when you say a body, what sort of body?"

Daimeh shot Xanoth a searching look. "A race known as the Rhajok'Don, you know of them?"

Xanoth's heart missed a beat. Ugoki!

"Yes." He swallowed thickly. "I know of them." Xanoth turned his face aside, blinking hard.

Daimeh frowned. "Are you all right?"

"His name was Ugoki and he was... very close to me."

"I'm so sorry," Daimeh said softly. Such a high price so many had paid! And how many more would yet have to pay before it was all done.

"His body was treated with respect, I assure you."

Xanoth nodded.

Daimeh waited for Xanoth to collect himself before saying, "So you know of the tablet?"

"I sent it... with the guidance of Anamai."

Daimeh was silent for a moment. "Thank you – it protected my people from the Amunisari by blocking their surveillance over us. I must thank Anamai when I see her."

"We have to find her first." Xanoth scrubbed his fingers through his hair. These Amunisari had to be Anamai's people; the people she begged him to save. But, if they were corrupt like the Zygeth? Could he even trust this boy? He sighed. One thing he did know – he trusted Anamai. "Why did the Amunisari banish you?"

"The tablet has great power and it's protecting Alkoryn. They wanted the knowledge it contained. I wouldn't give it to them." Daimeh sucked in a deep breath, releasing it through his mouth. They killed Elisaris, the woman I love." Daimeh's eyes welled for a moment.

"And they banished you because you wouldn't give them what they wanted?"

"Yes. The council only care for themselves and the evolution of their race."

Xanoth felt as if he had taken a punch to the gut. The Amunisari would not be coming to the Resistance's aid as he'd hoped – or saving the Rhajok'Don.

"You understand now why I must see Anamai?" Daimeh said. Xanoth nodded. "I need to retrieve my weapons first." He walked to the hatch, clanked it open and went through it.

* * *

When Xanoth reappeared again, he was once more dressed in his familiar attire: dark khaki leathers and a loose fitting, brown, hooded coat, with his composite bow hidden beneath it. Short black metal swords were strapped to his legs, knives decorated his arms and darts were hooked to his belt.

He walked over to Daimeh, who had shot to his feet.

"I was beginning to think you weren't coming back!"

Xanoth ignored him. "We use the ladder to go as high as we can," he said, passing him a useful combat knife.

"How do we know it's the right way?"

"Up, is always the right way to find the Zygeth," Xanoth said grimly.

They exited the Collectors' bay. Looking up, they could see a grid blocking their way into a tight shaft carved out of the rock. Behind the solid looking structure, an old metal ladder led upwards, where it disappeared into a dark hole. Xanoth hacked at the grid with his black-metal sword. It broke away easily and Xanoth stepped cautiously onto the incredibly high and creaky ladder. The ancient rungs protested but they held his weight. The crumbly, stone shaft was a very tight fit around Xanoth's wide shoulders as he forced his way through the opening and began to climb. Below him, dust and stones trickled down onto Daimeh, clinging to his auburn hair.

"It's going to be a squeeze," Xanoth called back.

For one wild moment, it was all Daimeh could do to keep himself from running, then he strengthened his resolve and, taking a tight hold of the ladder, he began to climb.

Midway up the dirty tunnel, Xanoth launched into conversation. "You know it's going to be tough up there? The Zygeth are relentless." His voice reverberated off the cylindrical walls.

Daimeh worked moisture into a dry mouth. "I understand – but I have you to watch my back, right?" he said, trying to inject some humour into the situation.

Xanoth sighed and continued climbing.

As they neared the top of the ladder, they were faced with another hatch, this one was more sophisticated than the last. It was made from the same material as all the outer doors of upper Kraag'Blitz... and it was locked. Xanoth discreetly placed his hand over the locking mechanism; the blue pulse jolted through his arm and an instant later the door opened.

"What was that?"

Xanoth cursed silently. "I needed to break open the lock," he said quickly.

Fortunately, as the hatch steamed open revealing an alien looking room, with what looked like walls and ceiling covered in intertwined pipes and tubes, both mechanical and organic, all their attention turned to the black, segmented tubing from which an eerie blue glow was seeping through the gaps. The pipes and tubing wriggled in and out between one another, the arteries and veins of the organic components commingling, creating a soft, red illumination. The rest of the room was empty but for a few metal storage crates. From somewhere, there came a disturbing, squelching sound echoing around the room. An overpowering odour of meat and solder hung like a palpable cloud in the air.

Xanoth dropped feet first into the unsettling room, quickly pulling a weary Daimeh up from the tunnel.

Daimeh brushed his hands and knees free of dust and webs, staring around himself in amazement as he did.

"I wasn't expecting this." Xanoth broke the silence as he walked over to a wall.

"It's... interesting," Daimeh said, circling.

Xanoth slipped his hand in between an artery and a

segmented tube. Grabbing the slimy organic ducting, he used one of his knives to slice it open. Blood spewed from the wound in regular pulses, splashing the wall. Xanoth stood back, watching it bleed.

"What are you doing?" Daimeh stared at the crimson cascade.

"I need to see how it reacts," Xanoth said. "I want to check something out." The mechanical pipes surrounding the injured area glowed brightly as blue jelly-like slime oozed and electrical sparks flashed as a thread of organic tubing wrapped itself around the bleeding artery, connecting the two halves back together. Under their gaze, the cut healed in seconds. "As I thought," Xanoth muttered.

"Self-healing?"

"Yes."

"Fascinating." Daimeh touched the wall, threading his hands between the pipes in awe.

Xanoth grunted. "Let's get moving."

* * *

Beyond the room they had found themselves in lay a maze of biomechanically engineered corridors. Wandering aimlessly, they tried every one of the many closed doors. All were locked and they had no way to open them.

"What are we doing?" Daimeh groaned. "If we don't get out of these corridors soon, we'll die here."

Xanoth could hear the fear and desperation in Daimeh's voice. "We'll find a way out, trust me." Xanoth had been in worse situations, besides, he had Anamai on his side.

They passed another score of locked doors before coming to a stop at yet another intersecting passageway. Daimeh rested against the wall. He looked both ways. "Maybe we should go back the way we came and choose a different route?"

"I agree," Xanoth replied curtly.

Retracing their steps, they began exploring alternative corridors. They had been walking for around five minutes when they heard the echo of footsteps ahead.

"A patrol," Xanoth whispered quickly. "Hide."

Slipping silently into an adjoining corridor, they waited. As the footsteps drew closer, Xanoth peered cautiously around the corner. To his relief he saw that the guards were enchants; he would be able to control them.

"Stay here," he mouthed at Daimeh.

Daimeh nodded and Xanoth leapt from his hiding place and tore towards the enchants to deactivate them.

Suddenly, Daimeh felt the sharp steel of a blade against his throat, and a hand covered his mouth... a hand he couldn't see. Yet the pressure of invisible fingers was undeniable. Just as suddenly as he had been ambushed, the hand, as well as the man it belonged to, materialised.

"Who are you and why should I not kill you now?" he asked.

Daimeh's answer was initially muffled by the stranger's gloved grip, until he removed it.

"I'm D–Daimeh," he stammered. Then, visibly collecting himself. "I've important information for whoever's in charge."

"What sort of information?" The blade snagged Daimeh's throat.

Daimeh flinched. "Information about the Amunisari, in the Golden Lands," Daimeh said, talking fast. The blade retracted in a flash and the ambusher released his grip. "I'll escort you myself."

Daimeh glanced at his attacker, gaping at the hooded and tattooed figure with cold, aqua-coloured eyes. That soulless stare told Daimeh everything he didn't want to know. One step out of line and this man would kill him without a second's hesitation. Grabbing his arm, his advisory dragged him through the corridors.

Having subdued the guards, Xanoth hurried back to the spot

he had left Daimeh, only to find no sign of him. Xanoth struck the wall with his balled up fist. He felt responsible for Daimeh, but the fate of more than one man might be dependent on him finding Anamai and learning what she could tell him. No matter how bad he felt, how guilty, he had to keep going and hope Daimeh could look after himself.

* * *

Grimly, Xanoth tramped down endless corridors similar to those he had already traversed. With no clear way to go, he picked his route at random. Finally, the labyrinthine passageways were exhausted and he found himself looking at a solid, metal door. He could see no lock. Gingerly pushing at it, he almost fell through when it swung open easily.

Daylight streamed into the doorway, together with the mist of water vapour, as it opened onto the lovely creek from his dreams. The jungle birds calling was the first thing he heard, then the wonderful trickle of the gentle waterfall. He looked to his left and there was the gradual meandering ripple of water. Anamai sat with her legs curled under her on a hillock of perfect, jade coloured grass. Her face was solemn, as always, as she beckoned him to approach.

Xanoth hesitantly walked across the soft cushion of lawn and sat next to her. His eyes met and held her soulful gaze as she took his hand firmly.

"Your honour is admirable," she said, smiling warmly.

Xanoth searched her glorious, fiery eyes. "Why've you brought me here?"

"I needed to see you – before you find me. I wanted to thank you for the great service you've offered me. I knew I could trust you to deliver the tablet to the Golden Lands." She tightened her grip.

"I know it was the right thing to do," Xanoth told her,

wondered if he really meant what he said or was just trying to convince himself. Despite himself and the seriousness of his mission, his hazel eyes devoured her delicate face, coming finally to rest on her full, sensual lips. "My sorrowful, Anamai, let me help you."

"It's too late for me," Anamai told him, a world of regret spilling into her voice.

Xanoth drew in a long, shaky breath. Her mouth said no, but her eyes were pleading, asking him for hope. He reached out, gently cupping her smooth, silky cheek. "I'll find a way," he vowed, his own voice ragged.

A single tear spilled from her eye and rolled through his fingers. He wiped it away with his thumb before stroking his hand alongside her jaw. Again, his eyes locked with hers. This was the moment he had longed for. For this instant there was nothing else beyond her lovely eyes, the depths flickering yellow: nothing but the warmth of her skin and the fierce longing to bury his face in her soft, clean smelling hair. He was afraid to move, to speak, in case anything that he did shattered this completeness he was feeling for the first time in his life. But he had to... *needed* to say it. "You're so beautiful," he whispered. And I want you, Anamai, I've always wanted you.

She took his hand, leading it to rest on her hip. Xanoth buried his fingers in her copper coloured mane, letting the gleaming strands run through his grasp. Resting his hand gently on the nape of her neck, he slowly guided her closer to him. Her lips turned up at the edges as she smiled coyly. It was the first time he had seen that coy smile and it was as if a veil had been lifted from his heart. A sweet tension thrummed in the air between them. Xanoth's breath came in short, sharp gasps as Anamai, a delicate colour staining her cheeks, her eyes, half-hidden by her long, thick lashes, glinting up at him like stars, drew him like pollen to a bee.

"I will help you," Xanoth murmured, lowering his head to

kiss her lips. She relaxed into his arms as naturally and easily as if she had always belonged there and he rolled her onto her back, supporting himself above her on his hands, his sandy hair flopping forward, and as they shared their first embrace, the cool, clear water of the creek sang to them its song of life.

15

Unexpected Outcome

The underdeveloped body of an Amunisari infant floated, suspended inside a chamber, blue gel surrounding it and holding it in place. Anamai stood with her arms crossed staring into the large circular cell. Progress was looking good this time, she thought. She tapped on the surface of the glass and a screen appeared showing the baby's vitals. Healthy.

As she closed the screen, she heard the door to the incubation chambers open and Ethen marched over to her, looking more disgruntled than ever.

"You've not shared all the research with me, Anamai."

Anamai could hear aggression in his usually dispassionate voice. "You have everything," she told him flatly, her eyes still on the helpless babe; a specimen, pinned there for them to probe, examine and, eventually, perhaps discard as worthless.

"I think you're lying to me."

"Why do you do this, Ethen? You're a good man." Anamai spun around to face him. "What we're doing is immoral."

Ethan glared at her. "I do my job. I don't have the luxury of being Ceolm's sister," he said snidely. "If I was to just stop working on this, you know they'd banish me."

Anamai flushed, his cutting remark hitting home. "One day," she said, her eyes boring into him, "you'll have to make a decision. How far are you willing to go?"

"I'll cross that bridge when I get there." He raised his eyebrows. "Now, how about the research?"

"Go away, Ethen. I don't have it." She nodded in the direction of the door. "Take it up with Ceolm."

"Fine," he said sharply before abruptly exiting the room.

Anamai did one final check of all the babies before returning to her residence for the night.

* * *

A clanking sound awoke Xanoth. He lay still, becoming aware of another noise: something that had the resonance of sludge moving through a pipe. Opening his eyes slowly, he saw he was lying on the sticky floor of a room with the, by now, familiar Zygeth wall structure.

"Xanoth!"

Xanoth shot upright, peeling himself off the floor. That was Anamai's voice; she was calling him! He scanned the room, recoiling in shock as his horrified gaze fastened on something that froze his blood, momentarily rooting him to the spot.

A biotechnical machine, embedded into the ceiling and angled downwards, filled his vision. "No!" Xanoth shouted hoarsely, his mind refusing to process what he was seeing. It was only when he felt the cold wall pressing against his back that he realized he had retreated as far from the nightmare staring down at him as he possibly could. "No, no, no!" he whispered, his voice cracking. His legs would no longer hold him up and he allowed himself to sink back down onto the floor. "No!" The wail tore from his throat as he reached out his hand in anguish.

Anamai was suspended from the ceiling by an array of mechanical pipes joined with organic material. Only her head could be seen, sporadic tubes holding her in place. A transparent dome covering, filled with red liquid, surrounded the beautiful face he had touched in his dreams. Xanoth's gut roiled, he swallowed hard, tasting the bitterness of bile at the back of his throat. His eyes squeezed shut but he forced them open again. He had to see: had to know.

Her body was criss-crossed by an outer casing of mechanical and organic pipes. The arteries pumping blood in and out of the machine and into the ceiling beyond. Xanoth stared aghast at what he was quickly realising was her life support.

"Xanoth, please, don't fear me. I told you it was too late for me."

Xanoth wanted to weep at the guttural, gurgling voice, so unlike his dream memories. His stomach churned again but he got himself back firmly under control. The physical was nothing like his dreams but the spirit of this amazing, incredibly courageous young woman was unchanged.

Hauling himself to his feet, he crossed the room to stand in front of her.

"Come closer."

Xanoth swept his gaze around the room, looking for something to help him do her bidding. Dragging an old filing cabinet over to the centre of the room, he tested his weight on a couple of rickety, half-rotted crates before piling them one on top of the other and leaping from them to the top of the cabinet. Very gently, he placed his hand on the domed shell surrounding her face. His hand sparked as he touched her. This close, the savagery of what had been done to her was unbearable. He could feel the pressure of unshed tears and he blinked hard. Her neck had been decapitated from her body. A network of pipes disappeared into the walls and nerves and arteries linked into her. Technological neck connections pulsed, interfacing her with the machine.

"Why?" he choked.

"To get the knowledge I hold."

Xanoth rested his forehead against the dome.

"They caught me returning from the hideout and imprisoned me here. They wanted me alive and under their control. To bleed me for my research."

Xanoth's head jerked back from the dome. "The hideout? The Resistance?"

"I started the Resistance, many generations ago," Anamai gurgled.

"Yes!"

"I formed the Collectors to oppose the man known as Zygeth."

Xanoth stared at her, silent, awed by the strength and determination of one, young woman.

"The followers of Zygeth industrialised the land and enslaved the Rhajok'Don to mine their power source, the crystalline blue rock known as lazulic."

"And the Resistance?"

"As the Amunisari in Kraag'Blitz have a meritocracy and I have the knowledge, I was able to achieve a high ranking amongst them. That gave me access to privileged material. The bunker you live in was hidden from the regular maps as it was disused. I decided to make it my base of operations."

"The Collectors didn't join you?"

"Not all of them. Your ancestors did, and a few other families. We started anew. We renovated the bunker into a suitable hideout."

"You're an amazing woman, Anamai," he told her, pressing his cheek against the glass casing.

"Xanoth." Anamai paused.

"Yes."

"They used my knowledge of cloning to build the Zygeth army. And now I am a machine whose sole purpose is to do their bidding."

For the first time since he had found her, sadness touched her face and clouded her eyes.

He shook his head. "I don't believe that, Anamai. You visit me in my sleep, and I know your heart's pure. You've resisted them, held onto your consciousness." He paused. "You showed me the Alkoryns, and that you wanted to save them, that's why you were banished."

"I... was unaware I had told you this," Anamai said, confusion flashing across her face.

"I see you in my dreams each night, living your life in the

Golden Lands." Xanoth said, surprised that she had no recollection of those times.

"Those memories are not for your eyes, Xanoth. I have been compromised. Someone is trying to use my memories against us. But, remember this well, Xanoth; only the Amunisari council is corrupt. The people are innocent!"

Her still beautiful eyes held his. "Don't forget that, but don't let it make you falter from the right path."

Xanoth glanced toward the door at the sound of rapidly approaching footsteps.

"Guards are coming," Anamai warned. "Quickly! Hold out your hand. I have something for you," she gurgled. A tube snaked out from between the pipes, wrapping itself around the hand with the blue capsule embedded, and jabbing a plate of some sort into it.

Xanoth watched as his skin moulded around it.

"It will help you against the Loyalists and adepts."

Xanoth glanced toward the door again, the footsteps sounded much closer now. Hurriedly unsheathing his two short swords, he jumped down and hid in readiness.

The door opened and Xanoth saw a Loyalist dressed in Zygeth armour. Before he could react, the guard was on him. The ferocity of the attack forced Xanoth to yield ground, his ankle twisted as he lunged awkwardly and he went down.

Hastily scrambling to his feet, Xanoth prepared himself again. As he raised his hand to ward off another deadly blow, the plate Anamai had given him suddenly grew warm, distracting him and opening him to attack. What the spirit was the thing doing? He needed all his focus and concentration! Anamai had said it would help him but it seemed more likely to kill him. Perhaps it was a weapon of some sort? If only he knew how to activate it. There must be a way; if he could just get a moment or two to work it out, he thought desperately, half his mind on blocking blows and half on how the plate might work. Abruptly, a blue substance shot forth, encapsulating his adversary, solidifying on contact.

Xanoth wiped the sweat from his brow with the back of his arm and heaved a sigh of relief. "Why didn't you just give me the bolts?" he asked.

"His armour would have just deflected them."

That same dispassionate, guttural voice. Xanoth forced himself to a calm he didn't feel. "I see."

"Find the cloning chambers! I will guide you."

Xanoth nodded, unable to speak.

"Destroy what you can. Once it is done, return to the hideout and prepare yourselves for an attack."

"An attack? We're no match!"

"The Zygeth will make their move on Amunisari in two days. They will be vulnerable when they do and it is a chance for the Resistance to achieve great things with small numbers. Trust me, Xanoth."

"I do." He hoisted himself back up to his perch on top of the old cabinet and rested his head against the dome one last time, then kissed it gently.

"Now go."

For a few moments, Xanoth fought the need to just sink down where he was and let whatever might be, come. But so much depended on him, so many lives would be forfeit if he failed. Steeling himself, he met her gaze. "I'll come back," he vowed, before dropping back down to the floor and quickly crossing to the door. He left without looking back.

* * *

With guidance from Anamai, Xanoth arrived at an arched doorway covered in a biomechanical network of veins and pipes. There was an oval red bubble in the centre of the door.

"Push it." Anamai's voice in his head urged.

Xanoth did as he was told and gently squashed the bubble, it bounced back and the tubes covering the doorway retracted away and the door skimmed open.

The first thing he noticed was the smell of fresh blood mixed with the mechanical smell of circuits and machinery. The air was close and moist.

In front of him was a vast, dark, underground chamber. The only light came from the pulsing of the synthetic blood, casting an eerie, dull, red stain. The room must have been a mile wide, Xanoth thought, as he looked at the rows and rows of stationary Zygeth enchant soldiers. There were thousands of them – and this was just one of the cloning chambers.

The blood machines!

They were suspended off the ground by a tangle of organic as well as mechanical parts, the arteries and synthetic pipes connecting to the machines. They hung like gigantic bats, covering every square inch of the room, the walls and the ceiling, as the charnel slime pumped into the armoured exoskeletons. Now he knew why they seemed moulded; they *were* moulded.

Looking up, Xanoth saw a number of doors, giving onto a narrow platform running around the walls, allowing access to the machinery. An enormous, throbbing bubble sat in the centre of each row, spider like veins visible through the semi-transparent, taut skin. That, Xanoth guessed, was where the main source of blood was coming from. He had to stop it.

Unclipping his bow from his back, he aimed and fired. His arrow struck the vesicle in the exact centre, tearing it open. A tide of red slewed from the opening, splattering everything and narrowly missing him. Almost as soon as it had been injured, the mechanical tubes activated and a blue spark played over the injury as slowly, the bubble healed.

Xanoth stared at the pulsating sac: what now? He scrubbed his fingers through his hair. Weariness hung over him like a heavy cloak but he had to get this done. He could give in to... a picture of what Anamai endured rose up unbidden. Hastily, Xanoth pushed it deep into the back of his mind and straightened his shoulders. Okay, if he couldn't bleed the thing, there was only one alternative left; he had to stop it from flowing. He examined the plate Anamai had given him, half-buried in his flesh. Gingerly, he aimed and focused. Blue stuff shot toward the bubble, covering it completely before hardening. Xanoth gave a grim smile of satisfaction as it ceased pumping. That should slow production down.

Abruptly, something slammed into his back. Xanoth spun around, above him were five enchants firing bolts at him. He hastily threw his grappling hook upwards, wrapping it around a drooping pipe. As he quickly shinned up the rope, he saw a hooded Zygeth, tattoos on his face; a Zygeth he was unfamiliar with. He wondered if it was one of the elusive adepts he had heard about. The figure raised its arm and Xanoth saw a slew of metal bolts launch from its wrist, heading his way at speed. One found its mark, piercing his arm and he flinched in pain, barely managing to hold onto the rope. Then three more of the strange Zygeth arrived. Xanoth was trapped and no match against them all.

"Drop down," Anamai's voice told him. "You can escape through the tunnels below."

Xanoth glanced down, it was quite a drop, but he trusted Anamai's judgement. Letting go of the rope, he fell. The next moment he was tumbling down a blood-drenched funnel and through a small exit hole in the bottom. He plummeted down a fleshy-walled tunnel, frantically trying to slow himself down and finding nothing to grab hold of.

At the bottom of a very long drop, gelatinous bodies, smooth and featureless, identical in shape and moulded to fit their armour, cushioned a fall which would otherwise surely have killed him. A glimmer of light from above glinted off the slimy bodies; rejects, he assumed.

Another body dropped down from the opening and fell onto him, eliciting a grunt of disgust. Xanoth scrambled free of the sticky mass and crawled towards another downward chute. Easing into the gaping mouth, he found himself sliding at an alarming rate, to topple out the other end, into a vast, open crater, tumbling head over heels down the high pile of bodies. He flailed his arms uselessly, trying to find a hold to slow his fall. His palm dragged squelching through the torso of one of the blood-filled sacks that barely passed for bodies as he careered past.

Xanoth's shoulders hit rock as he fetched up against the deep wall of the crater. Winded, he lay where he had come to rest. Looking up, he saw, a long way above the crater, a clear, starry sky. Wearily, he stumbled to his feet and began the arduous task of clawing his way back up the heap of bodies. Once he was close enough, he went for his grappling hook: that was when he realized he'd left it in the cloning room. Sighing, he leapt for the nearest ledge, caught it, hanging there, his muscles trembling. He swung his other hand further up and was relieved when his fingers found their target on the first attempt. Doggedly refusing to give in to his exhaustion, slowly, hand over hand, he hauled himself out.

Clambering over the edge, he found himself on the Stygian plateau. Kraag'Blitz silhouetted against the skyline like a dark sentinel squatted close by. Opening his compass, he marked his bearings. The spirit was with him this day – he wasn't far from where his orpid had dropped him. Having made his way back to the right place, Xanoth chanted loudly into the air. After a few minutes, his orpid arrived and landed gracefully, its claws scattering gravel. Gratefully, Xanoth mounted, turning his beast for home.

As he flew north from Kraag'Blitz, his eye was caught by movement below. What looked like the remains of a tribe was wandering northward, towards the tai-qay forest. Swooping lower, Xanoth saw they were Rhajok'Don. He frowned, wondering what they were doing so close to Kraag' Blitz. If they were found, they would be either imprisoned or put to death. Deciding he had better find out what was going on, he put down close by. As he strode towards them, he knew he must make a frightening sight, covered in blood and gore, his augmented arm on show. He was not at all surprised that the Rhajok'Don seemed terrified as they huddled together.

"I mean you no harm," he said hurriedly, speaking Rhajok'Don and raising his hands. His gaze travelled over the little group. "What are you doing here?" He jerked his head in the direction of Kraag'Blitz. "You must know what this place is!"

"We know!" A female Rhajok'Don called. We were imprisoned here – slaves to the Zygeth." She paused, then added, her voice cracking with a mixture of disbelief as well as relief, "They released us for some reason."

"Released you?"

"The guards came and told us to go, to head north."

Xanoth would have given his other arm to know why. What had happened to persuade a bunch of inhuman brutes to release their prisoners? But he was obviously not going to find the answer here, and his first priority had to be the safety of the small band of travellers. "I know somewhere you'll be safe," he told them, pointing towards the forest. "We have a Resistance group that way. I'll guide you." Giving the signal for his orpid to fly home, he set out at the head of the straggly, demoralized line.

* * *

One after another, the Rhajok'Don descended the ladder into the entrance chamber, Xanoth bringing up the rear. As soon as the door steamed closed behind him, the chatter of relieved Rhajok'Don overwhelmed the chamber.

Xanoth recognized the female who had spoken to him earlier. She stood apart from the others, sadness clinging to her like a shroud. Going over to her, Xanoth lightly bumped his chin with hers, familiar as he was with their customs.

"Welcome to Haven's Heart," he greeted warmly. "We need more Rhajok'Don around here."

Kinoko dipped her head in acknowledgement of his curtesy.

"What's your name, my friend?" Xanoth asked, determined to draw her out.

Her deep-black eyes crinkled at the corners as she gave him the ghost of a smile. "Kinoko, wife-to-be of Ugoki."

Xanoth stood stunned for a moment, a low, burning pain flared in the pit of his belly and his heart constricted.

He cleared his throat. "I... I know of Ugoki," he stuttered.

Kinoko's face lit up. "You do? Is he all right?"

"H–he isn't with us anymore..." Xanoth paused, buying himself some time – he would have to tell her, he knew. He just couldn't bring himself to say the words. "He left, to carry out a very important mission." Taking her hands in his, Xanoth forced himself to meet her eyes. "I'm so sorry, Kinoko. Ugoki died on his journey." Xanoth swallowed around the lump in his throat. "I met one of the recently banished. He'd found the body. I know from what he said that they treat him with respect."

Kinoko closed her eyes, her face crumpling as she struggled to hold back tears. "He was very brave," she said, holding herself proudly. "He died for a worthy cause."

"None braver," Xanoth affirmed. We'll hold a remembrance for him. I'll arrange it."

Just then a junior officer arrived at the scene.

Xanoth released Kinoko's hands. "Excuse me," he said. "There are things I need to see to urgently.

Making his way through the throng to the officer, Xanoth raised his voice over the chatter. "Corporal Taylor see that these Rhajok'Don are taken to suitable quarters and provided with food and water."

"Yes, sir."

Signalling to the Rhajok'Don, Xanoth waited a few moments

until they quieted. "Everyone, please follow this officer. He'll see to it that you're quartered and fed." As the weary troop was led away, Xanoth headed for General Connor's office.

Knocking briskly upon the General's door, Xanoth waited impatiently.

"Come in!" Connor called.

Xanoth pushed the door open, closing it again behind him. Approaching the desk, he saluted smartly. "Sir!"

The General put down the pen he had been writing with. His sharp gaze sweeping over Xanoth. "All right, man – spit it out!"

"I found a Rhajok'Don tribe running from Kraag'Blitz on my way home. I brought them back with me."

"A tribe? Running, you say?"

"They'd been released." Seeing the questions written on Connor's face, he held up a hand. "Don't ask me why, I don't know."

"Have they been accommodated?"

Xanoth gave a stiff nod. "Yes, sir, they have, sir."

"Good. Now tell me the rest."

Xanoth gave Connor a report on his mission, leaving out nothing. The General listened without interrupting until Xanoth had finished.

"I'm sorry to hear about Anamai, son," he finally said. "I know how much she means to you." He shook his head sadly.

"So," he scratched the side of his mouth as he reflected on Xanoth's information, "how do we know which Amunisari are friendly and which aren't?"

"They're not Zygeth, sir." They're prisoners. They can be distinguished by their white or bright clothing. Xanoth paused. "There's something else General, some important intel."

Connor grimaced. "Go on, soldier, spit it out."

"The Zygeth attack in two days."

General Connor shot to his feet. "You're telling me we're facing an attack in two days' time?"

"No, sir. They're going to attack the Amunisari, in the Golden Lands."

The General raised his hands and walked around the table. "Woah! Slow down, Xanoth. Are you talking about the Amunisari who were going to pitch in on our side?"

Xanoth sighed heavily. "They were never coming, General. But, the Zygeth will be left weakened when they march their army south."

"What's this?" Conner asked, noticing the new implant in Xanoth's hand.

"Anamai, when I found her, she gave me this, to help me escape."

The General stepped back reflexively.

"Don't you see, General," Xanoth pressed. "This is the biggest and best opportunity we'll ever have. I've seen their cloning chambers, they've tens of thousands of drones, all of which will be gone. Kraag'Blitz will be ours for the taking." He looked the General squarely in the eye. "We have to be ready."

Connor brought his fist down on the desk. "How? With what? We're a few hundred at most, and though I don't for one minute question our soldiers' bravery, we're no match for those… things!"

Xanoth raised his arm, displaying his implants. "I can take care of any enchants, that'll leave only the Loyalists to deal with, our soldiers are equal to them. We can do this, sir," Xanoth insisted. "We'll be able to live above ground, free the Rhajok'Don, build a new civilisation."

"What if?" General Connor turned away, pacing back to his desk before piercing Xanoth with a look, "the Zygeth win their battle? What if they double back to finish us off?"

"Why would they come back here?" Xanoth asked. All they've ever wanted is to leave this place."

"Point taken." General Connor was silent, thinking, then, "Prepare the men."

16

Fall from Grace

Displaying a strength never guessed at from his slender appearance, the adept threw Damieh across the smooth, polished floor and he slid up to Viktor's desk.

"I found him in the lower corridors, near the cloning facilities," the tattooed man said. "He had this on him." He tossed the backpack, sword and the knife onto the desk. "There was another intruder but I let the enchants deal with him."

Viktor pushed his chair back and stood up, the hem of his dark robe skimming the ground. Pulling back his hood, he drew a long, deep, breath before looking at the tattooed man. "Initiate a search for the other intruder."

"Yes, sire." The man turned on his heel and left the room.

Viktor slowly walked around the table. Kneeling down with his arms behind his back, he stared at Daimeh with russet coloured eyes. Lying on his front, Daimeh twisted his neck in an attempt to keep his aggressor in sight. Viktor pushed him onto his back. "How did you get here?"

"A l–ladder," Daimeh stuttered, "from the dwellings below." He inched away, striving to place a little distance between them.

"Stand up!" Viktor ordered and Daimeh hesitantly did as told. "What are you doing here?"

Daimeh knew he had to think quickly. "I want to join you," he blurted. Joining them was the last thing he wanted, but he knew they would kill him if he didn't offer them something.

"Join us?" The Chief Commander chuckled to himself. "Why would I want to hire you?"

"Er." Daimeh hesitated. "I've information – about the Golden Lands."

Interest flicked momentarily in the strange russet gaze. Viktor sat back down at his desk. "Tell me more."

"I'm from Alkoryn. A place where the sun doesn't set."

The information elicited a brief nod. "I know of the place."

"A message was sent over the seas. I think the Amunisari may know you're coming," Daimeh continued reluctantly.

"And their army?"

"They have no army to speak of, just city guards. They're unprepared, now's the best time to attack." A wave of despair washed over Daimeh. What was he doing? But he had to be convincing.

"I don't need an intruder to tell me when to attack." Viktor narrowed his gaze.

"Of course not." Daimeh lowered his head.

"Why should I trust you? You could be a member of the Resistance."

Daimeh pointed to the bag. "Look inside." He inched forward. "There are symbols to prove I'm from the Golden Lands."

Viktor opened the bag and laid the four amulets onto the table top. "These mean nothing, you could just be trying to infiltrate us."

Daimeh's mind scrambled for a way out, a reason to persuade them not to kill him. "I'm here because I want revenge against the Amunisari, just like you do. They killed the woman I loved. I'm willing to fight for you. I know we both want the same thing – the downfall of the Amunisari. Give me a chance and I'll prove my loyalty."

Viktor put his hands flat on the desk. "Even if that's true – what use are you to me?"

Daimeh nodded at the symbols. "Those symbols on your desk. Only one gives access to the Citadel in the Golden Lands and only Alkoryn blood can activate it"

The Chief Commander leant back and looked at Daimeh down his long, hooked nose. Pressing a button on his comm, he spoke into it. "Take this boy away and lock him in the dungeon until we have use for him."

No sooner had he finished than two guards entered the room and grabbed Daimeh's arms roughly. Panic sped through Daimeh like wild fire.

"W–what are you doing?"

"Putting you to good use." Viktor smirked.

* * *

The guards dragged Daimeh away. Once outside, Daimeh felt the sting of a syringe, then the world tilted crazily and plunged into darkness.

He came to lying on the cold, grimy, stone-flagged floor. His head throbbed and his mouth was so parched it felt as if someone had crammed it full of sand. His eyebrow was stinging and when he touched his fingertips to it, his hand came away bloody.

What had he done? Had he saved his life? He still wasn't sure. He pushed himself to this feet, then sat on the stone slab that served as a cot as his eyes adjusted to the gloom enough to take in the cramped, dirty dampness of his surroundings. As if drawn by a magnet, his mind clung irresistibly to thoughts of Elisaris and letting his head drop into his hands, he heard himself make a sound that might have come from the throat of a wounded animal. He wanted her back; he needed her. Only she could save him from himself. Shoulders slumped, defeated and ashamed, he wept into his hands.

* * *

The buzz of someone seeking entrance cut through Viktor's thoughts.

"Come in!"

The door skimmed open and in came an older man, dressed

in a long black robe, hands tucked into his wide sleeves. The fibres of his garment glistened in the light. Under a deep, finely stitched hood, his head was lowered. As he approached Viktor's desk he slowly raised his head.

"Master Xylos, a pleasure." Viktor stood up and respectfully bowed to his elder.

"Viktor. I hear you have an Alkoryn." The master moved with the conserved energy of one no longer young, yet his face had a smoothness that defied the stamp of age.

"I do," Viktor acknowledged. "We have him in the prison block."

"I wish to see him." Xylos stared at Viktor with his blue, flecked with green, eyes.

"Of course. I'll let the guard escort you." Viktor paused. "May I ask why?"

"I would like him as my personal servant," Xylos told him, the corners of his mouth twitching upward.

Viktor raised his eyebrows in surprise. "I see, I'll arrange for him to be brought to your room."

Xylos dipped his head. Slowly, he turned and gracefully left the room.

* * *

The guards had roughly bundled him from his cell. Now the door before him skimmed open to reveal exquisitely furnished yet modest quarters. From the little he could see, the accommodations were stamped with the owner's personality more than most rooms. Fine ornaments were on display, while beautiful paintings decorated the walls, all illuminated by carefully placed, elegant lamps.

"Allow him in and remove those bindings," Xylos ordered in the calm manner of someone used to being obeyed.

Daimeh was stepped into the room, his eye drawn to the

immaculate, textured metal walls, shining blackly. Something about one of the paintings seemed to tug at his memory. On closer inspection, Daimeh saw with a start that it was Galunda Bay.

"Leave us," Xylos told the guards, waiting for the door to close behind them before turning to Daimeh. "Take a seat."

Daimeh did as ordered, sitting down into a smoothly curved chair. Strangely, in view of the lamps, there was a candle on the table next to him.

Xylos sat in the chair opposite him. "You know they'll kill you when they're finished with you."

Daimeh was silent for a moment before nervously replying. "I do fear it."

"Oh, where are my manners? I'm Xylos, they call me Master Xylos as I'm the eldest," Xylos added speaking pleasantly.

"I'm Daimeh. How old are you?" he rushed on nervously.

"You want to know how old I am?"

"Er."Daimeh hesitated, wondering if what he had asked was considered impolite. "Y-yes. If you want to tell me."

"I'm over three millennia."

"How? How is that so?" Daimeh couldn't hide his astonishment.

"Our people, the Amunisari, live for millennia, some older than me, but we aren't part of the Zygeth," Xylos replied. "Yet when we're banished, they re-activate our ageing genes. So our numbers can be controlled."

"You're Amunisari?" Daimeh's amazement was growing by the second.

"All of the Zygeth were, once. I was banished over five hundred years ago and joined the military movement almost immediately. I was angry, perhaps foolish. But I'm here now."

"If your ageing genes are reactivated, then how have you been here for five hundred years?"

"The Zygeth have developed a method to de-activate the

genes again."

"So you can amass numbers?"

"Yes."

"Something puzzles me. Why are you so interested in me?" This had troubled Daimeh since he had entered the room.

"Now that is a good question." Xylos pushed back his hood to reveal his long, silver hair. "I was working on the Alkoryn project called Spiritual Influence. I know your people well. You may have noticed my painting of Galunda Bay."

Daimeh shot to his feet. "You were one of those who experimented on us?"

"I understand you're upset. But we never meant you harm. Please, do sit down."

Daimeh allowed himself to sink back onto the chair.

"If you know my people well, then tell me, why did you experiment on us?"

"We wanted to learn about life and how it evolves under manipulated circumstances. We seeded the Alkoryn race. Your people accepted religion as your guidance and developed a peaceful community," Xylos explained.

"Not all of us are religious," Daimeh told him.

Xylos inclined his head. "We expected that. It was all a part of the experiment." Xylos fell silent, then he said, "I can help you. I don't want them to kill you once you let them into the Citadel. I can provide you with technology before the army marches."

"You have a guilty conscious?" Daimeh asked.

"I do. I want to make amends, it's why you're here with me now."

"When do the Zygeth march?"

"Their army is ready, any day now they'll attack." Xylos stood up. "A drink?" He walked to a marble bench, also candle lit, and poured from a smoky glass decanter. The wine was dark purple with a fluorescent swirl at the heart of it.

Daimeh raised his hand. "No thanks, I don't drink."

"Oh, this isn't alcoholic. A fruity taste with a sting on the tongue." Xylos lifted his glass.

"No, thanks anyway." Daimeh was unsure of how far he could trust this man.

"If you're tired, there's a room through there for you." Xylos pointed to the doorway behind Daimeh. "Tomorrow they'll ask about you." He cleared his throat. "But don't worry, all will be fine."

"Then what do we do?"

"I'll show you how to use the refractor," he said, smiling as he spoke.

* * *

That night Daimeh lay in a simple bed, the head up against the wall. The room was windowless and again, although thought-fully furnished, it too was lit by candlelight.

As he rested, Daimeh let his is mind wander to thoughts of Elisaris and their time in the Elyon simulation. It had been the happiest day of his life. He doubted he would ever be as happy again. Tears blotted the pillow and he turned it over. Rolling onto his back, he stared up at the black, slanted ceiling. He tried to blank his mind but disturbing thoughts kept pushing their way in. Throwing back the covers, he leapt out of bed and blew out all the candles before climbing back in. His mind shifted to Lybas and his family.

Finally, after what seemed a very long time, he fell asleep. He dreamed as he slept and his dreams were all about his journey to the Golden Lands.

* * *

The next day Xylos entered Daimeh's room just as he was waking up.

"I heard you crying," he said as he put a glass of water on Daimeh's bedside table.

Daimeh cleared his throat. "I miss the people I left behind, my family."

"I know that feeling all too well." He bowed his head as if remembering his own losses. "Come, I have some fitting clothes for you."

Xylos dropped some dark, matt-black clothes onto the bed. "Join me in the other room when you're dressed."

Daimeh picked them up and got changed once Xylos had left the room. The tunic and trousers were a good fit and smelled fresh and clean. Ready, he walked through to the main room.

Xylos cast an appraising eye over him as he passed him a black, hooded robe. "Here, wear this also."

Daimeh wrapped the cloak around himself.

"Follow me and carry this." Xylos handed Daimeh a tray with a glass of purple liquid, the same drink as the night before.

He led them out of the room and into an empty corridor, coming to a T-junction, Xylos turned right. Daimeh, following, saw two Zygeth guards ahead. As they drew level, the guards stopped, put their backs to the black walls and bowed their heads as Xylos walked past. Daimeh realised Xylos had an important status amongst the Zygeth.

The corridor ahead began to ascend, then it spiralled around on itself. The slope wasn't steep and the two continued up and around.

Arriving at a shiny black door with a small panel next to it, Xylos gestured with his hand over the panel and the door slid open. Inside was a large, circular room with racks of weapons all the way around the outer wall. A round, black table stood in the centre.

"Come in," Xylos said. "You can take a look around."

Daimeh entered the armoury, heading straight for the weapons racks.

"This is one of many armouries throughout the upper levels of Kraag'Blitz," Xylos told him.

"It's quite impressive."

Xylos pointed to the safe. "What we want is inside there." He approached the safe, unlocking it with a gesture before opening it. "Here's the refractor," he said, taking out a small, palm-sized device, circular in design and silver in colour.

Daimeh eyed the device curiously. "How do I use it?"

"Keep it by your side at all times," Xylos instructed. "Press this small button when you want to… avoid detection. Go on, give it a try," he urged, passing Daimeh the little silver object.

Daimeh pressed the button and waited. Nothing happened. Then he heard Xylos chuckle. Glancing down to the floor, he drew in a startled breath as he saw his feet and legs had disappeared. Bit by bit he began to vanish. In a matter of seconds he was completely invisible.

Daimeh couldn't take in what was happening and couldn't resist touching his legs arms and chest to reassure himself they were still there. "This is outstanding," he said, astonished. "How does it work?"

"It refracts the light around you, about a foot ahead, so your body blends with the environment. It's proved very effective for our assassins," Xylos explained. "Now, make your way back to my room."

Daimeh puffed out his cheeks. "All right. Here goes."

Exiting the armoury, he waited for the two guards on patrol to turn and head away from him before he made his way silently through the corridor, down the spiral slope and into Xylos's residence.

A few minutes later Xylos arrived.

"I guess you like it," he said as he entered the room, unable to see Daimeh. "Look after it well, it'll save your life."

Daimeh reappeared, sitting on a chair. He glanced down at the device with a thoughtful expression. "Why don't I just use it to escape from here?" he murmured.

"Because deep down there's something you want from the Zygeth."

Daimeh was silent for a moment as he thought about what Xylos had said. "No – I just want to go home." He frowned as he stared at the refractor. Xylos was right, of course. He did want something from the Zygeth. He wanted vengeance, on Ceolm. He shook his head as if trying to dismiss the thought, yet a deep hatred welled up inside of him.

"You're right," he admitted. "I want my revenge. The Amunisari council must fall." He held the device up in front of him. "When do I use this?"

"When they ask you to use the final key to get into the gates of the Citadel. You use it then," Xylos said slowly.

Daimeh nodded. "I understand."

17

Miah's Mistake

The glorious Alkoryn sun brightly illuminated the quaint reception room of the elaborately imposing manor.

Daimeh's mother, Miah, sat on a highly glossed wooden chair, sewing Alith, her baby niece, a new garment in soft, cream fabrics. Perfect for her, she thought. Her shoulder-length, cinnamon hair was tucked behind her ears as she listened to her nephew, Oeradon, practising his lute in the other room. She could hear his slow melodies. He wasn't as outgoing since Daimeh and his mother, Cresadir, had left and his music reflected that. He spent every waking hour with his lute and many nights performing in The Fish's Flask. It would seem he had found his passion – or his coping method.

Suddenly Miah flinched as she pricked her finger with the needle. Annoyed with herself, she watched the droplet well up before sucking on it. On the table was a small piece of rag and she wrapped her finger in that. Leaning back into the chair, she gazed out at the rear gardens, remembering Daimeh playing on the grass when he was a boy. Her memories shifted to him as a teenager – always out roaming the beach. Inevitably, her thoughts turned to his leaving and her last moments with him. Giving in to her sadness, she sat, staring at nothing as the tears flowed. Struggling to control herself, she got to her feet, looking around the familiar room as if there lay some comfort, but there was none to be found. That was when she decided; she would go to his house. There, surround by his things, surely she would gain some peace. Miah made for the charming little room that served as a reading room. Bookcases lined one wall and a large window gave onto a sheltered corner of the garden. Her brother-in-law, Theo, was positioned by the window. As she neared him she felt the familiar twist of sadness for the shadow of the man he had once been. But now a new feeling vied with the sorrow. Now every time she looked at Theo she felt the sharp edge of fear – fear for Daimeh and for her sister, Cresadir. Stifling a sigh, she gently placed her hand on Theo's shoulder, managing a smile, she was never quite sure if he was looking at anything in particular, but she hoped he at least enjoyed the music. As always, there was no response and Miah crossed to where Daimeh's cousin was practicing.

Oeradon stopped playing, glancing at his aunt with his pale-blue eyes. "You've been thinking about him again," he said quietly. "It's been over six months." His clear eyes were troubled. "I wish they'd come home. I didn't think I'd miss them so much."

Miah felt the press of unshed tears. She blinked hard. "I... I'm very much afraid they won't be coming home, Oeradon."

"Don't say that," he ground out, shooting her a fierce look. "You don't know that."

Miah sighed heavily. "I think Daimeh's house is due a clean. I'll be there if you need me."

"All right, Aunt Miah."

* * *

Daimeh's front door led straight into the kitchen. Miah let herself in and sat herself down at the kitchen table, running her bright, arctic-blue eyes over the array of cupboards and fixings. It was all a bit dusty, yet everything was just as he had left it. Pushing herself to her feet, she went to a small corner cupboard and took out a dusting cloth. After wetting it under the tap, she began to wipe down all the surfaces. She decided to clean a bit more thoroughly today, she wanted to clean through the cupboards and have the place pristine for if... when he returned.

Going to another cupboard, much taller than the last, she took out a broom, bucket and some old sacks to collect any rubbish. As she cleaned around the kitchen, she bumped the larder door and it clicked open, a smell of stale food wafting through the gap. She needed to clear all that out too. Opening the door fully, she wrinkled her nose as the unpleasant smell intensified: rotting fish and mushy, decomposed fruit, as well as some of the baskets which were supposed to go to the fête. Miah chuckled, he'd said he had them all, she should have known better.

Unravelling a rubbish sack, she proceeded to bin the food. Pulling out all the baskets, she took them to the sink to be washed later. As she removed the final one, she saw a dirty cloth lying on the floor. It looked as if it was concealing something. Intrigued, she picked up the old rag. Beneath was an oblong, black tablet with a smooth surface. Lifting the tablet carefully with both hands, Miah examined it. There was nothing on either side. She frowned as she placed it on the table; what was Daimeh doing with such a strange thing? She would take it back with her, she decided.

* * *

A few hours later, Miah returned to Cresadir's manor, where her husband, Halgar and herself had been residing for the past six months. Halgar was on the roof, resurfacing it. He waved down at Miah and she waved back before going inside.

Oeradon was still strumming his latest tune when she strolled into the room.

"Do you know what this is?" she asked, handing the tablet over to him and perching on the edge of a chair.

Oeradon put down his lute and inspected the object. He shook his head. "No. No idea."

"Hmm."

At that moment, Theo turned his head and stared at the tablet. "Theo?" Miah said, astonished that he was showing awareness.

"He's looking at us!" Oeradon let out a short gasp before an incredulous smile lit his face. Putting down the strange object, he hurried to his father. But Theo's deep-grey eyes weren't tracking either of them; he continued to stare at the tablet.

"Seems he's only interested in that," Miah said, glancing at it. To further their amazement, Theo spoke. "Give it to me."

Miah's mouth opened as she tried to find what to say, she was completely stunned, her mind blank. Oeradon, too, just stared at Theo, not quite sure how to react.

"Give it to me," Theo repeated flatly.

Miah hesitated only fractionally before quickly getting up and fetching the tablet. She rested it in Theo's lap.

As soon as he touched it, it activated and golden fluid emerged from deep inside, forming the script that Daimeh had found. Abruptly, Miah realised just what the tablet was. Why, she wondered, had Daimeh kept it a secret? Was there more to their trip beyond the borders then had been told?

As Theo focused on the device, the irises of his eyes began to shine with the same golden glow as the script.

Miah stood up and edged backwards. "What's happening? Oeradon, take it off him."

The tablet sparked as Oeradon tried to grab the unknown object and his whole body flinched. "I can't."

Miah kept her distance, watching the glow pulse through Theo's body. "What do we do!" she wailed, increasingly afraid as the illumination intensified. It was as if light poured from every cell of Theo's skin, so bright she had to squint her eyes.

"We can't do anything," Oeradon said tightly. "We just have to wait."

"Please, stop!" Miah was frantic with worry.

Theo's head flopped back. "Your fate is in danger." The words sounded nothing like his normal speech.

As soon as he had finished talking, the magical and unnerving effect stopped and Theo resumed his usual trance-like state, the tablet slipping off his lap and onto the floor.

Miah rushed to Theo and checked his pulse before looking into each glazed eye. "He doesn't seem hurt," she said, relieved.

"Should I start writing a message to Granddad about this?" Oeradon was thinking ahead, he knew Ommaya had a right to know.

"Yes, please, Oeradon," Miah replied, picking up the tablet and placing it on the nearby table.

Oeradon left the room and pulling a chair closer to Theo, Miah sat with him for a few minutes before retrieving the tablet and carrying it over to the tall, wide bookcase and placing it securely between two thick, hardback books. Returning to Theo, she looked worriedly into his grey eyes, wondering what was going on in there.

Leaning forward she kissed his cheek just as Oeradon returned with parchment and pen.

Smiling wanly, Miah took them from him setting them down on the table. "Now, let's write this letter."

Dear Father,

I have found an object at Daimeh's which he had kept secret for some reason and it initiated a surprising reaction from Theo. He spoke to us and....

She finished the letter, explaining everything that had happened, then, placing it into an envelope she took it to the post-box just outside the mansion.

* * *

There was a blinding flash as the whole room lit up from the wall sized screen. It ceased as quickly as it had started. When he was sure it was safe to do so, the technician lowered the arm he had quickly thrown up to protect his eyes from the glare and stared, stunned, at the screen, which now showed a top-down view of Alkoryn, instead of a bare landscape.

"It's back," he mumbled aloud. "Ceolm needs to know about this." Quickly he activated his comm, but it only buzzed. Whatever it was that had just happened was interfering with the systems. Grabbing his long, white jacket, he bolted from the surveillance room.

* * *

Ceolm, leader of the Amunisari, scratched absently at his pitted cheek and smoothed down his unruly black hair as he waded through his correspondence. He was less than pleased when the inexperienced technician was ushered into his wide office. He glanced up at him out of crystal-blue eyes with flecks of white in the iris. "Yes, what is it?"

"I was run-running th-through the surveillance and…" he stuttered nervously, awed at this close encounter with the great man."

"And?"

The technician hesitated, a little worried about what Ceolm's reaction would be. "And Alkoryn reappeared, but just for a few minutes. It's gone again now."

Ceolm closed down all his screens and stared at the tech. "Are you sure?" he asked, there was always the possibility that a new technician was prone to make a mistake.

"I have it all on record, sire." He inched forward as he spoke.

"Very well. Show me.

The technician waved his arm at the wall and a screen appeared. He tapped in a few symbols and a bare landscape materialized. "You'll need to look away for a moment," he warned, pausing the footage. "There's a very bright flash." He resumed the footage and they both looked away quickly. Once the flare was over they turned back to see Alkoryn on screen. The technician paused the footage again. "There it is."

Ceolm stood up and walked towards the screen. "Interesting. How did this happen?"

"I don't know. There was a power surge and it just appeared. You can see there's an illuminated patch there." He pointed to Cresadir's manor. "I'm not sure what it means."

"I wonder." Ceolm returned to his seat, tapping his fingers on the desk, thinking. "We took a man called Theo a few years ago and used an experimental chip on him, implanted into the occipital lobe. It was intended to give us feedback on Alkoryn's day to day functioning. There was also a mechanism integrated into the chip, to ward off any discussions or attempts to explore past the boundaries."

"How did it work?" The technician asked, curiosity overcoming his nerves.

"We heightened all of the subject's senses, so he could monitor his close vicinity. He lost all functionality as a person and was simply used as an information tool. The idea was that, depending on how effective it was, we would infiltrate more of the islands with the devices." Ceolm lowered his hands and clasped them in front of himself.

"Was it effective?"

Ceolm nodded curtly. "For some time, yes. Then we lost connection when Alkoryn disappeared."

"I see," he murmured, "and you think the tablet at Alkoryn reacted with the chip and gave us this opportunity?"

"I do." Contemplation washed over Ceolm's face, "We must send someone to retrieve it."

"But, the shield's active again – we can't enter."

"Ah." Ceolm grunted, preoccupied. Then his eyes sharpened and he swept his cold gaze over the young man before him. "Don't be so hasty," he said, a thin smile twisting his mouth. "I believe I might know someone who can breach the shield."

18

Awake

Just the motion of her breath was noticeable as she lay perfectly still and peaceful beneath a single sheet. Her face was so pale it was almost the colour of the sheet covering her and her lips were blanched and dry.

Ceolm's wife, Eleanor, wearing the typical Amunisari white robes, stood by Cresadir's bed as she had done each evening for the past several months. Her faith for her own people had dwindled and she felt she was a prisoner in her own home. Her husband kept her under constant supervision and she was expected to treat the clone of Elisaris as if she was her real daughter. Eleanor had retreated into a shell, her life taken from her.

Taking Cresadir's hand and patting it, she whispered, "We'll be free one day. I promise." She let go of Cresadir's hand and moved her butterscotch coloured hair away from her face before quietly leaving the room.

* * *

The dim light reflected off the smooth white walls as Cresadir slept. Her bed stood in the middle of a small, rectangular room, with nothing else in it other than a monitoring screen embedded in the wall. The machine emitted a series of regular beeps as it kept track of Cresadir's pulse.

Suddenly, the beeping quickened as Cresadir's hand twitched almost imperceptibly. Beneath the closed lids, her eyes moved rapidly from side to side. Her breathing rasped and she mumbled wordlessly. Suddenly, she spluttered and jerked upright, her eyes wide open, staring at the opposite wall.

Her sight was blurry and she blinked hard until it cleared some. Where was she? What was happening to her? Her mouth was so dry her lips were stuck together and she worked to raise some moisture in a throat as arid as dust to enable her to peel them apart. The more she tried to think the less she understood: everything was gone – lost in some kind of mind fog. Cresadir! That was her name! She was sure of it! The small victory helped calm her panic. Another name floated into her consciousness. "Tristan," she whispered.

Determinedly pulling herself over to the edge of the bed, Cresadir managed to shuffle around until she succeeded in getting her feet on the floor. Groggily, she tried to stand up. But her legs refused to hold her up and she slumped to the floor, groaning as she landed on her belly. Helpless and frightened by her weakness, she lay for a moment, moaning as she looked up at the seemingly impossible goal of the door. Bracing herself with her arms, she pushed upwards, using the bed as balance. Wearily she managed to haul herself onto two feet and shuffled towards the door. Falling against it, she banged on it weakly, then, as panic surfaced once more, gradually getting louder. Drawing on the last reserves of her strength, she shouted, "Tristan!"

* * *

Ceolm accompanied Tristan on the way to the observation room. "She was calling for you when they found her." He glanced at Tristan as he spoke.

"Do you think this means the treatment worked whilst she was asleep?"

"Yes, I believe so." Ceolm scratched at his cheek. "Of course, she won't be accustomed to living amongst us, but she should have most of the memories we want her to have."

When they arrived, a doctor was already with Cresadir.

"She's been awake for about thirty minutes now."

"I just want to go home," Cresadir pleaded.

Then her toffee coloured eyes found Tristan in his neat white top and trousers and a joyful smile lit up her face. "Tristan, oh my goodness, I'm so pleased to see you," she said opening her arms, anticipating a hug. "When can I see Kiara?"

Tristan hurried to her side, pulling her into his embrace. "Don't worry about anything, darling – it's all fine now. Kiara's at home with Olivia. You'll join us, just as soon as you're well enough, and be with your family."

Ceolm permitted himself another tight smile. What Elisaris had done, sedating Cresadir all those months ago – her motives may have been to sabotage their efforts, but it would seem it had worked in their favour. The long, induced sleep had made the treatment even more effective. He nodded almost imperceptibly at the doctor and the man quickly followed him out of the room.

Once outside he said, "It's been a success."

"Yes. I think she'll be fully compliant," the doctor rushed to reassure him.

"We can even go on that holiday we talked about," Cresadir said, squeezing Tristan tightly. She had remembered a conversation she'd had with him.

"That would be lovely." Tristan was careful to wipe away any trace of triumph at how well the implanted memories were working before looking directly at her with his almond-shaped, crystal-blue eyes.

"How long have I been asleep?" Cresadir asked.

"Two months." Tristan brought her hand to his mouth and placed a kiss on her skin. Adopting a frown he said, "We lost you to a coma not long after you had the accident." He paused. "What's the last thing you remember?"

"I remember being at the incubation chambers." Cresadir looked thoughtful. "Then, I saw Kiara… After that it's a blur."

"Do you remember back to the accident?" Tristan probed.

Cresadir thought hard. "Just a flash. The doctor told me it was a power surge."

"What about before?"

Cresadir shook her head. "It's all a bit fuzzy. I'm sure I'll remember more as time goes on."

"All right, Tristan, we need to do some more tests, could you wait outside please?" the doctor in charge said.

"Yes, of course." He bent to kiss Cresadir's cheek. "I'll head back to the apartment, dearest – make sure everything's ready for you to come home." Turning away, he quietly left the room.

* * *

The doctors continued monitoring Cresadir until later in the day. Progress was good, there had been a marked improvement in her condition and she was more alert and responsive.

"She certainly seems less confused, more active too," one doctor quietly said to the other.

"I think she can probably go home."

"I concur. I'll go and tell our patient the good news."

Cresadir was overjoyed to be going home, back to her baby.

A nurse was summoned to wheel Cresadir back to her room. Minutes later, the hover bed had been detached from the monitoring equipment and Cresadir was on her way.

"If you need anything just get in touch," one of the doctors said, patting her shoulder.

* * *

The comm activated and Tristan answered; a baby was wailing in the background.

"Cresadir's been discharged," the nurse informed him.

Opening the door, he saw Cresadir struggling to her feet. Giving Tristan a quick cuddle, she made her way to the bedroom, drawn by Kiara's fitful crying.

"There, there, shush, Kiara." Cradling her daughter, rocking her gently in her arms, Cresadir walked back through to the lounge area.

"She calms down so much quicker with you," Tristan said, giving Cresadir a big wide smile.

Cresadir frowned. "She hardly knows me." She kissed her daughter's soft cheek. "But that's going to change," she said, smiling as she sat down next to Tristan. He put his arm around her and gestured for the cube to activate.

"I was thinking," she said, snuggling closer to him, shall we take that holiday we planned before Kiara's birth? We were going to go to Galia weren't we?" she asked, stroking Kiara's blonde hair.

"Well, it's only a couple of hours away," he replied, signalling for the channels to change. *You're not to go away. I need Cresadir for another duty.* Ceolm's voice sounded in his head via the implant all Amunisari were given at birth.

"Er." He hesitated.

"What is it, Tristan?"

"You know what? Kiara's still very young, maybe we should wait a few more months?"

Cresadir looked disappointed. She got to her feet. "Let me just put her back to bed."

Tristan nodded and Cresadir disappeared into the bedroom.

She returned looking thoughtful. "Perhaps you're right," she said. "Perhaps we should wait a while first."

* * *

Later that day in the circular council room, four council members waited for their leader to speak.

"As you all know," Ceolm began, "we've pinpointed where in Alkoryn the device is hidden. We must prepare to send someone to retrieve it."

"We know it can't be one of us," one of the council members interrupted. "We can't breach the barrier."

"I'm aware of this," Ceolm snapped, impatient at the interruption. "We can use Cresadir. Although she now has Amunisari genes, she's still Alkoryn." He began to walk around the table. "She can enter Alkoryn without any difficulty."

"How do you propose we get her there?" Salvador asked. "She won't want to leave her family and we don't want to lose her trust in us."

"Any suggestions?" Ceolm asked.

A third councilman raised his hand. "We can make it part of her therapy."

Ceolm stopped pacing. "How?"

"Tell her we need to do a transmuting liquescent simulation with her, to see how strong her memories are." The councilman stood up. "She won't even know we've sent her anywhere."

"Hmm." Ceolm scratched at his chin, he had almost completed a full round of the table. "Interesting idea." He cocked his head. "I think I like it." He sat back down in his chair.

"She'll need something to deactivate the device once she gets there," the fourth council member spoke up. "And she'll need augmented vision to help her find it."

"I can get my technician to sort that out," Salvador said. "It'll be no problem."

The fourth man nodded.

Ceolm pushed his chair back from the table. "I'll escort Cresadir to augmentation," he said, "and let's put this plan into action."

* * *

Arriving at Cresadir's apartment, Ceolm activated the comm. "Cresadir, it's Ceolm here. I've come to discuss a new therapy which could be very helpful to you."

He waited as the door skimmed open. "Come in!" Cresadir called.

Ceolm entered the lounge area and saw Cresadir lying on the settee cradling Kiara.

"Sorry to intrude," he said.

Cresadir smiled warmly. "If there's something that can help me get back my memories then it's no intrusion." Sitting up, she said, "Please sit, make yourself comfortable. Let me put Kiara back into the other room."

"What is this new therapy?" she asked returning.

"We'd like you to take part in an experimental procedure that we believe will have a greatly beneficial effect for you," Ceolm explained.

"What sort of therapy is it?"

"We'll test a transmuting liquescent simulation on you. We'd like you to follow the instructions you'll be given when you're in the simulation," Ceolm lied.

"And what exactly will this do for me?"

"You'll be in a place that isn't familiar to you and what we would like to see is how you form new memories from a new setting. It's about strengthening your memory to its previous state," Ceolm improvised.

"I see, well, when do I start?"

"As soon as possible would be best."

Cresadir thought for a moment. "I'll need to contact Tristan to look after the baby."

"Don't worry about Kiara," Ceolm told her. "I'll make all the necessary arrangements. I'll return in twenty minutes," he said, walking to the door.

* * *

Twenty minutes later, he was back, having already sent along someone to look after Kiara.

"Are you sure you'll be all right, Olivia?"

Olivia smiled. "We'll be fine, won't we, Kiara?" She gently bounced the baby in her arms.

Arriving at the observation room – a simple room with panelled walls and a single hover chair at the centre, machinery suspended above it, Cresadir sat in the reclining chair.

"We want to just augment your vision a little before we put you into the transmuting liquescent chamber," the doctor explained. "Just lay back as far as you can."

He injected her with anaesthetic before gesturing a virtual screen down over her head. A translucent projection of her brain appeared in front of him. He tapped in the areas of the brain he wanted to enhance and they lit up in red. Positioning the translucent image over Cresadir's brain, he stepped clear. The image lit up with one bright flash and then ceased glowing. Cresadir was now completely asleep.

"I've programmed her to wake a few minutes after she lands, sire," the doctor said.

Ceolm grunted. "I'll arrange the pod. I want her to arrive during low-sun. I'd rather she didn't have any encounters."

19

Secrets Revealed

It was low sun over Galunda Bay and the dyak bats were squawking between themselves. Her hand reflexively clenched the warm sand as Cresadir gradually awoke. She lay on her front, slightly buried in the sand, away from the tide and in the easternmost dunes of Galunda Bay, just outside the invisible protective barrier that surrounded Alkoryn.

Spluttering sand from her mouth, she used her arms to lift herself to a sitting position before wiping the rest of the sand off her face. It's so real, she thought, gazing at the beauty of the bay. Locyan palm trees to her right, the mile long stretch of the bay in front of her with white, pristine sands. The temperature was a little colder than she was used to and she had never seen the sun so low, it glowed with an orange tint.

Standing up, she kicked the sand with her light boots, she had hardly ever seen sand, she wondered if it was like this in reality. Brushing herself off, she realized she was wearing clothes she had never worn before – oddly different to the usual Amunisari design: tight fitting bottoms with numerous straps around the legs and a tight top, also with straps around the arms. The material was very thin and soft to the touch, with a slight silvery glimmer. There were pockets on the thighs and Cresadir quickly checked inside them. There was a small, square device in her pocket, somewhat nondescript, it looked like a chip of some sort. She slipped it back in place.

What should she do now? Was she supposed to do something – go somewhere? She had no idea what, if anything, was required from her or which direction to head. All she knew was that she was in an unbelievably real simulation.

"H–hello?" she said cautiously.

"Hello, Cresadir, I see you're awake, a male voice answered."

"Yes. What do I do?"

"I'll activate your on screen HUD and enhanced vision."

For some reason Cresadir failed to understand, his cold voice made her uneasy.

Her vision flashed and when the flash cleared, she could see a small map overlaying the beautiful landscape of the bay, and a directional marker.

"You follow that beacon," the voice instructed.

"When you get to the destination, you'll find a device of some sort, you'll see it highlighted on your HUD. You're to press the chip in your right hand trouser pocket against it. You shouldn't see any people, but if you do, it's just a glitch in the simulation. Now go. You'll hear from me again once you get there."

Cresadir obediently began her walk over the sands of Galunda Bay, finding herself stopping often to gaze out over the blue-green ocean. Although she kept reminding herself that it was just a simulation, the place tugged at her heart in an unexplainable way. A soft breeze wafted the scent of salt and seaweed her way and Cresadir breathed deeply, feeling a sense of well-being that she could not remember feeling for a long time. She wondered how many other simulations there were, and if they would have the same striking effect on her.

* * *

Some time later, Cresadir arrived at the outskirts of Lybas, pausing to take in the five quaint houses to her left before walking on. The marker on her map directed her right and she continued towards what seemed to be the village centre, a circular, paved area, topped off with a circle of shrubs and plants. Here the houses were more elegant and arranged in circular rows, reminding her of the ripples she had stood and watched as they spread across the surface of the bay. As the voice had told her, there was nobody around. Cresadir continued along the street carving its way through the houses straight ahead, until she reached a gravel path. Still faithfully following the marker, she turned left, up towards a small hill at the back of the village and an elaborate manor straddling the top. The low light cast long shadows from the houses across her path as she walked.

As Cresadir got closer to the manor, her vision locked onto a small, oblong shape which lit up with a golden glow.

The door was open and Cresadir walked straight in and through the main hall, into a short corridor, then to one of the reception rooms. The object she was searching for was on a bookcase. Cresadir didn't hesitate, making her way to where the object was secreted she reached out her hand, only to hear, behind her, the sound of a plate smashing.

Miah was frozen, staring at the back of the intruder. Feeling as if she moved in slow motion, she grabbed the butter knife from where it had fallen and held it in front of her.

"Who are—" she broke off as the intruder turned around. "Cresadir?" she whispered, gaping at her sister. "Oh my goodness! You're home!" She glanced around the room. "Where's Daimeh?"

"You're just a glitch," Cresadir said, removing the tablet from between the books and taking the chip from her pocket.

"I'm your sister, Miah," Miah told her. She glanced at the strange object she had carried home from Daimeh's house, which was now firmly in her sister's grasp. "What... what do you want with that?"

"I don't know you. You're not real."

Miah's heart was beating hard. Something was terribly wrong here. She tried again, "Cresadir! I'm your sister! Look at me!" she insisted, grabbing her arm. "You look so young – what – what's happened to you?"

Cresadir shrugged her off. "Go away! You're not real!" she

shouted, pushing her away.

"You... don't remember me?"

"I don't know you! Go away!" Cresadir pushed her away with both hands.

Miah stumbled back, crying. "C–Cresa? Why are you doing this? B–be careful with that. We don't kn—"

Cresadir, ignoring her sister, pressed the chip firmly against the tablet. A blinding blast of light came from it, causing them both to hastily mask their eyes. Cresadir's whole body lit up brightly. The illumination abruptly cut off and Cresadir collapsed to the ground in a heap. Her body ceasing to glow as quickly as it had started.

Miah ran to her sister's side. Thank goodness, at least she was breathing. What in spirit had happened to her? Why was she acting like this? Why didn't she remember her? Laying Cresadir on her side, she ran upstairs to wake Oeradon.

* * *

"Sire, we have surveillance again. It worked." The technician leant back in his chair looking at Ceolm.

"Excellent!" Ceolm stood up from his chair. "What about Cresadir?" He pointed at the screen. "Is that her lying there? And who's that running up the stairs?"

"The device had some kind of effect on her. We're trying to contact her but it appears she's unconscious," the technician said. "And she." He pointed at Miah. "Is her sister."

"No one should've been around," Salvador added from the back of the room. "It was unforeseeable."

"How can this have been a success if Cresadir is unconscious and the device is still in Alkoryn!" Ceolm stormed.

"But we can continue the observation on Alkoryn," the technician said calmly.

"We need that object of power, there's a war coming!" Ceolm

snarled.

Salvador frowned. "Do you still think the banished will have the numbers for an attack of any substance?"

Ceolm jabbed his finger into Salvador's chest. "The banished will be stronger than you think. Don't underestimate them. They have Anamai, our most advanced scientist."

"That was your choice, to banish your sister," Salvador said, narrowing his blue eyes.

Ceolm stalked towards his desk and sat down. "She deserved it," he said coldly.

"Sire, should we not concentrate on the Alkoryn situation at hand?" the technician said hesitantly.

Ceolm raised his hands into a triangle under his chin and nodded. "Yes." He stared at the map. "Did we give Cresadir a mind control chip?"

"No, sire," the young man admitted.

"But we can contact her?"

"Yes."

"Then we'll just have to wait and contact her when she wakes."

"What about the Alkoryns?" the technician queried.

Ceolm favoured him with an icy smile. "We'll just have to be more convincing than them."

* * *

Miah came running down the stairs and into the reading room with Oeradon close on her heels.

"Mother!" Oeradon ran to Cresadir's side. Kneeling down by her still body, he shook her gently. "Mother! Wake Up!" he called.

"Let's get her to bed," Miah urged."

Together they managed to get Cresadir up the stairs and into the bedroom and gently laid her down. Miah closed the drafty window.

Oeradon sat down on the other side of the bed, his eyes never leaving his mother. "I'm staying here until she wakes," he said.

"So am I." Miah sat herself down on the other chair.

* * *

"Why does she look so much younger?" Oeradon whispered to his aunt.

Miah shook her head, frowning. "I don't know. Questions will just have to wait until she wakes up.

"It's been hours," Oeradon complained.

"Well – we just have to be patient. You need to check on your father. Take your time – make sure he has everything he needs."

Oeradon stood up and walked over to the door.

Just then Cresadir started to moan and roll from side to side.

"She's waking up!" Oeradon said, hurrying back to the bed.

* * *

The cold, male voice inside her head was the first thing Cresadir was aware of.

"Cresadir, you must wake!"

Rolling onto her back again, she slowly opened her tawny eyes, blinking rapidly. "W–where am I?"

"You're home," Miah told her, while at the same time the inner voice said, "You're still in the simulation. There was a problem."

"I–I found the device... the odd tablet," Cresadir said aloud.

Oeradon looked at Miah. "The tablet? It's in the other room."

"These people aren't real," the voice said firmly. "We need to get you out of the simulation."

Cresadir pushed herself up into a sitting position. "You people aren't real."

"Why do you keep saying that, Cresa? We're your family!"

Miah struggled to keep her voice level and not give in to the panic surging through her at her sister's strange behaviour. "I'm your sister and Oeradon's your son."

A look of confusion flashed across Cresadir's face. "I don't have a son," she insisted, "and I need to get back to my husband and daughter."

Oeradon glanced at Miah, bewilderment and hurt in his eyes. "What's she talking about?" he whispered.

Miah shook her head. "I don't know, let's just keep talking to her."

Cresadir gazed around the bedroom. "I... have I been here before? It feels like... I know it from somewhere."

"Of course you know it! It's your bedroom, you've spent the last twenty years sleeping in this room." Miah smiled as reassuringly as she could.

"Ignore her!" The voice was back. "The simulation's bugged."

"But it's so real! It feels so real."

Miah gave her sister a warm smile. "Of course it's real, Cresa," she said, stroking her lower arm. "Oeradon, would you mind getting the painting from the main hall?"

"On it," he said, rushing out.

"Cresa, who's your husband and daughter?"

"Tristan and Kiara – we don't live here." Cresadir said uncertainly. "It's a simulation. But something seems to have gone wrong."

Miah reined back her frustration. "Nothing's gone wrong. This is where you live, and you say yourself that it feels real."

"Do not listen to her!" The voice had become threatening.

Just as Cresadir was about to say something, Oeradon arrived back in the bedroom with a large, family, landscape painting. It was almost the size of a doorway. Propping it up on the bottom of the bed, he waited.

"That's me," Miah said, pointing, "and Daimeh next to me, with you stood there."

"I... I've seen Daimeh before." Cresadir squinted as she fought to remember. "We... were camping. In a ravine... we'd just encountered a giant worm."

"Was that on your journey?" Miah said, wanting to keep Cresadir talking, recalling.

"Stop what you're saying and do as ordered!" the voice raged.

Cresadir thumped the side of her head. "Go away!" she screeched.

Miah and Oeradon jumped up, staring at her and each other in confusion.

"Not you!" Cresadir reached out to them. "There's... someone in my head." She tapped her temple with her finger.

"It's all right, Cresa," Miah said soothingly. "Would you like to meet the rest of your family?" She pointed to a man standing next to Oeradon in the painting. "This is our father, Ommaya."

Cresadir lifted herself forward and touched the painting. "Father," she said. She stared at Miah and Oeradon. "I... remember... the secret library."

Miah laughed. "Yes, yes, we were all there."

"Cresadir, you must follow protocol for this therapy to work. The simulation is trying to trick you."

The voice had calmed down, yet Cresadir still ignored it. "Where's Tristan? I presume this was done before the baby was born?"

Miah hesitated. "Er." She decided to pretend he wasn't there that day. "He–he couldn't make it for the first draft, so we had to leave him out of this one."

"I see." Cresadir frowned. "And I look older, no thanks to the artist."

Miah giggled.

"Who's that stood next to me?" Cresadir pointed to the man to her left.

"That's our brother, Alfrit, next in line to be monarch," Miah told her.

"Hmm, Alfrit. He was from Spiritmist?" Cresadir was recalling her family quite well. She felt a warmth flow all over her. "I must go to Spiritmist."

"What? Now?"

"Yes, actually. I recall Aedolyn's Promise is there." Cresadir frowned. "For some reason I feel impelled to go there... as quickly as possible."

"You can't go to Aedolyn's Promise!" the male voice shouted.

"And why not?" Cresadir shouted back.

Miah and Oeradon exchanged worried looks over the painting.

"How are you going to stop me?" Cresadir demanded.

The voice was silent.

* * *

"Sire. She remembers parts of Alkoryn and she wants to go to Aedolyn's Promise," the flustered technician informed Ceolm.

Ceolm sighed heavily. "This is going to be a problem. I should've known she'd be drawn to the temple once she remembered it."

"How so, sire?" Salvador asked.

"The experiment we're doing on the Alkoryns is called Spiritual Influence. We built Aedolyn's Promise before we allowed the Alkoryns to settle there. There's technology inside that temple that emanates a signal to the Alkoryn people. We were testing how susceptible they would be to influence from an almighty power. We created their docile, controlled society," he explained. "I didn't think Cresadir's implants would have any connection to it."

"Yet she's drawn to go there," Salvador observed.

"This could get very complicated," Ceolm muttered. "It places the whole experiment in jeopardy."

"We should send men to retrieve Cresadir and the device,"

Salvador suggested.

"Sire! We've lost communication! We're being jammed!" The technician's chair swivelled as he quickly ran to another terminal.

"What?"

"Something's interfering! There's nothing I can do!"

Ceolm slammed his fist against the screen. "Fix it!"

* * *

A new voice, gentler, somehow familiar, spoke in Cresadir's head. It was her own voice, she realized with surprise.

"You need to go to Spiritmist," it said. "There are many answers for you there.

There's technology in the obelisk, it's the same technology that's in you."

"How do you... I... know that?"

"You'll see when you get there."

Cresadir leaned forward and cradled her head. Miah and Oeradon just watched, afraid they would make things worse if they interfered. Whatever was going on was beyond their comprehension.

Abruptly Cresadir threw back the covers and got to her feet. "I'm going to Spiritmist. I have to!" She found her boots and pulled them on. Looking at Miah and Oeradon, she said, "I'll be leaving now."

"Wait!" Miah called, hurrying after her.

Cresadir spun round. "Do not follow!"

"When will you be back?" Miah asked, on the verge of tears. "We miss you, Cresa!"

Cresadir closed her ears to Miah's pleas and continued walking, feeling her suit vibrate as she did. Glancing down, she saw her hands disappear in front of her eyes. "What the...?" To her astonishment, her hands, forearms, arms and shoulders had all vanished. Nor did it stop there, whatever was happening to her kept happening, until, within a short space of time, she was completely invisible.

"Leave the house and head west, towards the ocean," her own voice instructed.

Well, Cresadir decided, her own voice was a whole lot nicer than the sterile, male voice she had been listening to previously. She shrugged, doing as told.

* * *

The sun had begun to rise in the sky, casting a tranquil silver ribbon of illumination across the ripples in the ocean. Cresadir stood at the water's edge and let the waves trickle over her boots.

"You must find a boat," her voice spoke in her head. "Take one of the bay houses' boats."

"You want me to steal it?"

"Yes."

Against her ethics, Cresadir walked towards the nearest boat, climbed into it and set a course for Spiritmist.

* * *

The Amunisari observed Cresadir find a boat to travel to Spiritmist.

"She's being drawn to the temple," the technician said.

"I can see that," Ceolm snapped. "You just concentrate on maintaining the link. I'm going to be very unhappy if we lose it again – and you won't like that, believe me." He drew in a deep, calming breath. "It's the technology – it's the same, and just as it drew her to the object of power, it'll draw her to the obelisk."

"Do... do we just let her go?" ventured the technician. "She might shut it down."

"She won't if she knows what's good for her people," Ceolm

said grimly.

* * *

Arriving on the east side placed Cresadir behind Aedolyn's Promise. In front of her was a steep embankment covered in boulders.

"You'll need to climb," the gentle voice instructed.

Cresadir was an agile woman so climbing the boulders was no real challenge for her. As she arrived at the front of Aedolyn's Promise, its magnificence overshadowed everything for a moment. Pressing herself flat to the wall, she peered around to the front of the building.

"There are guardians at every doorway," Cresadir projected her thoughts at the inner voice.

"You need to take them down."

"What?"

"Just a quick knock on the head will do it," the voice told her calmly.

"But?"

"It's the only way, Cresadir. They can't see you, remember."

"Ah! I forgot that for a moment. Should I not just steal past them?"

"They'll see the door move. It'll just cause complications," the voice said.

Cresadir sighed and looked at the ground. *"All right."*

Emerging from behind the wall, she moved cautiously, careful not to disturb any pebbles or stones that would give away her presence. Positioning herself behind one of the guardians, she steeled herself.

"Use plenty of force," the voice directed.

Cresadir lifted her fist high, intending to bring it down on the back of the man's head.

"Find a weapon!" her other self instructed.

A weapon! And just where was she supposed to find that?

"Over there – on the left."

A stone, roughly the size of her palm lay just a few steps away. Retrieving it, Cresadir hoisted it above the guardian's head, bringing it down as hard as she could. He dropped to the ground unconscious. Relieved to see he was still breathing, she dragged him the short distance and sat him up against the wall. "Sorry," she muttered. This will give you a little more dignity.

Her other self laughed drily. "And if someone spots him, they might just think he's snoozing and leave him to it."

Cresadir moved warily down the central aisle of Aedolyn's Promise. Sunlight streamed through the high windows illuminating the interior but she hardly noticed, her attention all on getting to the domed, central room without alerting anyone who might be around. She had dropped the stone at the scene of her crime and even invisible, she would rather not risk another encounter. As she approached the high obelisk the light spilled onto its marble surface, falling onto a golden, glowing hand print at the bottom of the pillar. "I guess it's only visible to me," she whispered to herself.

"Correct," her inner voice replied. "I think you should place your hand there."

Stepping closer to the obelisk, Cresadir slowly stretched out her hand and placed it onto the glowing impression. Immediately the glow began to spread, as if infecting the rest of the obelisk.

"What's happening?"

"Wait, soon you'll see."

Suddenly, Cresadir was bombarded with flashes of images and thoughts.

Her head being tilted forward, then a pain in the back of her neck.

"That was Elisaris implanting you with a chip. It's how I'm able to talk to you. She wanted you to have the council's knowledge."

"I... remember Elisaris."

Images and thoughts rolled across her mind, one after the other.

"They tricked you," her other self said. "This isn't a simulation. Where you are now is real and this is really happening. This place, Alkoryn, is your home. I know you're confused. You don't know who to believe. But you must follow my guidance. I'm trying to save you, Cresadir."

Cresadir stood, rooted to the spot, as the secrets of the Amunisari were revealed to her.

She saw how they had lied to her. She saw Daimeh and herself journeying to the Citadel and being taken away. The Amunisari wiping her memory and trying to integrate her. Tears pricked her eyes as Tristan and Kiara were revealed for who they really were: a deceiver and a clone.

Her stomach churned. "I'll never see her again."

"She's safe," the voice told her gently.

Images of her childhood in Alkoryn, her family and friends flashed before her eyes: her trip to the borders, last year's fête, her stealing the amulet all raced through her mind. Then she was with the Amunisari admiring the obelisk. A moment later she remembered herself with her pseudo-husband, Tristan, and her baby.

Images of her son and Miah came to mind. *"My sister and Oeradon."* She smiled. Then another thought. *"Daimeh!"* Sadness filled her again. *"Theo... he was manipulated by the Amunisari!"* Her eyes widened. "There's a chip in his head!" she burst out. Realising she had shouted, she quickly scanned the area – luckily, no one had heard. *"I can cure him."*

"Alkoryn was an experiment, this obelisk controls us. This whole temple was built by the Amunisari. Aedolyn's Tears... they're just another device."

Cresadir's whole world was falling apart. Her whole life, everything... all of it was built on her faith, her complete trust and belief. And it had all been just a lie.

"The experiment was called Spiritual Influence. It was

intended to test a society with a high religious belief in order to see how it affected their social development, amongst other things."

"The obelisk controls us with signals." More memories: A place she had never seen before. A sizeable area inside a sophisticated building with similar gleaming white architecture to the citadel; the walls engraved with symbols, all of which glowed an aqua-blue. Inside the image, she turned around. In front of her was a huge window, outside she saw the magnificence of a planet rotating amongst the stars, on one side light, one side dark, the glorious sun beaming onto the light side. She knew it was her home world.

"This is Solnyx," the voice said. "This is where you are."

Cresadir saw the threat to the Amunisari, and what the tablet had said.

The images suddenly stopped.

"What do I do? Deactivate the obelisk?"

"Ask yourself, is it doing any harm?" the voice said.

Cresadir shook her head. "No. It's not," she said aloud. "But it has manipulated us. Yet we are peaceful... and we thrive."

"Yes, peaceful. Do you want to disrupt the status quo?"

"I'll do what's best for my people and leave it."

"You're making the right choice."

"Where do I go from here?"

"You reconnect with your loved ones. I'll guide you to the right path and help you expose the Amunisari council for who they are."

Cresadir took her hand away from the obelisk. Turning, she walked back down the aisle and out of the temple. As she walked past the guardian, still slumped by the wall, she saw he was beginning to stir. Quickening her pace, she continued down the embankment, arriving at her small boat. The memories and grief clamoured at her for attention but she pushed them aside and climbed in, setting sail for Lybas.

20

Return to Port Draclyn

The five houses abutting onto the bay were almost fully visible on the horizon as Cresadir rowed back towards Lybas.

Bermel was out on his fishing boat, he cast his net into the sea as he watched Cresadir approach.

"Cresa, is that you?" he called across the breeze.

Cresadir smiled and waved. "I'm back," she said.

Bermel's boat wobbled as he stood up. "Ma'am it's so good to see you. You've been missed greatly," he told her, peering at the rear of the boat.

Cresadir guessed who Bermel was looking for. She steeled herself. "I'm sorry, Daimeh didn't return with me."

"I–I don't understand," he stuttered.

"No one will," she told him sadly.

Bermel found himself abruptly done with fishing. He turned his boat around and headed for home with Cresadir following him to his mooring. Tying up her little vessel, Cresadir said, "I need to see my son and sister, so for now, a good day to you, Bermel."

"Yes, certainly," he gave a stiff bow of the head.

Standing, watching Cresadir striding away until she was just a small smudge against the horizon, he shook his head. She's come back different, he thought.

* * *

Cresadir retraced the same route back to the manor that she had trodden earlier. Opening the door, she let herself in.

"Oeradon, Miah!" she called with some trepidation.

There was no answer.

Following the faint sound of a lute, Cresadir continued on to the reception room, where Oeradon was playing a delightful, slow paced, somewhat melancholy tune.

He glanced up as she entered. "Mother! I–I didn't know if I'd ever see you again. Are you all right? Where did you go? Why did you just leave yesterday?"

"Ssh, my dearest. All's well with me. I know who I am now," Cresadir said softly, opening her arms.

Oeradon's smile lit up his whole face. Putting his lute aside, he hugged his mother tightly. "I've been so worried."

"I apologize for who I was last night," she murmured, stroking his back lovingly. "Where's Miah?"

"She's upstairs, sleeping."

"I need to see her," Cresadir said, reluctantly letting go of Oeradon.

She started up the stairs, Oeradon trailing close behind.

* * *

Miah was drifting into sleep when Cresadir stuck her head around the door.

"I'm… so very sorry, Miah," Cresadir said slowly.

Miah pushed herself up into a sitting position.

"I've changed," Cresadir admitted, crossing to her sister. "There are a lot of things you may find hard to comprehend."

Miah slipped from the bed and grasped hold of Cresadir's hands. "Tell me."

"Miah." Cresadir tightened her grip. "Daimeh won't be coming home."

Miah's face blanched and her eyes rolled up in their sockets.

Oeradon sprang forward and between them, he and Cresadir softened her fall and lifted her back onto the bed.

Cresadir sighed. "I'll get her a drink for when she wakes."

Oeradon, his own face troubled, perched next to his aunt,

gently stroking her brow with the back of his hand.

Miah slowly came back from the deep, dark hole she had fallen into.

Hot tears welled in her eyes and rolled silently down her cheeks.

A big, calloused fist closed around her arm.

"We'll get through this, Miah," Halgor said.

"We'll do what we've done over the past six months," his voice cracked but he ploughed on. "We'd already accepted that Daimeh might not return to us." He leaned over, gently wiping the tears away from her cheeks.

Miah slowly lifted her gaze and stared at Cresadir, sat next to her.

"Is he dead?"

"No."

Her eyebrows raised hopefully. "Where is he?"

Cresadir flinched. "He's in a place far from here... a place he can't return from."

"Where did you go for all those months, Cresadir?" Halgar asked.

"We found the Golden Lands, the place from our myths—"

"Aedolyn!"

"No. We met a race known as the Amunisari."

"And this is where Daimeh is?" Hope shone in Miah's face.

Cresadir wished she could say something that would give comfort to Miah and Halgar, but she owed them the truth. "We were interrogated and separated. I believe Daimeh's imprisoned there."

"Well, why can't we rescue him?"

Cresadir cupped Miah's hand with both of hers. "The Amunisari are just too powerful."

"Then how are you here?"

Cresadir looked away from the accusation in her sister's gaze.

"They did something to me, tried to turn me into one of them. They brainwashed me and sent me back here on a mission to deactivate the tablet."

"I found the tablet, in Daimeh's larder," Miah said, pushing herself into a sitting position, "and brought it here. Theo asked for it."

"Asked?" Cresadir's head whipped around. "Must be the chip in his head."

"I was so shocked, Cresa, I just handed it over and he just..." she paused, "lit up."

"They would've monitored that, it's probably why they sent me back," Cresadir said thoughtfully.

There was silence for a few minutes, then Miah said,

"You were different last night, you said we weren't real."

Cresadir drew in a sharp breath. "I was under the impression it was all a simulation. And they'd messed with my mind so much I didn't recognise you."

"But you do now?" Miah asked, narrowing her eyes.

Cresadir nodded. "Yes. I was drawn to the obelisk at Spiritmist by a device implanted in me." She pointed to the back of her neck. "A woman, Elisaris, put it there. She helped me. I activated the obelisk and was given knowledge of everything that had happened to me, and complete knowledge of the Amunisari. I remember everything now and I understand things I knew nothing of before." She hesitated, afraid that what she had to say might make Daimeh's loss even harder to bear for her sister and Halgor. "I–I know how to cure Theo." To her delight, both of their faces filled with pleasure for a moment before sobering again.

"So what are you not telling us, Cresa?" Miah asked, shooting her sister a shrewd look. Seeing Cresadir's surprise, she added. "You're troubled – it's not hard to see."

Cresadir hesitated. "Nothing's as it seems," she said finally. "The Amunisari have control over us, and I fear that Alkoryn's in danger."

"What kind of danger?" Halgar asked.

Cresadir gave a tight smile. "That's just it – I don't know yet. It's something to do with the tablet, it was protecting us somehow. That's why they sent me back to deactivate it. That's what I was doing when you saw me, Miah." She sighed. "Of course, I didn't know what it was for, until after my trip to Spiritmist."

"Our people have no way to defend ourselves against such superior technology," Halgar confirmed, shaking his head. He looked at his sister-in-law. "I take it their weapons will be equally superior?"

Cresadir nodded.

* * *

A small, fluorescent pink bird fluttered down next to Oeradon as he was taking a breath of fresh air in the gardens. The bird bounced along the grass until it was at his feet, then hopped on the spot, staring up at him with intelligent eyes. Oeradon knelt down and held out his hand, palm up, and the little bird dropped the tiny roll of paper it carried in its mouth into his hand. Oeradon quickly unravelled it. He read for a moment, then ran back into the house and up the stairs.

His deep voice could be heard as he ran. "It's grandfather! He's left for Port Draclyn. He wants us to meet him there in a day. He wants us to bring the tablet," he finished as he reached the doorway.

Cresadir glanced at Miah. "Father knows about the tablet?"

"I told him after Theo's episode," Miah said hastily.

"All right, we should get prepared to leave. Oeradon and I will go."

"We all should go," Halgar said.

Cresadir shook her head. "No, you need to stay here and take care of Theo." For a moment she looked very vulnerable and fragile. "I so wish I had time to attend to him now, but I need to be here after it's done – just in case." Then she squared her shoulders. "It'll just have to wait until I return. Besides, Miah's in no shape to go anywhere."

For an instant it looked as if Halgar would argue, but then he nodded. "All right."

Cresadir crossed to the door and they heard her going down the stairs. Halgar helped Miah to her feet.

"We'll pack a few things," he said.

"I'll get the glennies." Oeradon called as he clattered after his mother.

* * *

Cresadir hurried back to the reading room where the tablet still lay as it had fallen, on the carpet in front of the bookcase. Picking it up, she inspected it. It was smooth and blank with no markings, turning it over, she saw the chip she had installed to deactivate it. Digging her fingernails into the side, she did her best to pull it free. Two broken nails later, the thing hadn't budged. Cresadir fought off a wave of despair. Alkoryn was at risk because of her, and she didn't know how to fix it, but giving in would solve nothing. Shrugging off her emotions, she made her way outside.

* * *

Waiting patiently for her was Oeradon, mounted and with a glenny by his side. Halgor ran out of the manor, with Miah arriving shortly after.

Cresadir exchanged a long look with Halgar and Miah before she reached out for her bags. He passed her two modest satchels; they would travel light. Cresadir tossed one to Oeradon, who skilfully caught it and wrapped it over his shoulder. She waved and hoisted herself up onto her glenny. They were ready to ride.

Her sister and husband-in-law stood at the doorway to the manor and waved them off.

* * *

They led their mounts out of Lybas. The soft sands of the beach giving way to rocky ground as they approached the white cliffs. The sure-footed beasts traversed the cliffs as they continued along the cliff top.

They had been riding for about twenty minutes when, suddenly, two assailants appeared from thin air. Both wore white cloaks and carried staffs. In two swift strides they were upon them, one knocking Oeradon out of his saddle, the other pressing the sharp point of his staff to Cresadir's throat.

"We want the tablet."

Cresadir, shocked, afraid to move in case she found herself speared like a fish, sat helpless. The first ambusher grabbed Oeradon by the neck and carried him over to the cliff edge.

"Give me the tablet," he barked.

"Don't!" Cresadir cried, terrified. "I'll give you it. Just put my son down."

The Amunisari lifted Oeradon away from the rocks and dropped him onto the grass. The other man thrust his staff close to Cresadir's face as she carefully dismounted. Taking the tablet out of her baggage, she passed it to the Amunisari.

Between one breath and the next, they were gone.

Cresadir and Oeradon stared numbly at the spot where they had been.

"Are you all right, Oeradon?" Cresadir asked. Tears flooded her eyes but she would not allow them to fall. If she gave in now, she was finished. She would turn tail like a whipped dog and run home and she could not allow herself that luxury. Too many sons – and daughters – lives depended on her getting her information to her father.

Oeradon gave a shaky laugh. "Not something I ever want to experience again, but, yes, I'm fine. Relax mother."

"There was nothing we could do," Cresadir said, shaking her head.

"I take it they were Amunisari?"

His mother nodded, still shaken.

"What did they want with the tablet?"

She sighed. "From my recent insight into the Amunisari I'd say they want to draw power from it – perhaps use it as a defence for themselves." She paused. "Come, Oeradon, mount up. We need to get to Port Draclyn as soon as possible."

* * *

Later that day they arrived at the crescent. They slowed, drinking in the view sweeping down to the picturesque Port of Draclyn. Dozens of marvellous square-sailed ships were docked at the port and other, smaller ships, weaved in between the larger ones. They descended down the sloping street, past the shanty houses and onto the cobbled road. The closer they came to the town centre, the more elegant and outstanding the buildings were. Lovely two-storey houses lined either side of the thoroughfare, some with shops on the ground floor. They reached the well-kept and lush garden, and as they rounded the curve, the harbour came into view, followed by the hotel they had stayed at when visiting the fête.

Oeradon pointed. "That's where grandfather's staying."

Cresadir nodded and they trotted onwards through the shadowed street, flanked by high town houses, the raised brick edges catching the light from the gleaming sun.

She felt a sudden shiver up her spine and quickly turned her head, searching the quiet street. But there was no one to be seen. Yet she couldn't rid herself of the feeling that they were being watched. She scanned the area one more time.

"What's wrong?" Oeradon asked nervously.

Cresadir's tawny eyes were concentrated as she listened carefully for any movement.

"There's someone here. I'm sure of it."

"Are you sure you're not just a little jumpy after the ambush?"

"I'm sure!" She nodded, certain. "We're being watched." She paused. "Let's keep going."

* * *

They arrived at the quaint hotel, it hadn't changed since their last visit. Yet, the spritely man, Annard, was not there to greet them this time, and instead, there stood Ommaya, holding the door open. He was dressed in leather-stitched trousers and a flouncy shirt, an attractive man even into his sixties.

Cresadir and Oeradon dismounted and tied their glennies to the surrounding fence before Cresadir dashed over to her father and hugged him tightly.

"Oh Father! I thought I'd never see you again." Tears once more filled her eyes.

"Somehow I knew you'd return," Ommaya said, patting her back soothingly. Loosening his hold, he turned his attention to Oeradon, gripping his hand and pumping it up and down.

"Where's Daimeh?"

"He didn't come back with me." Cresadir didn't want to say that, as far as she knew, he was imprisoned.

"He will though?"

"I don't know," she admitted, heavy hearted.

Ommaya sighed deeply. His greying, shoulder-length hair dislodged from behind his ear as he momentarily lowered his head. His eyes bleak, he bade them enter.

* * *

In the main lounge, they seated themselves comfortably on a firm, leather settee with a strong, high back and wide arms.

Ommaya cleared his throat before opening the conversation. "What's this tablet all about?"

Cresadir thought carefully. Her father had no knowledge of where she had been or of the Amunisari and their corruption. She opened her mouth to speak but Oeradon took the initiative. "It was stolen on our way here."

Cresadir looked at her son. "Slow down, Oeradon, Father doesn't know what it is yet."

"Aunt Miah found it at Daimeh's house, hidden in his larder." Oeradon edged off his seat in excitement. "Dad touched it and he lit up and pulsed with gold."

His mother put her hand on his leg. "I'll explain," she said looking at Ommaya. "I presume Daimeh found the tablet at the bay, with the body. There must've been a message for him to leave the tablet as it protected Alkoryn."

"From what?" Ommaya quizzed.

"From the Amunisari."

"Who?"

"Let me explain, Father." She paused, gathering her thoughts before continuing. "Daimeh took a copy of the scripture and map, and that's what he showed us. I know what it says, as the Amunisari prosper, Stygia conspires. Time is short. As the darkness is coming."

"The Amunisari?"

"They're the civilisation who live in the Golden Lands. They could be considered as deities by us. The scripture was a message to them, a warning so to say." Cresadir clasped her hands on her lap. "A warning from who or what, I don't know.

"Oeradon mentioned the tablet was stolen, by who, these Amunisari?"

"Yes, the tablet holds great power and they want to utilise it."

"All right, I think I understand." Ommaya nodded his head

whilst stroking his thin goatee beard.

Cresadir went on to explain her time with the Amunisari, the manipulation, and their attempt to integrate her. She explained the so-called 'therapy' to trick her into stealing the tablet for them and her visit to Spiritmist to unlock all her memories and more. She told him about the Amunisari's technology and the things they had done to her, implanting a chip into her head which allowed her to do 'magical' things.

Ommaya listened silently, without interruption. His blue-grey eyes focused on Cresadir's face as she spoke.

"We're in grave danger then," he acknowledged, troubled.

His daughter looked at him silently, the terror in her eyes telling all.

21

The March

Viktor descended down the grand staircase to witness his mighty army marching out of the cloning chambers and through a door to Stygia. Tens of thousands of soldiers could be seen, stretching far into the distance.

Viktor made his way through the door to the outside world and waited as his squarm was brought over. Squarms, a native species of large lizard, stood low to the ground and were covered in thick brown fur. The beasts were both sure footed and fast and Viktor wasted no time in mounting. Many of the enchants were already mounted, awaiting his signal. Viktor nodded to the soldier on his right and the sound of the battle horn cut the air. Viktor urged his lizard forward and the army rode out in formation.

Daimeh, chained inside a cramped, low-ceilinged cage that hovered slightly above ground as it was dragged behind an enchant found himself confined to a sitting position.

As the last stragglers were emerging, Viktor rode his group of enchants to the back of the army.

"Bring Nis'Ka," he ordered, his voice as hard as stone.

Loyalists unlocked another door and Nis'Ka walked out and made his way to Viktor's side.

"You'll be my bodyguard," Viktor informed him.

Nis'Ka nodded obediently.

Once more urging his mount into action, Viktor set off, Nis'Ka easily keeping pace beside him. They were to head south, over the ice plains of the South Pole, then north, to approach the Golden Lands from above. The massive Zygeth army swarmed over the land like a black cloud, dust billowing with each thunderous stride of their uniform tread. They travelled hard and they travelled fast, pausing only to allow the men a few hours rest and some sustenance before continuing their march.

* * *

A week into their journey and the sky was darker and the air cooler as the icy wind started to blow in from the south. Daimeh shivered inside his cage. The bars were covered in a white, powdery stuff that glinted in the light of the sun and was so cold it hurt his fingers when he touched it. Although he had read of the phenomena, it was the first time Daimeh had seen frost.

"May I have some blankets? Please," he called to his driver. "I'm so cold."

The driver glanced back at him but said nothing before returning his gaze ahead.

Were they going to let him die? Daimeh thought bleakly as he rubbed his arms in a vain attempt to generate some warmth.

As the army advanced, the ground turned glacial and slippery. The usual haze of the sun was just a tint below the horizon. The sky was blacker than Daimeh had ever seen it. He tried to concentrate on the stars and nebula above to distract him from the pain of the cold.

Soon gusts of icy wind swirled small flurries of white flakes in through the cage bars. Daimeh's skin was turning a pale-blue and frost clung to his eyelashes and hair.

"I'm going to die here, I'm no use to you dead," he called to the driver.

The driver continued to ignore Daimeh but catching the attention of a nearby rider, he beckoned him over and whispered something to him. The rider nodded and galloped away to Viktor.

"Sire, the boy needs protection from the cold. We need him alive and he's not looking good," he reported.

Viktor signalled a man wearing thick, black clothes, stitched into a light armour. His face was cracked and there was blue shining through from the cracks. At the signal, he turned his mount and rode to Daimeh. As he approached, he rubbed his hands together until they started to glow, then, from his wrist, he fired a golden blast which shot in between the bars and stuck to the cage floor, where it grew in size, warming the space inside the prison. Daimeh sighed as his cramped muscles began to relax in the welcome heat. The frost on the bars started to melt and after a few minutes, he was almost back to his usual olive skin colour.

Daimeh looked to the strange rider and nodded a thank you.

* * *

When he next awoke, huddled close to the glowing heat source, Daimeh's back was covered in snow and exposed to the raging blizzard. The ground beneath the hovering cage lay buried under a thick, white blanket which the soldiers were forced to trudge through. The choking darkness weighed down on him.

Daimeh blinked hard, clearing the sleep from his eyes. He blinked again, bumps of snow were appearing, small mounds with holes in the tops, placed as if consciously organised.

The blizzard cleared and Daimeh heard a commotion from the ranks. Squeezing his head through the bars, he could see soldiers fighting at the front lines, their swords glowing through the haze and darkness. Daimeh cursed, too far away to be able to see what they were fighting.

A split second later and a luminescent, wriggling creature jumped from one of the lumps of snow, straight into his cage. It happened in a flash and before Daimeh had time to gather his wits there was an overgrown maggot writhing around on the floor, its frightening jaws snapping instinctively. Daimeh sprang into action, kicking at it, but it grabbed his boot with sharp, dagger-like teeth. Luckily, the boots he had been given were strong enough. He booted it with his other foot, then kicked it up against the cage bars. The thing split into two, with the front end half stuck to the bars. Daimeh stared as it continued writhing for a moment before finally lying still.

The strange creatures were everywhere. They clung to soldiers, forcing the army to a halt as they fought the things off. Looking up to the sky, Daimeh saw hundreds more, falling like deadly rain. The soldier next to him had a dozen gripping to his armour.

He peered through the bars again, trying to see what was happening ahead. Through the mayhem, Daimah could just make out what looked like small hills immediately beyond the front line.

Without warning, a huge, chitinous, glowing monstrosity sprang from a hillock, another massive bug following close behind. The things let out a piercing shriek, half-scream, half-hiss, as if about to explode. Instead, the bugs covered the distance between them and the army in two enormous bounds.

One thundered down next to his cage, squashing two Zygeth, killing them instantly, Daimeh had no doubt. Another flew overhead, landing on another small group of soldiers. The surrounding men unsheathed their swords and started to attack the beasts but it was soon apparent that the rough textured, off-white shells, each plate overlapping the last, formed a tough exoskeleton that the weapons simply bounced off. Even the terrible blue gel only succeeded in burning a small hole but was unable to penetrate any deeper.

Daimeh tucked himself at the back of his cage and watched as the immense bugs reared up, before heavily pounding back down to the ground, knocking the defensive soldiers off their feet.

Quickly, the Zygeth developed a strategy; two men attacking from the side, whilst one soldier baited the beast, causing it to rear up. Once the vulnerable underside was exposed, the other soldiers flanked it and brought it down. One had fallen... the others would follow.

Finally, the battle was done. Carcasses lay as far as the eye could see: bugs and soldiers both, and the army continued its trek, over the small mounds, onwards to the Golden Lands.

* * *

Little could be seen as the army pushed through the abrasive winds, blowing one way, then suddenly changing direction to punish them from another side. The only illumination was from the blue luminescence of the enchants' armour and the glowing heat source Daimeh was huddled next to. He was still a long way from being warm, but at least the object kept him from freezing to death.

The army marched for hours across the vast tundra, the weather unrelenting and the hazy sunshine almost completely extinguished by the horizon.

The winds had died down and sheer darkness was upon them as they approached the southernmost point on the planet. The sky was a flat black in which the stars shone with a crystalline intensity, all the constellations clearly visible. But it was the nebula which drew Daimah's eyes again and again. Its orangey-red colours a burning brilliance, the coral coloured wisps of gas seeming to be nebulas of their own.

Daimeh gazed upwards; for a few minutes, he was oblivious to his predicament, imagining images in the stars.

The snow thinned as they continued through the South Pole, they were heading northwards now and after another few hours the gleam of sunshine returned. As the days passed, Daimeh watched the sunrise over the horizon. He had missed its beauty even more than he had realized; its mesmerizing orange light reflecting off the ice patches; its heat warming his soul, warming his cold heart; it was a shining beacon of hope.

The squelching of the army's footfalls as they marched told

him without needing to look that the snow had melted. Fluffy seeds drifted past his cage and Daimeh knew their northward journey was well underway.

Another week passed and the army came to a halt as the sound of a horn echoed through the ranks. Soon a few mouthfuls of dry bread were thrown into Daimeh's cage; he guessed the Zygeth were resting. The clones, of course, didn't need to rest and were simply standing around, waiting to set off once more. Daimeh was confused. Looking around, all that lay ahead of them were towering cliffs, surely too high for an army of tens of thousands to climb.

A short time later, the horn sounded again and the gruelling march continued. The army heading straight towards the cliff wall. Daimeh heard the distinctive fizzle of Zygeth bolts and realized that their intention was not to go over, instead, they meant to go through. They intended to blast a tunnel through the rock face, not knowing or caring how thick the stone would be.

In an unbelievably short time, the army reformed into orderly lines to pass through the tunnel.

A few weary hours later, Daimeh and his escort reached the tunnel entrance, and then there was darkness again. Daimeh craned his head to watch the diminishing sunlight as they headed further into the tunnel. Heavy footsteps echoed throughout the enclosed space and the air was close and sticky. Dust pouring into Daimeh's lungs caused him to cough periodically and he had trouble breathing, his eyes watered and his clothes stuck to his body with sweat. Finally, to Daimeh's intense relief, a weak light began to dilute the dark; they were nearing the end. Emerging from the tunnel, he was greeted by a desolate sandy landscape. The sun beat down on the cracked ground and Daimeh saw little sign of life. At first, as he looked, the massive plateau shimmered here and there indicating what he thought were pools or lakes of water. Then he realized that it was all illusion, glistening mirages in the distance.

As the army moved on, the dust from the tunnel cleared, giving way to the choking dust stirred up by their passage. The white sun glared down, the cloudless sky shimmering with its heat. Daimeh's bones welcomed the climate he was used to, but his eyes hungered for the grassy surroundings of Lybas village.

* * *

Daimeh came awake to the sun sitting high in a cloudless sky. The north was approaching. Around him, the arid plain had given way to lush grasses and tropical greenery. He estimated another day of marching would bring them to the Golden Lands. The thought was like a hot potato lodged in his innards. Just what would happen when they arrived? How would he escape? His anxiety gnawed at him and he stealthily checked he still had the device Xylos had given him. But that only served to give rise to more questions. What if it didn't work? If he didn't become invisible, the Zygeth would surely kill him on the spot. Daimeh shook his head trying to dislodge the disturbing ideas as the rocky ride brought them ever closer to their destination.

* * *

As they travelled further across the savannah, delicate clouds started to form, with wisps of pure white lining the pale grey underneath. A fresh, fruity breeze pleasantly blew between the bars of Daimeh's cage. He recognised the smell: overripe berries from the jungle. *The jungle!* Craning his neck as far as he could, he spied ahead. His sense of smell had not failed him, the army was indeed approaching a jungle. From a distance, its density of growth was astonishing. Tall palm trees poked out of the top of the verdant canopy and the lush vegetation was a variety of greens, the lower undergrowth blanketed with herbaceous, wide-leaved bushes, interspaced with blooming fruit plants.

The army reached the outskirts of the jungle and without pause ploughed into it, effortlessly pushing their way through nature's obstacles, ignorant of its hazards, determinedly advancing towards the Citadel.

22

Time to Retaliate

Hundreds of orpids flew from the nearby cliffs and flocked above the tai-qay forest. Xanoth stood by the side of a hatch and watched soldiers of the Resistance exit one after the other. Men and women dressed in military clothes, tight, black utility trousers and matching thick, close-fitting, black jackets with many pockets, harnesses across their chests to hold their weapons and radios.

The crackle and rustle of leaves grew louder as more and more personnel poured out above ground; their faces expressing fearless determination; each one ready to lay down their lives.

Spreading out across the area, they awaited their turn to chant for their orpid, watching as the creatures touched down gracefully beside them, before quickly mounting and lifting off to join the formation circling above.

* * *

The smog of industry was upon them the minute the small army came within sight of the industrialised skyline.

"We stay as high as we can," Xanoth called across the sky.

Aiden broke from formation and flew up next to him. "Do you want me to take a few men to the east?"

Xanoth nodded tightly. "Yes." He paused. "A hundred at least."

Xanoth's second in command veered left and signalled to the men he wanted with him to follow. Flying away east, they were soon lost in the smog.

Xanoth looked to Avaeth, his next in command. "You fly these men straight south, to the centre of Kraag'Blitz," he ordered, pointing at another group of soldiers.

He gave a signal to the men he had picked to join him. "I'll head west."

Avaeth nodded compliance.

Having gathered his men, Xanoth cut away right, entering the smog. He coughed as the smoke seared his throat and lungs and hurriedly lifted his facemask to cover his mouth and nose.

Raising his arm, he signalled to his men to slow down as he pulled out his binoculars, scanning the area. It was hard to see clearly thanks to the pollution, but he did manage to locate Zygeth adepts manning the tops of factories and prison blocks. Glancing around further, he caught a glimpse of the central team just beginning to enter Kraag'Blitz, weaving between the chimneys and buildings. Unintentionally, Xanoth had used them as bait; they would be sitting ducks if they flew any further in. Frantically, he grabbed the radio. "Halt there," he shouted. "I see adepts close by. I don't want you to continue until I give the order."

"Yes, sir."

The team stopped and hovered in the air, awaiting their next command.

Xanoth signalled to his men and they silently moved deeper into the smog, approaching the adepts from the side.

Xanoth's heart stuttered as he saw that the adepts were looking directly at the oncoming orpids; they knew they were there. Xanoth's thoughts scrabbled for some way out as he led his men into what seemed like a pre-emptive trap.

"Stop!" he ordered quickly. But even as the words echoed in his ears, it was already too late.

As Xanoth's team came within reach, the adepts jumped off the building, their cloaks hardening as they swooped over the orpids, firing darts. Several orpids were hit, tumbling screeching from the sky, taking their riders with them. Other adepts leaped onto the orpids, grappling with Xanoth's soldiers, knocking them out of their saddles to plunge to the depths of Kraag'Blitz. His eyes on his men, the first thing Xanoth was aware of was a weight crashing down. Instinctively, he flattened along his ride's back, letting his weight carry him low to the side. As the adept lost his hold on him and fell, Xanoth pushed at the strange material of the cloak, setting him into a spin. He used the weapon Anamai had given him to solidify and drop a few from the sky, watching with satisfaction as they plummeted towards the ground like rocks.

"Attack!" Xanoth screamed over the radio.

Aiden's team flew in from the east, releasing a hail of arrows through the smoky air, some found their mark but failed to stop the adepts and they continued their murderous attack on Xanoth's men. Once Aiden's men were close enough, they ordered their orpids to attack. Aiden's orpid swept his tail through the air, ripping a hole in one adept's cloak, causing him to drop from the sky.

"We're at a disadvantage in this smog. Fly lower!" Xanoth shouted.

Underneath the smog visibility was better and the odds more even. But that didn't last long. Looking downwards, Xanoth spotted Zygeth ground troops preparing to fire.

Xanoth contacted his central team. "Take your men to the Rhajok'Don camps," he ordered, free as many as you can. We need ground support."

He watched as the platoon commander directed her men north, to the slave camps. Through his binoculars, he could see the Rhajok'Don attempting to bring down the barricades, they, too, were ready to fight.

Landing and quickly dismounting, Xanoth's soldiers ran towards the first buildings. Unsheathing their swords, they attacked the dozen Zygeth guards in front of the gates. A brief skirmish took place, at the end of which the guards, all except for one needed to open the gates, lay dead. As the gates opened, hundreds of Rhajok'Don poured from the camps and headed for the centre of Kraag'Blitz.

The team leader smiled grimly. "Let's go, there's more work to do." A short time later, they stood back as the last slave camp gates swung open, releasing the remaining Rhajok'Don.

From above, Xanoth could see hundreds of charging Rhajok'Don heading straight towards the Zygeth soldiers, who, distracted, firing at the orpids, were unaware of what was heading towards them.

The Rhajok'Don reached the Zygeth and threw themselves into battle, using their horns to toss their enemy into the air, their heavy feet trampling them into the dust. The Zygeth, caught by surprise, were initially overcome by the onslaught and a small number went down and stayed down. But too many slowly got to their feet and aimed their swords at the Rhajok'Don. Bolts were fired and many Rhajok'Don, enveloped in the goo, dissolved almost instantly.

Bitterness flowed like acid in his veins as Xanoth watched the slaves fall. Although the Rhajok'Don fought for a good cause and died with honour, it was nothing short of wholesale slaughter.

More adepts had joined the battle, leaping off the top of the buildings, but this time Xanoth's men were prepared and their orpids landed on them, turning their own tactics against them, and forcing them to the ground.

Below them, the fighting was in full flood and a surprising number of Rhajok'Don were managing to dodge the death bolts. The Resistance were also clashing swords with the enemy, while a number of soldiers fired arrows into the Zygeth ranks.

The orpids who had brought down the adepts held onto their prisoners with their sharp talons and, even when the occasional one managed to escape the ferocious claws, the riders were there to cut them down.

The Zygeth now found themselves outnumbered and began to pull back. Xanoth spied their commander signal to the soldiers at the rear and saw them break away and run towards the main buildings.

A few minutes later a series of explosions ripped through the buildings, followed by a massive rumble under the battlefield, and Xanoth saw one of the tall rock formations begin to crumble. The structure fell as if in slow motion, boulders breaking away and crashing to the ground. Slowly the building slid down and a colossal boom could be heard as it hit the earth. Seconds later a blast of dirt and stones bombarded the battling armies, forcing them to the ground and burying those closest under the debris.

More explosions were heard as another towering formation began to rumble.

Anamai! Anamai was in there! He had to save her! That was the only thought in Xanoth's mind as he ran towards the building she was imprisoned in.

"Xanoth! Don't!" Aiden shouted. "You'll never make it back in time!"

Xanoth kept running.

Seconds later, a shock wave smashed into him blowing him off his feet and covering him in debris. Xanoth wasted no time in digging his way out and, scrambling back to his feet, he continued his dash towards the building.

An enchant guard was blocking his entrance through the main door. Xanoth ran at him, raising his hand, he took control of the guard, commanding it to open the doors.

Xanoth dashed inside, the cloning chambers were just below him. He used the guard, who was still under control, to open further doors for him until he reached an elevator. Stepping inside, he pushed the down symbol. As soon as the doors glided open on the biomechanical corridors, he burst out of the lift and ran in the direction of Anamai's holding chamber. Hurtling into the room, he stood doubled over for a moment, pulling air into his starved lungs.

"You cannot save me, Xanoth," he heard her say.

Straightening, Xanoth looked into the eyes of the only woman he would ever love.

"You must go now," she insisted.

"I won't leave you," he told her, panting, still short of breath. Unsheathing his sword, he hacked at the pipes.

"Xanoth, stop," she insisted. "I will die here. It was always my destiny."

That mechanical voice, without timber or inflection, tore at Xanoth's heart. He shook his head, blinking back the tears that were blinding him. "I won't leave you!" he shouted, pulling the veins and tubes away.

A moving tube projected from Anamai. She held his hand, preventing him from further destruction.

"It will kill me. It is my life support," she said calmly.

"I'll take you straight to the hideout. Doctor Kaelan will save you. I know he can," Xanoth's voice betrayed his longing.

More explosions ripped through the building, the force almost knocking him from his feet. "No!" he yelled. "No – not now – not yet!"

"It is too late," Anamai said weakly.

Xanoth raked his hands through his hair. Everything in him, his very soul urged him to keep going, to keep striving. But his mind couldn't hide from the truth. He gave up on freeing her and instead wrapped his arms gently and as best he could around her encapsulated body. "I want to kiss you one more time," he said, looking into her sad, fiery eyes.

"Smash the glass."

Xanoth raised his sword and drove it downwards, breaking the capsule. He watched as the red fluid drained out and down her body. The pipes in the wall began to break and spew blue matter and blood around the room as the ceiling dropped a little.

"My heart's yours, Anamai," he murmured. "Whatever happens, wherever we go, I'll always love you." Unashamed, he let his tears flow as he moved his face close to hers and covered her mouth with his own. Cupping her face, he held his kiss as the walls fell around them and until they were both crushed under the rubble of the collapsing building.

The collapse of the building hurled more boulders and debris across the battlefield.

Glancing up, Aiden witnessed the full force of the demolition. "Xanoth!" he screamed, his voice breaking. There was no way that his friend could have survived the chaos. Losing focus, he lost balance and was forced to give way to his opponent. He bared his teeth in a feral smile as he allowed his anger to build, moulding it into a white-hot fury. Swinging his sword wildly he slashed and sliced at the armoured Loyalists, drawing blood with practiced ease. His friend might be gone, but his death would not go unavenged. His rage was so powerful he took down five Zygeth single-handedly before running out of breath and retreating away from the front-line.

The Zygeth army was dwindling and the bodies were piling up, the troops unable to hold back the force of the Rhajok'Don and the Resistance combined. Step by step they retreated back towards the rubble that was all that was left of the buildings. Finally, the Loyalists recognized defeat and put up their swords. The enchants were dead and the adepts had all been crushed by orpids.

"No mercy!" Someone shouted from the rear ranks, pushing his way through to the front, where he was joined by another few Resistance members ready to dispense rough justice.

"Stand down, soldiers!" Aiden ordered. "These are regular men, they just chose the wrong path. We'll be taking them prisoner."

For a moment, the ringleader stood his ground, then, "At least let me chain them," he muttered.

Aiden nodded permission.

* * *

As the dust settled, the only structures left standing were the factories, the huge, towering rock formations were nothing but big mounds of dirt and rocks. What remained now was for the factories to be shut down and the smog cleared.

Aiden ordered a group of around fifty men to spread out, sweep the buildings and destroy the machinery.

He pointed to a young soldier whose combat fatigues were torn and smeared with dirt and blood. The young man was bleeding from the arm and his face was haggard and worn, as were all his people. "Gather some men, soldier. I want you to retrieve all the bodies you can find. Our men and the Rhajok'Don deserve an honourable ceremony."

The young man saluted. "Yes, sir."

Aiden saluted back, staring towards the demolished edifices. His throat constricted at the thought of Xanoth's body trapped inside. He didn't want to leave him in his dusty grave, but he had neither the men nor the equipment to dig him out.

He watched as bodies were dragged from the battlefield and laid next to each other respectfully. Walking along the rows, he honoured each one individually.

* * *

For the first time since before he was born, the chimneys had ceased spewing chemicals. A new hope rose on the air and flowed throughout Kraag'Blitz; a feeling of rebirth as gusts of fresh air rushed through the buildings, heralding the winds of change. It would take some time for the toxic cloud to dissipate, but the process had begun.

A female Rhajok'Don approached him. "Thank you," she said in her native tongue.

Aiden nodded.

"What do we do now?"

"Do as you wish, rebuild your home here with us or go your own way. You're free now," Aiden told her gently. His smile fading as her bemused expression showed him that this truth had still not registered. "You're free," he said again.

Finally, she nodded. "Free… Yes." She gave him a small smile, almost as if her facial muscles no longer remembered how to perform that simple task. "Most of us wish to be as far away from here as possible," she said. "But I know a handful who wish to help with rebuilding, to turn Kraag'Blitz into something special."

"Gather those who want to stay, Aiden said, "Let's get things rolling."

The Rhajok'Don nodded before walking away.

* * *

The immense bonfire illuminated the whole area at the junction between buildings. The silhouetted flames danced and flickered against the scarred and pockmarked brickwork as the thick, black smoke carried the spirits of the fallen upwards into the still air, towards the stars and nebula that they worshipped. Rhajok'Don circled the funeral pyre, crouching, arms outstretched in front of them, paying their final tribute to their lost comrades. The Resistance stood behind them, heads bowed in respect.

23

Fallen

The click of heels from rapid footsteps could be heard as an edgy scientist rushed through the corridors of the white citadel. Reaching Ceolm's office, he buzzed the comm and asked permission to enter.

The door opened and the scientist dashed through.

"Sire, our coverts have recovered the tablet and we've begun reverse engineering," he said quickly.

"What progress do we have?" Ceolm asked.

"Well... err, well, presently we have nothing. The technology's more advanced than ours. We need more time."

Ceolm's pockmarked face washed with anger as he pointed to the images of the approaching army. "Look!" he shouted. "We have no more time!"

"But... sire, t–the technology... I researched it... and the last time we did this kind of work, the project was led by a woman known as Anamai."

Ceolm sighed and closed his eyes. "So, she sent the message to warn us, yet at the same time compromised our experiment. Clever woman."

"We can't utilise its power."

The leader of the Amunisari placed his hand over his face. "Very well," he mumbled. "I fear for our people."

* * *

The sound of the horn reverberated through the ranks and the army stopped as instructed. There was a commotion at the back as soldiers shuffled to create an aisle for Viktor and his Commanders to walk down. Daimeh followed them with his eyes. Through the bars, he saw what they were heading towards. In the distance, around an hour's march away, atop a large, sandy embankment, the Amunisari Citadel appeared strangely vulnerable, with little in the way of defences. Its landmark sky sphere and imposing dome were clearly visible and its white-washed walls sparkled in the sunlight.

Daimeh squinted, peering ahead he could see Viktor talking with his subordinates, who then pointed back towards Daimeh's cage. A sub-commander nodded and rode towards Daimeh, once close enough, he beckoned Daimeh's escort to move.

Daimeh stared from side to side as they travelled up the aisle. The soldiers were perfectly still, not a single pair of eyes glanced towards him. Arriving at the head of the army, his cage was placed next to Viktor, who threw a small bag into the cage causing Daimeh to flinch.

"We'll need you soon," Viktor said sharply.

Daimeh picked up the bag and opened it, inside was the amulet key to open the door to the citadel. His nerves got the better of him and the amulet slipped from his unsteady hands. Snatching it up again, he realised he had been trying to put the task ahead at the back of his mind. Now the moment had arrived and he could no longer ignore the fact that his death might be at hand.

Daimeh looked out of the cage again, his oval, green eyes focused on the Citadel and, to his surprise, it had vanished.

"They've activated the barrier." One commander said to the other. "They must have spotted us."

Viktor grinned savagely. "Don't worry." He threw another bag at Daimeh "We have a second key." He looked down at Daimeh. "And the boy knows where to deactivate the barrier."

Daimeh slowly nodded.

Viktor raised his hand and the horn sounded once more. Immediately the army marched forward.

* * *

"Release him from the cage and chain him," Viktor ordered.

The door was opened and a guard, roughly grabbing him by the scruff of the neck, dragged him from the cage. Daimeh half-jumped, half-fell onto the soft grass. Familiarity crossed his consciousness. He remembered this part of the jungle from his journey to the citadel from Alkoryn. He recalled the artificial plant. Daimeh stared fearfully up at Viktor, he wasn't sure if he should move or not, then his chains were yanked fiercely from the side.

"Well get on with it!" Viktor ordered. "Go! Deactivate the barrier!"

Attached to a leash, Daimeh immediately began searching. His memory was patchy and under pressure he couldn't remember where the plant had been. His mind worked feverishly as he searched, looking for possibilities, the when and how to try for escape. Would he still be leashed at the doorway? It seemed likely... and how was he to escape then? His legs, shaking from lack of exercise and long confinement in a sitting position, gave way and he slipped in the bushy undergrowth. His guard forcefully dragged him to his feet, scowling at him. A few minutes later, he spotted a patch of grass he remembered falling in previously. For some reason it was softer, the blades finer than the rest, Daimeh recalled being struck by its difference to the surrounding greenery. It's west he thought, setting off in a shambling run in that direction. He was starting to recognise more and more; there was the plant that he had pricked his finger on, and a little north from there was the unnaturally swaying plant he was searching for. He hovered the amulet over its stalk... and the keyhole appeared, glowing on the surface. Daimeh allowed the two to magnetically connect. The barrier disappeared and the Citadel was once again visible. Its tall, daunting architecture not as intimidating to Daimeh the second time around. As he was dragged back to his cage, he admired the irregular angular panels laid in glossy, white walls and the unforgettable glass dome in its centre. The cage door swung closed, the guard making sure it locked.

Viktor stared at the citadel, he gently nodded his head. "Soon the Amunisari will be no more, and we'll have our lands back," he said. "Years of preparation, all for this moment. And I'm going to savour it.

* * *

The walls of the surveillance room displayed footage of the army amassed outside the Citadel. Only Ceolm and Janus, one of his council members, were present in the room.

"Sire, the barrier's down," Janus said. "It's like when those Alkoryns arrived."

Ceolm frowned, putting his hand to his forehead, he whispered, "The keys."

"Guard!" he called, slamming his fist down onto the table.

The door opened and a guard entered. "Yes, sire."

"Get my wife," Ceolm ordered.

The guard nodded and executing a smart turn, hurried from the room.

Ceolm turned to his councilman. "I believe my wife's betrayed us. She insisted on Daimeh being banished, and clearly, our enemy has him and the keys to our citadel."

"What are we going to do?"

"Prepare the city guards at the gates." Ceolm switched to another screen and tapped in a command. An overview of the volcanic landscape appeared and the blue gargantuan was visible. "The Protector is needed. Send a signal. He brought the boy and his aunt here, now he can help defend us."

"Yes… Yes." Janus rushed to a bench in the middle of the room and pressed a button on the communicator. "Contact the gargantuan. We need him under mind control, do what you can."

* * *

The army marched to the front gate and halted outside, their numbers spreading out into the forest behind.

Viktor dismounted and approached the cage. He unlocked it and reached inside for Daimeh.

"I'm sure you know what to do," he said.

"What then? You'll kill me?"

Viktor was silent as he dragged Daimeh to the ground. "The chains won't reach the gates," he said, unlocking them. He pointed along the front line of the army. "If you try to escape you'll be shot down."

Daimeh's fear filled heart was racing, but he was confident. Viktor's men wouldn't get a chance to shoot him.

Viktor hooked his hand under Daimeh's arm and hauled him forward into the sand. As the scared young man slid in the grainy dust he felt around his belt for the refractor, breathing a sigh of relief to find it still there. Climbing wearily to his feet, he began to shuffle towards the gate.

* * *

The corner of Ceolm's mouth twitched spasmodically as he watched Daimeh make his way towards the citadel. "Are the guards ready at the gate?" he asked, his eyes still locked to the screen.

"Yes, sire."

"I want them to attack immediately."

"Understood."

The door opened and Eleanor entered, escorted by a guard. She bowed her head in submission before speaking, her long, blonde hair flowing over her shoulders. "You requested me, sire."

Ceolm stared at her for a long moment before sighing and beginning to slowly move towards her.

Eleanor sensed something was wrong and knelt on one knee. "I hope I've not upset you, sire."

"Why did you want to banish that Alkoryn, Daimeh?"

Eleanor's eyes widened. "Because... because he didn't deserve to die, she stuttered."

"Look at this," Ceolm demanded harshly.

Slowly, reluctantly, Eleanor looked at the screen. She recognized Daimeh immediately, and the key in his hand.

"He has the key, Eleanor." Ceolm's voice was as smooth as silk and as cold as a lake in the depth of winter. "Now, how, Eleanor, do you suppose he got that?" A cruel smile flitted across his face. "Do you suppose someone gave it to him? A little pipila perhaps?"

Eleanor stayed silent.

Ceolm launched himself at her, grasping hold of her arm. Dragging her over to the screen, he jabbed his finger at the image of the key. "*You* gave them to him!" he hissed, his face flushed with anger as he stared furiously at Eleanor, shaking her viciously as he spoke.

There was fear in his wife's beautiful blue eyes but Eleanor met his gaze, refusing to be cowed, her defiance infuriating him even further.

The first blow sent her reeling, staggering backwards, but she managed to stay on her feet. The second punch, to the ribs, doubled her over. His fist hammering into her skull sent her to the floor, clasping her hands over her head to defend herself.

Ceolm struck her again and again, delighting in seeing the effects of his work as her face swelled, eyes reddening as cuts bloomed on her clear skin. He heard himself laugh as the first scream tore from her throat and laughed even harder as more followed. This time she would learn her lesson – he would see to that. Never again would she betray him by so much as a thought.

Janus watched in horror, his face ashen. He didn't dare help her, if he tried, he too would be punished and he could not expect anything as lenient as a beating; his sentence would be death.

Finally, Ceolm allowed Eleanor to slip from his grasp and slide to the floor where he gave her one final kick to the stomach. He towered over her as she lay motionless, blood leaking from her nose and mouth.

"Will... will she be all right?" Janus risked asking the question.

Ceolm stared at him with hatred in his crystal eyes. He didn't say a word as a vein visibly throbbed on his forehead.

Janus instantly knew he had gone too far. Hesitantly, he looked back to the screens and with a shaking hand pointed to Daimeh.

Ceolm composed himself, clearing his throat before resuming his position, watching the footage.

* * *

Daimeh was upon the massive, intricately engraved door. The creamy, marbled texture gleamed and, in the centre, an area glowed; the counterpart to the amulet. Daimeh glanced behind him and saw the army of Zygeth, thousands of glimmering blue eyes staring at him. Taking a deep breath, he held the amulet over its keyhole, then felt under his belt, placing his finger over the small mechanism hidden there. He allowed the amulet to magnetise and pull a little in his hand, then he let it go. It slotted perfectly into the engraving.

The door immediately split into five segments, and as it did so, he quickly pushed the button on the device and disappeared from sight.

The sections of the door opened fully, and in front of him were hundreds of Amunisari guards, lined up facing the doorway, their staffs pointing in his direction. Just as the firing began, Daimeh threw himself onto the gritty sand. As the golden bolts shot over his head, they lifted his hair and blew the sand into little dust swirls around where he lay, the loud whistling noise piercing his eardrums. He scurried to the nearest wall and placed his back up against it. Having found a safe spot just inside the Citadel, he watched as the onslaught unfolded in front of him.

Rows of Amunisari guards, no match for the Zygeth, were firing relentlessly through the gate towards the oncoming army. Their armour moulded perfectly to their bodies without any visible joins, a flexible metal, no doubt based on the transmuting liquescent technology he had witnessed on his previous visit. Projecting from the off-hand were translucent golden shields, covering them from head to toe and deflecting the flesh eating blue bolts raining down on them from the enemy.

Daimeh had managed to escape, just as planned. Now he had to find Cresadir. He knew his mission would not be easy, although the battle distracted his jailors and invisibility lent him a great advantage. Daimeh slowly got up onto his feet. Staying low to the ground, he dashed off into the Citadel.

* * *

The horn trumpeted loudly as the Zygeth army advanced forward, step by brutal step, towards the gate. In the front line, a row of enchants who, as a single, unstoppable barrier, were deflecting the golden bolts while allowing the shots from the rows behind them to penetrate easily. They continued to push forward.

As the enemy drew closer, the guards atop the citadel began to amass. Below them, the Zygeth army stretched as far as the eye could see. They commenced firing, managing to take down a few hundred or so Zygeth. Continuing their rapid fire, their energy bolts burned through a few hundred more soldiers. The commander shouted an order and they combined their fire to create one, immense stream of light which shot what looked like massive balls of golden energy at the Zygeth. Whole areas of the ground were blasted, leaving behind small craters. The Zygeth scattered, as if panicked, but the force held together enough to keep on firing their terrible weapons at the guards on the walls, their shots precise and deadly. A number of Amunisari fell to the pestilent blue bolts. Still the remaining guards stood their ground, firing steadily. The Amunisari had the vantage point, but they did not have the brute force.

The guards at the gate held their defensive position, but soon the army would be upon them and their numbers were too small to win in close combat.

The commander of the Amunisari guard glanced up to the balcony, at the council members. "Where's the gargantuan? We need it now!"

One of the councilmen activated his personal communicator, a small tablet device. Moments later he shouted down, "Hold them for a few more minutes."

The commander waved his men to give ground, allowing them some more time.

* * *

Daimeh stared around him at the chaos, behind the guards, he could see civilians running in many directions, some had children in their arms, others holding hands. The young Alkoryn decided to mingle with the crowd and take advantage of the opening and closing of doors to look for Cresadir. He passed a room he recognised as the breakfast room, and a sudden image flashed into his brain: the second door Ceolm had always retreated through after breakfast.

Daimeh cautiously entered the room, passing the same oblong, alabaster table. Moving slowly to avoid alerting anyone to his invisible presence, he tried to activate the door Ceolm had disappeared through after eating, and, to his surprise, it opened. He ran down the adjoining corridor, to a junction with an illuminated double arrow, the symbols made no sense, so he randomly picked the left corridor. He was half-way down the hallway when one of the doors at the end skimmed open. Out walked a guard, with what appeared to be a robed council member following him. Daimeh inched past them. Just as the door was to close, he glanced through the doorway. Inside was a massive circular table with six chairs arranged around it: the briefing room. He hastily turned around, knowing she wouldn't be there.

The councilman was heading straight ahead so Daimeh decided to follow, not having to worry about accessing doors would be a big help.

The next one opened on command and the councilman strode through, followed by his guard. Daimeh rushed forward, just squeezing through the doorway before it closed.

"Sire, we should make our plans for escape," the man said.

On the floor against the far wall was Eleanor. Daimeh barely contained a gasp when he saw her, covered in blood and unconscious. He couldn't go to her yet, helpless for the moment, he tucked himself into a corner.

"Is Elisaris protected and ready to go?" Ceolm asked.

Again, Daimeh barely stopped himself from letting go a gasp. *Elisaris!* He couldn't believe what he had just heard. He saw her die! His breath came short and fast remembering that day and he fought to steady himself. "I'll depart with her," Ceolm continued, turning towards the door.

Maybe she had survived? Or was it just her preserved body? A glint of hope washed through his heart. He stood, torn, desperately wanting to follow Ceolm, yet held by the need to save Eleanor. Whichever he did, he would lose one. Elisaris was dead, his common sense insisted. There was nothing he could do for her now. But he could help Eleanor, who might lead him to Cresadir.

As the door closed on Ceolm and his companions, Daimeh's heart gave a sudden lurch. What if she was alive after all? Even as the thought tormented him, he knew it was already too late for him to go that path; the door had closed. Hurrying to Eleanor's side, he tried his best to shrug off his thoughts about Elisaris.

Regaining visibility, he took Eleanor into his arms, her head on his lap. "Eleanor! Eleanor please wake!" Eleanor's head slipped to one side.

Daimeh shook her gently. "Eleanor, please! I need you."

He glanced around the room for anything that could be of use to him. A small glass of water sat on the desk. Quickly reaching up, he grabbed it, splashing it onto her. This time she roused a little.

"Eleanor! Wake up, we're in danger."

"Mmmh," Eleanor mumbled, turning her head to the other side.

Daimeh shook her gently again and slowly, she began to open her bruised eyes.

"Daimeh! Is it you?" She raised her hand to his face.

Daimeh smiled, relieved. "Yes," he said. "Yes, it's me." He frowned. "Did... he do this to you?"

"Yes." Her voice was dull, heavy with pain.

"I'll kill him," Daimeh vowed, jaw clenched.

Eleanor struggled upright, immediately noticing the screens. "Oh!" She stared at Daimeh wild eyed. "We're under attack!"

He nodded. "The Zygeth are close to breaking through the front gates. I'm here to find Cresadir."

"Oh, Daimeh!" Eleanor wasn't quite sure how to tell him, and there was no time to think, to find the best way to say it. "Cresadir's gone. I'll explain later," she told him, seeing his shocked expression. First, we must get to the escape pods. Come, help me get up."

Daimeh got her to her feet and together they crossed to the door. Eleanor's arm was over Daimeh's shoulder but she used her other hand to gesture the door open.

Daimeh looked carefully up and down the corridor before they stepped out into it.

24

Exodus

A thunderous roar cut across the skies, momentarily drowning out the buzz and hiss of weapon fire. Many Zygeth paused in their onslaught, distracted by the deafening noise.

The Amunisari, knowing what the mighty bellow heralded, took advantage of the opposing army's distraction and continued firing, managing to bring down some of the Zygeth front-line.

The creature's wingspan alone blew a breeze over the army, and as they peered upwards, an immense beast dived down towards them. Its body was a deep cerulean-blue, fading to a bright turquoise at the extremities. It stretched out its man-like hands, snatching up dozens of soldiers before soaring high into the sky again, crushing the Zygeth before dropping their mangled bodies on top of the rest of the soldiers. The army ceased firing on the Amunisari and focused their weapons onto the gargantuan. Their bolts found their mark but were harmlessly absorbed by its thick skin as it circled the sky, before once more roaring towards the army with such force that it knocked soldiers off their feet. The giant landed with a slide, shaking the ground and crushing Zygeth like ants. Swarms of adepts climbed onto its feet, grappling their way up its legs. Their daggers would not suffice, so they used their poisoned darts to penetrate the creature's skin. A few darts from one soldier would not achieve anything, but thousands of darts must have some effect. More adepts hurried forward, scurrying up the beast's legs. The gargantuan shook its body, managing to dislodge a good number, but the swarming adepts were too much for the creature. It screeched before pushing itself off the ground, flapping its enormous wings.

Once air-bound, the beast gave a last, piercing screech before wheeling away from the fight.

The respite was over, the Zygeth army continued to advance, each step bought with the blood of the Amunisari.

Again, the guards at the gate were forced further and further back.

"There are too many. They'll reach the Citadel!" The commander shouted to his guards. "We must hold them long enough for our people to evacuate! Take up the defensive position."

Immediately, the Amunisari ducked behind their shields, creating an impenetrable barricade by allowing the energy to meld forming one continuous cover. The guards at the top of the walls continued shooting.

The Zygeth front line had reached the gate and were almost inside.

"Hold them!" The Commander shouted.

The Amunisari guards stood firm and slowly, moving as one, they began to push back against the relentless fire, their shields absorbing the blue bolts, forcing the Zygeth to almost a halt, giving all they had to try to buy precious minutes for the civilians to escape.

* * *

Daimeh and Eleanor made their way through the gardens, Daimeh supporting her as she stumbled along. He could see she was in a bad way, unsteady on her feet, her breathing laboured.

"This way." She pointed to the rear doorways, where hundreds of panicking people jostled each other in their need to escape. "The evacuation pods are through there. But first..." she said, pulling them aside.

"Eleanor! We need to hurry!" Daimeh said, scanning the doors worriedly, unsure of what still lay between them and escape. They were already moving at a slower pace than the others who were fleeing for their lives.

Eleanor ignored him, making her way over to a small room to the side of the exit doors. Opening the door, she shuffled over to a locker, one of several stationed around the room. Reaching into it, she pulled out a robe and thrust it at him. "You'll need this."

Daimeh nodded, quickly pulling it on over his clothes. They joined the throng of people again and, eventually, they reached the doors. Beyond them was an enormous semi-circular enclosure with pods moving from left to right around the walls.

The people ahead of them were frantically climbing into the moving pods and as soon as they were strapped in, the door would close and the vehicle would disappear behind the far wall.

Daimeh and Eleanor ran to the nearest empty capsules and he helped her in before jumping into the one next to her. The door shut and he stood in darkness, except for the blue hue of the light between the cushions. The pod was the same kind that had brought him to Stygia and the all too familiar feeling of anguish rolled over him.

A small jolt and the capsule moved forward, continuing for a short time until coming to a sudden halt. It rumbled as it lurched backwards. Daimeh heard a low humming which gradually got louder, until it was a deafening whir, vibrating the entire vehicle.

He could hear a beeping from outside, its tone climbing higher with each beep, until it held the highest note and the pod released, shooting upwards. Daimeh felt the tug of gravity pulling him downwards. Abruptly lightheaded, he fell into a deep, black pit.

* * *

"They're at the gates, sire." One of Viktor's subordinates informed him, lowering his binoculars.

The group stood at the back of the army, watching from afar, Nis'Ka by Viktor's side.

Just as Viktor glanced at Nis'Ka, a huge shadow fell over them as the gargantuan shot towards them. Instinctively, the Rhajok'Don threw himself at Viktor, pushing him from his mount and onto the ground, covering him completely with his own body. The gargantuan was upon them, just metres off the ground, it flew past at speed, grabbing the unfortunate Zygeth who had stood with them before he could so much as react.

As the creature headed in the other direction, Nis'Ka released Viktor, who nodded his thanks.

"Bring it down, Nis'Ka," he ordered. "You know where the implant is."

The Rhajok'Don nodded back. Rising to his feet, he touched a button on his gauntlet and a circle of steel wire popped out of a compartment. Twirling the lasso over his head, he waited for the great flying beast to make another swoop, watching it circle above his head before beginning its dive towards him. Nis'Ka flung himself to the side, dodging the creature's powerful hands. Pressing more buttons on his gauntlets, Nis'Ka let fly more thin wires, each one topped by a hooked barb.

The beast screamed in pain and rage as the barbs bit into his flesh but Nis'Ka hauled himself up onto the immense arm and began his ascent to the head.

Wind rushed past him as he climbed up the body, using the thing's cracked skin to gain traction, mercilessly digging in his fingers and boot tips. The gargantuan roared again and tried to shake him loose, but Nis'Ka was too strong. Reaching its neck, he crawled around to position himself at the back of its head. Unsheathing his small, double edge scythe, he waited until the crackle of power ran down the blade before slicing through the tough, blue skin. Thick, turquoise blood splattered from the wound as the gargantuan roared, frantically shaking its head from side to side. Nis'Ka swayed with the movement but managed to keep his grip. Plunging his hand into the laceration, he ripped the skin apart even further. He climbed into the wound, slicing his way through the muscle and tissue until he reached the skull. Using his augmented vision, he quickly pinpointed the implanted chip.

The gargantuan lost height, dropping to the earth like a stone, squashing more Zygeth. Another wave of adepts advanced up its feet, their poisonous darts completely covering the beast.

Nis'Ka pounded his fist against the back of the creature's skull until he cracked open an area between two plates. Thrusting his hand into its brain, he grabbed the chip, ripping it from the connecting tissue and pulling it free. The gargantuan flung back its head, screaming in agony. The poison was doing its work, the chip removed, the giant was no longer under mind control and impervious to the effects of the darts. One enormous leg toppled, bringing the behemoth to its knee, quickly followed by the other leg, plunging it to the ground where it lay, attacked by Zygeth from all directions. Its man-like face was twisted in pain, its broad, flat nose gushed blood, its wide mouth was pulled back from its teeth and its white eyes were glazed over.

Nis'Ka clambered out from under the skin as more soldiers poured across its head. Using his steel lines, he made his way down the creature's unmoving carcass, knocking off some of his allies as he went. He didn't care. There was only one thing on his mind.

His powerful body thudded heavily to the ground and he barged through the crowd of soldiers, towards the front-line.

Behind him, the gargantuan mustered some final strength and pulled itself up to fly away in defeat.

* * *

The Amunisari were still holding the Zygeth back but it was plain that they couldn't hold out much longer. The Zygeth army had breached the gate area and it was only a matter of time until the sheer numbers overwhelmed the Amunisari shielding.

Inevitably, the guards were forced backward under the pressure.

"They're climbing over! Detach the shields!" the commander shouted as Zygeth soldiers climbed onto the domed shield. The guards quickly peeled away from each other, leaving them vulnerable behind their individual protection once more. "Keep pushing!" The commander spurred his men on even though he knew it was a losing battle.

From a distance, he saw the Rhajok'Don approaching, standing well above the Zygeth soldiers he made a formidable enemy.

Nis'Ka pushed aside his own men as he trampled through the army.

The commander stared, wondering what was coming his way. He recognised him as a Rhajok'Don but could see he was some kind of mutation or super-soldier. He tightened his grip on his weapon, making a hasty peace with spirit.

Nis'Ka reached the gate and joined the front-line Zygeth. Quickly the Amunisari's defence collapsed, their ranks decimated as Nis'Ka raged through them. A few remaining guards from the back ran forward to make a last stand, firing at the Zygeth and Nis'Ka. Their golden bolts taking down a few more Zygeth, but it was hopeless.

Nis'Ka, untroubled by the Amunisari weaponry, thrust himself through the fighting, grabbing guards by the throat, crushing their windpipes before dropping their bodies to the ground. Those out of reach, he skewered with his deadly assortment of arsenal. The Amunisari guards fled into the citadel as the Zygeth poured through the gates, stampeding over the fallen bodies.

Nis'Ka picked off the last few guards as they ran with the bolts from his gauntlets, the bodies slumping to the ground.

* * *

Ceolm and his daughter, surrounded by guards, hurried through the corridors towards their private pods. Behind them, screaming could be heard, and the sound of many booted feet.

"They're inside," Ceolm said. "We must hurry." He passed his daughter forward to his guards. "Take her first. I'll hold them back."

Elisaris turned to him. "But, Father?"

"Go," he growled, grabbing a staff from one of the guard and signalling another to follow him.

Elisaris was quickly escorted the rest of the way as her father and a single guard stood their ground.

Zygeth were spilling into the wide passage. The Amunisari guard projected his shield and held it up to protect the both of them as two Zygeth launched themselves at Ceolm. Their attacks were repelled by the shield, but now the guard was out of position and Ceolm found himself flanked by two more Zygeth. Grimly, fighting for his life, he managed to deflect the attack himself.

More Zygeth were pouring into the corridor. One of them, an adept, secured a grappling line to the ceiling. Shinning up it as agilely as a born tree-dweller, he used his advantage point and his poisonous darts to kill Ceolm's guard, leaving him alone – against a dozen Zygeth.

Desperately, Ceolm fired at his enemy, but the adept effortlessly dodged his bolts. Ceolm swung his staff at the surrounding soldiers, but again, they easily avoided the sharp blade. He knew his time was coming to an end, he was outmatched and his limited fighting prowess put him at a distinct disadvantage.

Still he was determined to take down as many of the enemy as possible. He was so focused on the Zygeth in front of him that he lost all track of those behind. The blade pierced his back just under his left shoulder blade and penetrated his chest. Ceolm gasped in pain, the staff slipping from his grasp as he fell to his knees, keeling over onto his side. Struggling, he tried to rise but he was suddenly so weak... and cold. He started coughing, blood spraying from his mouth, the red drops forming a pattern, almost like a cluster of red stars, on the white tiles. Sinking back against the floor, powerless to stop the enemy as they marched past him, he took his last breath staring at Zygeth boots.

Elisaris was climbing into one of the capsules when a commotion broke out as the Zygeth swarmed into the room. A chill ran down her spine as she realized that her father must be dead. She pushed the thought to the back of her mind for later. Now she must concentrate, she must escape! She would not let her father's sacrifice be for nothing.

As her guards worked to keep the soldiers at bay, she allowed the capsule to carry her away.

* * *

The army had completely overrun the citadel when Viktor strode through the undefended gate. Bodies lay in a pile at the opening and he and his remaining commanders had been forced to clamber over the mound to gain entry. It was a similar scene inside, the dead lay scattered everywhere, while congealed blobs of blood gave testimony to those unlucky enough to be consumed by the blue gel.

They advanced through the decimated gardens and towards the untouched sky sphere.

Reaching the top Viktor looked up at the glorious sun. The beacon of their existence was once again his. He laughed as he glanced down at the incredible Citadel. "It's all ours now," he said, smiling proudly. "We're home."

COSMIC
EGG
BOOKS

Cosmic Egg Books
FANTASY, SCI-FI, HORROR & PARANORMAL

If you prefer to spend your nights with Vampires and Werewolves rather than the mundane then we publish the books for you. If your preference is for Dragons and Faeries or Angels and Demons – we should be your first stop. Perhaps your perfect partner has artificial skin or comes from another planet – step right this way. If your passion is Fantasy (including magical realism and spiritual fantasy), Metaphysical Cosmology, Horror or Science Fiction (including Steampunk), Cosmic Egg books will feed your hunger. Our curiosity shop contains treasures you will enjoy unearthing.

If you have enjoyed this book, why not tell other readers by posting a review on your preferred book site. Recent bestsellers from Cosmic Egg Books are:

The Zombie Rule Book
A Zombie Apocalypse Survival Guide
Tony Newton
The book the living-dead don't want you to have!
Paperback: 978-1-78279-334-2 ebook: 978-1-78279-333-5

Cryptogram
Because the Past is Never Past
Michael Tobert
Welcome to the dystopian world of 2050, where three lovers are haunted by echoes from eight-hundred years ago.
Paperback: 978-1-78279-681-7 ebook: 978-1-78279-680-0

Purefinder
Ben Gwalchmai

London, 1858. A child is dead; a man is blamed and dragged through hell in this Dantean tale of loss, mystery and fraternity.

Paperback: 978-1-78279-098-3 ebook: 978-1-78279-097-6

600ppm
A Novel of Climate Change
Clarke W. Owens

Nature is collapsing. The government doesn't want you to know why. Welcome to 2051 and 600ppm.

Paperback: 978-1-78279-992-4 ebook: 978-1-78279-993-1

Creations
William Mitchell

Earth 2040 is on the brink of disaster. Can Max Lowrie stop the self-replicating machines before it's too late?

Paperback: 978-1-78279-186-7 ebook: 978-1-78279-161-4

The Gawain Legacy
Jon Mackley

If you try to control every secret, secrets may end up controlling you.

Paperback: 978-1-78279-485-1 ebook: 978-1-78279-484-4

Mirror Image
Beth Murray

When Detective Jack Daniels discovers the journal of female serial killer Sarah he is dragged into a supernatural world, where people's dark sides are not always hidden.

Paperback: 978-1-78279-482-0 ebook: 978-1-78279-481-3

Moon Song

Elen Sentier

Tristan died too soon, Isoldé must bring him back to finish his job... to write the Moon Song.

Paperback: 978-1-78279-807-1 ebook: 978-1-78279-806-4

Origin

Colleen Douglas

Fate rarely calls on us at a moment of our choosing.

Paperback: 978-1-78279-492-9 ebook: 978-1-78279-491-2

Perception

Alaric Albertsson

The first ship was sighted over St. Louis...and then St. Louis was gone.

Paperback: 978-1-78279-261-1 ebook: 978-1-78279-262-8

Readers of ebooks can buy or view any of these bestsellers by clicking on the live link in the title. Most titles are published in paperback and as an ebook. Paperbacks are available in traditional bookshops. Both print and ebook formats are available online.

Find more titles and sign up to our readers' newsletter at
http://www.johnhuntpublishing.com/fiction
Follow us on Facebook at https://www.facebook.com/JHPfiction
and Twitter at https://twitter.com/JHPFiction